LEGACY

LEGACY

THE GIRL IN THE BOX
BOOK EIGHT

Robert J. Crane

LEGACY
THE GIRL IN THE BOX
BOOK EIGHT

1st Edition

AUTHOR'S NOTE
This book is a work of fiction. Names, characters, places and incidents are products of the author's imagination or are used fictitiously. Any resemblance to actual events or locales or persons, living or dead, is entirely coincidental.

Layout provided by Everything Indie
http://www.everything-indie.com

To my kids:
No matter how many books I write, rest assured that the stories I
most care about are yours.

Acknowledgments

1. The Editorial Department - Heather Rodefer, Carien Keevey, and Paul Madsen all gave this book a thorough readthrough before I handed it off to the illustrious Sarah Barbour (http://aeroplanemedia.wordpress.com/) for final review. Every one helped make the manuscript stronger by their actions, and infinitely more readable.

2. The Cover - Karri Klawiter (ArtbyKarri.com) seems to have done her best work yet, producing something that is absolutely amazing. Kudos to her.

3. The Formatting - Nicholas Ambrose has once more handled the formatting duties, taking my rambling words and putting them onto an actual page.

4. The Narration - Though she hasn't done the audiobook for this one yet, I wanted to take a moment and give a shout-out to Annie Sullivan, who has diligently been working to turn Sienna's adventures into audiobooks over the months since Enemies came out. She truly has captured the spirit of our heroine.

5. The Home Front - To my parents, my in-laws, my wife and kids - my thanks for all you do to keep me writing.

Chapter 1

Forest of Dean, England
November 1467

Wolfe was on the hunt, sniffing for blood. He could smell prey in the distance, through the trees. The dirt was fresh after a light rain, and he loped along on all fours, following his nose. The chill of early fall was upon him, the low-lying gullies covered in a light mist. The smell of humans was all the same to him, all stink and filth, but under it was the blood. *Glorious blood, delicious meat,* he thought. *Serving one purpose and one alone—to feed me.* The pressure on the pads of his feet and hands was subtle as he went springing along, the way he was meant to. His clothes flapped in the breeze, making him long to tear them off. *Tear off all this civilization, the stink of the city, leave it all behind. This is how it was meant to be—in the woods, in the wilds, running them down one by one. Though slaughtering a whole houseful at once has its advantages ...*

There was only ambient sound around him, the noise of the forest. He heard a faint whistling ahead of him, some farmer's tune. *Yes, tell the Wolfe where you are.* He slowed, felt his muscles slacken as he started to creep. He listened, straining his ears to hear. *There. Prey. Food. Taste.* He ran his tongue over his jagged teeth, letting the points poke at him, savoring the sharp sensation on the sensitive skin of his tongue. *Soon we'll tear the flesh from bones, soon we'll rip the screams from a mouth.* He could smell only one, a man, or possibly a boy. *Either would be sweet, but young, soft, supple skin is better than old and rangy, worn down from life. If there were an entourage, then I might have a lordling. They're always so plump and delicious and scream in all the right ways, releasing the Wolfe's tension before they die.* He felt the throbbing, lower, the excitement of a short hunt about to reach its conclusion and of the relief that would bring. *The tension will subside with the thrills of the flesh. And it's been a long day since the last one ...*

He slowed further, now choosing his footing carefully as he made his way through the brush. His clothing no longer whipped in the breeze; his motions were controlled. The surprise was part of the thrill, starting things off right with a good scream. Then more screams, fueled by the anticipation, really—the fear, an opening tease of what would be coming. By the time he was finished, his clothes would be dripping red unless he removed them first. He took his shirt off carefully, listening over the rustle of the cloth to make certain that his prey didn't escape. The whistling continued, now only a hundred feet away through the brush, unceasing.

Wolfe undressed completely, leaving the clothes he'd taken from a shopkeeper's window in a small pile on a knotty tree stump. He felt the air coarse over his naked flesh and thrilled to it, felt the smile split his face. Sometimes, in these moments before the torment, he became so excited he could hardly control himself when it began. This time would be different, though. The forest was so large yet so sparsely inhabited everything had to be savored because he didn't know when he'd meet his next prey. He started forward again, listening to the whistling.

He padded over rough ground, closing the distance. There was a path ahead, and the whistling seemed to be come from it. He came over a short rise covered with new growth, saplings and heavy brush, and caught a glimpse through the branches. There was a man, indeed, hair long and around his shoulders. He wasn't plump but neither was he rangy, Wolfe could see from the back. A cloak protected him from the chill and the low, mournful tune which he whistled was almost like a dirge; it made Wolfe's smile dim. It was always sweeter when they were happy before the surprise came. It tasted better, somehow.

Wolfe crept over the rise, careful not to disturb the branches as he passed. He was whisper quiet, not a sound made as he slipped down the slope. His toes landed on the muddy path and he felt the sensation of it oozing around his feet. It made him think of blood, of how he sometimes tracked it after a kill. It heightened his anticipation, made him throb again.

He was only ten feet away, one good leap, when the man in the cloak turned, head cocked curiously. Wolfe froze, and the smile he'd felt building seeped away. There was no surprise on the fellow's face, but he smiled in greeting until he took in Wolfe's nakedness.

"Hello, there," the man said. "You're a bit underdressed." Wolfe looked down at his nakedness, his excitement plainly beginning to dissolve. "I say, walking naked in the woods in this weather would seem a bit of an odd choice."

Wolfe looked up, felt what had been his smile only a moment before turn into a sneer, a snarl. He looked at the man—medium height, brownish hair navy cloak that covered his clothing. He was tanned and had plainly spent his fair share of time out of doors. Not a tender lordling, that much was certain. The disappointment was palpable. Wolfe let out a little hiss.

"Are you quite all right?" the man asked again, head still cocked. He looked down at Wolfe's chest. "You are a hairy fellow, aren't you?" His hand came up to indicate Wolfe's front. "And large, save for ... that trifling area, there. Though I suppose it's not trifling for everyone, but a fellow as coarse and disgusting as yourself likely doesn't allow for it to see much happy use." The man's curious look had turned into a wicked smile.

"It teases the Wolfe," Wolfe whispered and felt a seething fire run through his brain. "It mocks."

"Indeed," the man said with a nod, apparently pleased to see the subject of his jest had gotten the joke. "Yes, I was insulting your manhood with that one, though I wondered if you'd be bright enough to catch it. You have the look of a man who's been in the woods entirely too long. Perhaps you haven't heard any complaints because you've switched to animals? Because I don't know if you realize this or not, but running down the King's deer for unsavory practices is a crime—"

"It shuts its mouth!" Wolfe hissed, holding off the urge to spring. *Intimidate. Make him fear us, savor that for a few minutes before we start, regain the sweetness before we start to make him scream ...*

The man raised an eyebrow. "'It'?" He looked down again. "That doesn't look large enough to have a mouth, now does it? Rather like a caterpillar crawled up your leg, actually, then retracted—"

Wolfe sprang with a howl of rage. *Wolfe will make him pay, make him scream, make him suffer for the insult.* He watched during his long arc through the air, waiting for it to register on the man's face that he'd made a horrible mistake. Death was coming for him now, death and so much worse—things that would make him scream and cry before it was over, beg for an end that would be slow to arrive, that would be savored ...

The fist hit Wolfe in the side of the head with enough force to interrupt his landing; he'd jumped and led face first, hands extended toward the man, but his momentum was halted with brutal force. He felt his jaw take the brunt of the punch and break—actually break! A follow-up kick sent Wolfe flying until he hit a tree and snapped the trunk with his back, bringing the whole thing down with him. He landed on his left arm, the shock of the impact making his forearm go numb, something that hadn't happened in well over a thousand years. His head hit the ground and bounced off an exposed root, stunning him. He looked up to see the tree he'd broken lying next to him; its trunk had snapped in the middle, the jagged splinters of a section of wood two feet in diameter jutting out unevenly from the top of it.

"Manners," the man said quietly over the ringing in Wolfe's ears, which sounded as though an abbey's bells were pealing in his head.

Wolfe snarled and lunged to his feet. *Strong. Meta.* He felt blood run down his chin and tasted it in his mouth. *Wolfe's own blood. Precious.* He held himself back, looking for the opening. The man stood still, regarding him, cloak opened to expose one arm and one arm only. "You ... you're a meta," Wolfe said, the low hiss overcoming the still-noisy humming in his ears.

"You really aren't terribly bright, are you?" The man stood, looking down his nose at him. He wasn't any taller than Wolfe, but that was the way Wolfe saw him; imperious. "I assume in those years of working with your brothers that you were never considered the brains of the operation."

"Who are you?" Wolfe let the snarl escape and fidgeted, his shoulders moving left and right, his toes keeping him up on the balls of his feet, ready to spring if an opening presented itself.

"Just a man," came the reply. Wolfe watched calm brown eyes follow him, but the man was still, completely so, absolutely unconcerned about him. *Lucky. Had to be luck. Wolfe was slow, too slow, not expecting a meta, that's all. No one is faster than Wolfe.* He clenched his fist, felt the points of his nails dig into his nearly impenetrable skin. *The suffering will be even greater for this one ... Healing will allow this to go on and on ...*

"Don't," the man said calmly, and just the slightest hint of a smile turned up one corner of his mouth.

Wolfe leapt, the rage taking over. He came in lower this time with a perfectly aimed forward spring that was fueled by anger. He saw the stranger's face so close, his hands extended ...

A fist met him and Wolfe flew again in a low, lazy arc. The

world grew dim around him, as if he'd landed in one of the low areas and been wrapped up in the fog. He hit the ground and rolled twenty feet, his ribs slamming into a tree. He blinked his eyes and realized he'd gone unconscious for at least part of the flight and after, as there were now broken branches and leaves matted in his hair. Blood ran freely down his chest. *I ... don't remember that happening ...* A face appeared, leering down at him, hovering just above his and almost out of reach. Wolfe's hand came up but the man grabbed his wrist, putting pressure on it greater than anything Wolfe could recall. The sound of bones snapping filled his ears and an exquisite pain filled the rest of him. *Is this ... what it feels like ... when I ... ?*

"You won't forget this, I trust?" The man knelt down, and the sound of fracturing bones got louder for a moment as Wolfe felt his elbow break as well. "I'm going to give you enough pain so you remember it. I don't know that I'll ever cross your path again, but I want you to recall, to tell others, in case they do. Tell them I beat you. Tell them I broke you. Let them know that I was the one who did this to you." The man smiled, and Wolfe felt a sick feeling in his stomach as the man's hand retracted. He felt the pain—the weakness—shoot through him, forcing him to stay down like one of his own prey. "Time to start building my own legend, I suppose."

"Who ... ?" Wolfe croaked. "Who are you?" His voice came even raspier than was usual for him, struggling as he was for breath. A searing pain in his ribs flared as the man kicked him, causing him to float through the air again and regain consciousness, this time in a bed of thistles.

"I suppose I should tell you, since I am building a reputation," the man said when he realized Wolfe was awake again. *Is that the look I have when they wake up? It is such a sweet moment ... how ... how am I ... ? This is all wrong, not supposed to be the one being watched, looked at, stood over while in agony ...* "You wouldn't know my old name, so I suppose I'll need a new one." The man stood up straight, put his hand over his mouth, tapping his index finger idly upon his upper lip as he thought. "Something ... distinctive. Something that gives me my due, that lets you know who I am." He leaned over again. "See, I stand apart from all of you. I'm different. I don't want what you want, or what the others want. I don't need anything. If you'd left me alone, we never would have met because I wouldn't have bothered to seek you out."

"Who ... ?" Wolfe heard himself rasp again, "... are you?"

"Good question," the man said, and looked around. "Wait. I think I have it. I'm apart from you, from the others, from these countries and monarchs. I'm my own man—a man apart, really." He smiled. "A man unto himself, independent of all others." He nodded. "Yes, I think that will do nicely."

Wolfe blinked at him, and blood slid into his eye, causing him to close it. "What ...?"

The man looked down at him, as though he'd forgotten Wolfe was even there. "Oh, yes. If they ask ..." He peered down, then smiled. "As badly as I've hurt you, I suppose it's more of a 'when' than 'if' ... When they ask, tell them ..." He slammed a fist down into Wolfe's ribs, causing him to sit up violently, a noise of shattering bones breaking filling his ears over the sounds of his own screaming. *How? How? Wolfe is ... unbreakable ...* The smell of his own blood, for once, was thick in his nostrils, mixed with the greenery of the forest. His vision was clouded, and the screams of pain in his own head were so loud he almost missed what the man said next. Almost, but not quite. And it stayed with him for all the rest of his days.

"Tell them it was Sovereign who did this to you."

Chapter 2

Sienna Nealon
Now

The handcuffs were heavy on my wrists: heavier and stronger than ones I had encountered before. I stirred, moving my hands, and heard the clink of the metal rattling as I shifted position. My chair was made of the same metal, and I was staring at four blank walls of old concrete. Even if I could get loose of the handcuffs, those walls would hold me in for a time.

I stirred again, rattling the cuffs. There were two pairs on my wrists and two rounds of ankle cuffs keeping my legs from doing much moving. The smell of stale, heated air filled the room, annoying me. An FBI agent named Li had ambushed me at Customs in the Minneapolis airport with a SWAT team arrayed in front of me like a firing line. If I had moved or done anything untoward, he would have smoked me. So I let them cuff me and haul me off in the back of a van, against my every instinct.

I studied the empty room that they had placed me in. I'd been here waiting for at least two hours, according to my internal timekeeper. After years of being imprisoned in much tighter confines than this, I had developed a pretty decent sense of time. I stared at the one-way mirror in front of me, giving it a hard look that I hoped would convey my dissatisfaction with my current predicament without giving away the fact that I was deeply, deeply nervous. I kept my hands still, my eyes as slow in their movements as I could, left my face expressionless, and just sat there like I was at the dullest event I could possibly be attending, all while experiencing a bout of lethargy. I based my performance on the workers I had seen at the DMV when I'd gotten my driver's license. I hoped it worked.

I kept my breathing calm and controlled and poured my energies into keeping the voices in my head calm and orderly, not in a cacophony.

This was a surprise, Zack said.

Ya think? I asked him in reply, all sarcasm. I didn't have to speak to do it now, I just concentrated hard on forming the thought behind the words, and I could feel him in my head, receiving it. I had just gotten my metaphorical ducks in a row, had a plan of action, and there I go getting jailed. I'm a regular 24601.

All the Little Doll's past sins have come home to roost like chickens, Wolfe said, and I could sense his grin. *But not as tasty.* I shut the mental door on him, not impressed with his attitude. While it was by no means perfect, I had a mental image of holding pens for him and all the others, perfect little boxes that I was familiar with from the time I'd spent in it. I'd built one in my head with a thought and threw the voices in my mind inside whenever I needed a respite from them.

If anyone has any brilliant ideas for escaping, I said, *I'm all ears.* I frowned. *Or brain, since I'm not actually listening to you.*

If you were all brains, you wouldn't have let yourself get caught, Eve Kappler said with a malevolence all her own. I rolled my eyes before I caught myself and the sound of her little box getting slammed shut followed. I thought I could hear her screaming in protest somewhere in the distance, but that faded quickly.

You're at their mercy now, Roberto Bastian chimed in. *Gonna have to wait to see how they want to play it.*

They haven't come in to question you and it's been hours, Zack said, and I could sense his thoughts swirling around, mixed with my own. *That's ... unusual.*

What are the odds I walk away from this through legal

means? I asked the question.

I heard a cackling from Bjorn and slammed the door on him as well. You'd think one of them would learn from the others, but apparently I got stuck with some real dumbasses. Which was unsurprising, given that my luck always seemed to run in a southerly direction.

Not good, Zack answered me, and I could feel him cringe. *Agent Li ...* I sensed his hesitation at the use of Li's name, *... is a pretty serious guy, and he read the charges to you right at the outset.* There was a pause. *He's definitely not bluffing. He's terrible at bluffing.*

"Wait," I said aloud then shut myself up after a quick, darting look around the empty holding room, as though I could see anyone looking at me. Stupid. *You know this Agent Li?*

Zack's hesitation was short-lived, but it spoke volumes. *He was my roommate at the University of Minnesota in my junior and senior years. He doesn't mess around. Smart, capable, and straightforward. Like I said, he doesn't bluff. If you haven't already been charged with the crimes he listed, then they'll be filed shortly. I'm just surprised he hasn't come in to question you yet, especially given that he seemed to know that you're a succubus and that you murdered five people.*

Including you, I said. *He accused me of murdering you.*

There was a quiet in my head, the three who were left uncaged not wanting to say anything. Finally Bastian broke the awkward tension. *Well, technically, you did—*

I slammed the door to his box, and he took it like a man, no bellyaching. I could almost see Gavrikov and Zack staring at me from the mirrored surface of the one-way window that I was facing. Their ghostly forms were standing nervously behind me. *So, how do I get out of this?*

Zack's face got a strained look. *Just wait. Play for time. Where you are right now looks pretty damned untenable, especially with those cuffs on.* I stirred again, putting some pressure on the cuffs, but I couldn't get any leverage on them at all. Certainly not enough to find out if I could damage the metal. *Since you probably can't beat the system—Li said you wouldn't be getting a lawyer—that leaves escape, which you can't really do at present. Which means you have to wait until they give you an opening. Be ready for it.*

I felt my eyelid twitch from the tension. Only the littlest part of me wanted to cry, but it was still a powerful call. I felt desperate at the thought of losing my freedom, having it taken away from me by these men. The fact that my entire subsection of the human species was being wiped out at this very moment and I was the only one organizing a resistance made it all the worse. I took a breath that was far more ragged than I would have liked and tried to stabilize my breathing, slowing it down, calming myself. It was working for now. I damned sure wasn't going to cry here, though this was potentially scarier to me for some reason than the idea of being in a fight that could kill me. If I died, it was all over. But murder was a life sentence, and at eighteen years old and with a metahuman life span, that was potentially a very, very long time to be imprisoned.

I wanted to punch the walls, to break the concrete, to shatter the glass in frustration, but I held back. Reckless anger had gotten me here, after all. I thought about the people I had murdered, whom I'd been accused of killing. Really, Li didn't know the half of it. Parks, Clary, Eve, Bastian and Zack were just the tip of the iceberg for me lately. Thankfully he didn't know about my recent activities in London or they would have probably added another dozen to the charges.

I blinked. *I forgot about those guys over in England. Breandan, Karthik, Kat, Janus and ... Reed. And Scott!* I felt a surge of panic, wondering if he was still waiting outside the airport for me. I questioned my internal timekeeper again, wondering if I had really been sitting in this chair for two hours. My ass answered me with extreme discomfort in both cheeks as I shifted my weight around. There was no more comfortable position, unfortunately, just this one. And this one sucked after two hours.

They'll be all right, Zack said. *They're a resourceful bunch.*

I felt my expression waver, emotion almost breaking through the facade. *They need me. There's no way they can fight Weissman and Century without me.*

I could almost see Zack's wan smile in the one-way mirror. *Maybe they won't have to. Or maybe they'll be able to do it. Reed could rise to the occasion and take over.*

I raised my hands and rubbed my face. "No," I whispered. *There's something about me that make me important. That makes me a threat to Weissman, that makes me important to Sovereign. They need me for ...* I started to shrug but stopped myself and feigned a stretch, *... something.*

But you don't know what, Zack said calmly.

And I won't find out sitting on my ass in this cell, either. I shifted in my seat again. There was no comfort to be had there.

But you can't get out right now, Zack said, trying to be reassuring.

I felt my internal temperature rise. *People are dying. Metas are dying, right now. They're being wiped out in South America, and probably North America soon. We don't have time to be sitting here. I don't have time to waste, to throw away just staring at ghostly faces in the mirror.*

His faint smile vanished. *Well, there's nothing you can do—*

I could rip apart this chair, I said, letting the anger build in my mind, *snag it behind my back and heave it through the damned window, following behind it by a second and pounding anybody in the next room to mutton.* I visualized it, jumping through the air and slamming into someone with my shoulder, rolling to my back and using my meta strength to launch back to my feet while striking someone with a vaulting kick as I did so. Then turning with both hands balled tight into fists, smashing them into someone's gut, sending them flying into the concrete wall where their skull smashed into paste—

You ready to kill cops? Zack asked me, snapping me back to reality, to the cell, to my ass still sitting sore on the chair. *You ready to murder men just doing their jobs—*

Them doing their jobs is keeping me from doing mine, I raged at him and saw him start to fade. *And the stakes are a hell of a lot higher for the world if I don't get out than they are for them if I stay here.* There was a dull roar of blood rushing in my ears and I knew my expression was far from calm, now.

But you can—

Forget it, I said and slammed the door on Zack, locking him away. *I'm not in the mood to argue with you.* I took another breath, steeling myself to carry out my plan of attack, when something Janus had said before he'd been wounded came back to me.

... a monster wouldn't care ...

I slowly relaxed my muscles, resting my backside on the chair, certain my expression was still surly. I heard the clink of the handcuff chains as I released tension I didn't even know I'd put into them, letting myself go slack and going back to controlling my breathing. Breathe in, breathe out. In through the nose, out through the mouth. Just like Mom taught me. I looked inward and saw Aleksandr Gavrikov still there, the only one I hadn't locked away in the recesses of my mind. He was quiet, dead quiet. *Well?* I asked him. *You got anything to say?*

He regarded me carefully in the mirror and shrugged, his faint outline showing me a face I hadn't seen in reality in something close to a year, since the day I'd absorbed his soul with my own hands, taking it into my body, my mind. *There is not much to say.*

I stared back at him and tried to release the tension in my jaw, which was set tight. *True enough. Not about this, anyway. It's time to wait, I guess.* I took another breath in through the nose and out through the mouth. *Want to talk about something else?*

He nodded then looked around the room. *Maybe we could talk about Klementina?*

I slammed the door on him, prompting a howl that faded quickly. It took me a few moments to get my annoyance under control after that, some more breathing exercises. In that time, I realized that I was at least fortunate in one minor way. If I'd had Gavrikov's sister's flat, skinny ass, I reflected as I shifted in my chair for the thousandth time, my backside would be even more sore than it already was.

I stared at my reflection in the mirror and wondered how long I would have to wait. The mirror seemed so big and I so small now, with the others gone from it. Still, I sat there, watching my empty expression, my dull, disinterested eyes, staring at the girl sitting in the middle of the holding cell, all alone.

Chapter 3

The sound of the lock shifting open caught my attention about an hour and a half later. My eyes diverted to it from my reflection, which I had been wordlessly focused on for the intervening time. The room's air was warm and stuffy enough that I was beginning to notice how ripe I was from the flight; how toxic my breath had gotten from not having a chance to brush my teeth in twelve hours at least. I was tempted to blow a big breath right in Li's face if it was him coming in.

It wasn't. Another man stood in the door, a taller one, powerfully built, African-American with greying hair at the temples and just a little scattered throughout the rest of his short-cropped cut. He wore a suit, which, unlike Li's, wasn't cheap, and his tie was a little crooked. The door shut behind him and he waved at me where I sat on the chair, hands cuffed in my lap. "Don't get up," he said with a hint of a southern accent. I stared back at him and started to say something but he cut me off. "Or uppity, for that matter, at least not until I've had a chance to introduce myself."

I gave him the cool glare, trying to pretend I was uninterested. Facing five murder raps and the threat of no trial, I was actually very interested in what he had to say, which was counterintuitive. After all, Agent Li had essentially painted a hopeless picture for me. Not necessarily the smartest move, putting someone like me into desperation mode. My questions got the better of me, though, even as I started to formulate a plan that involved using my guest as a human shield to help facilitate my escape. "Go on," I said without emotion.

"I'm Robb Foreman," he said, taking a step toward my chair.

If he was concerned about me being a threat, he hid it well. "Does my name sound familiar to you?"

I shrugged. "Are you the junior senator from Tennessee?" I didn't follow politics closely, but I knew the names of some of the notables, and he was definitely one of them. His name kept getting mentioned as a contender for the next presidential election.

"The very one," Foreman said, nodding his head. "I've come a long way to speak to you, Ms. Nealon."

"Question," I said, stopping him before he could get going. "What's to stop me from taking you hostage and using you as a human shield to walk out the front door?"

He grinned with a certain warmth. "You could always try it and find out, though I don't think you'll find the consequences agreeable or to your liking." I didn't love the sound of that, but I didn't say anything to it. After a moment, he went on. "Like I said, I've come a long way to see you."

"You could have 'seen' me from the other side of the glass," I said, nodding my head at the one-way mirror. "According to your Agent Li, this will be a common view of me pretty soon. He seemed to indicate I was heading toward—what do they call it nowadays? Oh, right—indefinite detention."

Foreman gave me a slow nod, his lips pursed. "That is a possibility. Murdering Parks, Clary, Kappler and Bastian?" He let a low whistle. "Cold-blooded. Premeditated. You can't even argue crime of passion on those because you planned it all out."

"Maybe I could argue self-defense," I said, keeping myself from showing emotion.

He gave me a slight shake of the head. "Never hold up in court, not with the evidence of the poison still in Parks's system or the elaborate means you used in that construction site to take out Clary." His face twisted, and I could see the discomfort exuding off him. "These are not the acts of a person who could argue self-defense."

"You didn't say Zack's name." I said it quietly, so quietly it was almost inaudible.

"No, I didn't," Foreman said, not taking his eyes off me. Mine came up and caught his, though, and I saw him smile in acknowledgment. No one could have heard me to be able to respond to it. No one human, anyway. "Yeah, I'm a meta," Foreman said, still smiling, but it was a tight one. "My wife is meta. My daughters are metas."

I stared back at him and something dawned on me. "That's why you're not scared to be in here alone with me."

He shrugged. "You're strong, but you're handcuffed, and you've got all your flesh except for your head covered. Under those conditions, I feel pretty comfortable that I could win a fight with you."

I held my hands up and clinked them as I pulled them to maximum extension. "What about without the cuffs?"

Foreman's eyebrow rose slowly. "I wouldn't care to chance it." He waved me off. "I'm not here to talk to you about a brawl for it all."

"Then what are you here to talk to me about?" I looked away again. "Here to give me the rundown of my crimes, like the Ghost of Christmas Past? Because I know what I've done, since I was there—"

His eyes danced and he cut me off. "I'm not here to talk about your past. I'm here to talk about your future."

I let my tongue roam over my back teeth as I bided my time, trying to wait for him to go on. He didn't, and my patience ran out, quickly. "According to Li, my future is the inside of a cell. And not five minutes ago, you made mention of that fact as well—"

"It's one possible future," Foreman agreed and took a step to his left, leaning against the edge of the one-way mirror. "It's hardly set in stone, though. There are ... other possibilities." His hands came to rest in the pockets of his jacket.

"Oh?" I kept my eyes on him then let them flicker to the mirrored glass, wondering if Li was behind them. "And what are those? The other possibilities?"

One of his hands came out of his pocket, something clenched within his fingers. He tossed it lightly, and it skittered across the table to come to rest in front of me. I didn't take my eyes off of him to look, though, I kept right on him, watching him watch me. He smiled, just a little at the corner of his mouth, a faint tug of the muscles, and he nodded his head at what he'd tossed at me.

My curiosity got the better of me and I broke away from his gaze to look. There was an open leather case resting on the table, a simple bifold that resembled a wallet. There was identification inside, something terribly familiar, something I'd used before. My picture rested inside, along with the letters FBI emblazoned across it. I sighed, and looked back up. "If you're going to charge me with impersonating an FBI agent, you're kind of wasting your time, aren't you? I mean, five murders—or four, or whatever—I think they'll probably keep me in jail for a long enough time, don't you? Assuming you even used the court system." I muttered the last bit.

"Maybe, maybe not, given your longevity." He ignored my last comment. "But you don't think I really came all the way here from Washington to discuss the fact that you have a fake FBI ID, do you? I mean, people commit those kinds of crimes all the time, they don't get a senator coming to them to talk while they're in stir."

"So what do you want?" I asked again, and all the fatigue of my trip, the tension from having been arrested and put into custody when I'd felt above the law, all of it came rushing down on me and I snapped at him. "What do you want from me in order to keep my future from being the one where I spend the rest of my life—which may end up damned short depending on how current events turn out—in a jail cell?"

"Look at the ID again," Foreman said gently.

I rolled my eyes. At a U.S. Senator. "I've seen it before. I've been carrying it for almost a year now—"

He cleared his throat. "No, you haven't." I glanced down. "You've been carrying one that says 'Sienna Clarke' on it. This one says—"

"Sienna Nealon," I breathed, reading my name off.

I looked up at Foreman, and he was smiling warily at me. "We seem to have something of a crisis on our hands here," Foreman said, and his smile disappeared. "Something about the extinction of all metakind? Well ... the U.S. government just lost its unofficial metahuman policing apparatus a couple weeks ago ..."

I blinked in surprise. "The Directorate?"

Foreman nodded, put a hand against the wall, and proceeded to lean heavily on it. "So ... how'd you like to avoid prison time by serving your country and helping us out of this mess?"

Chapter 4

I stared at him, not quite sure what to say. He stared back then spoke. "What are you thinking right now?"

"That old saying, 'Fool me once, shame on you, fool me twice, shame on me,' comes to mind."

"Have we fooled you before?" Foreman asked, folding his arms in front of him as he leaned next to the window.

"Not you, specifically," I said, "but one of your employees, apparently, since you just admitted the Directorate was your metahuman policing unit."

"Unofficially," Foreman said with a smile. "It generated its own revenue, had no ownership ties that could bind it to the government, and didn't share a single employee with us."

I puckered my lips and moved them to the side, contemplating. "But you gave them sanction?"

He bobbed his head. "We gave Erich Winter the latitude to do what needed to be done in that department. We provided him with full access to our databases, allowed him to use our agencies to create covers for his operatives, opened the door for him to do insider trading with government intel so he could keep the Directorate funded, and gave him a free hand to do what we couldn't after the Agency was destroyed. Imagine our surprise when he went rogue on us." Foreman gave me an unsubtle look. "I suppose you know a little of what that feels like."

I felt a subtle pressure of my teeth grinding together. Except it wasn't subtle at all. "Yes. I know what it feels like to be betrayed by Erich Winter."

"Like I said, we're in a bind." Foreman pushed off the wall and drew up to his full height. "See, we've read the tea leaves—

also known as the screaming of every single intelligence agency with any intelligence at all, planetwide—and we know the basics of what's happening in the meta world right now. But knowing what's coming without having the means to stop it is pretty damned useless."

"You want me to join you so I can be the means?" The weight of the handcuffs seemed to have vanished.

He nodded his head by inclining it sideways. "It'd be awfully tough for me to fight Century all by my lonesome."

"Give it a go," I said. "It could be fun."

Foreman grinned. "I don't think so." The smile vanished. "I'm not fond of the idea of giving a murderer an out, but I like it a lot better than the idea of walking into a fight with an organization composed of a hundred of the world's mightiest without at least one top-scaler on our own side. Especially when that top-scaler seems to be one that Century has taken a keen interest in for some reason. No, I like to hedge my bets, gamble as safely as possible."

I let it get quiet for a minute while I thought about what he was saying. "If I jump through your hoops and join your little version of Directorate, Part Deux ... once this is over, I get to walk free?"

Foreman looked suddenly wary. "You'll be given a pardon for any laws you may have broken while in the Directorate's employ and afterward, specifically with regard to the murders of M-Squad and Zack Davis because in a legalistic sense you did kill him, even if you didn't do it in a moral sense. You'll also be given a lot of free rein in the performance of your duties, meaning if you accidentally were to cause a civilian death in the course of fighting off this Century plot, or if you were to kill every single one of the members of that organization, you wouldn't be charged with those crimes—though you will be subject to oversight."

He paused, and I couldn't help but see the appeal of what he was offering. Still, I said nothing. He spoke again. "Let's think about this for a minute and assume somehow you broke out of custody sometime in the near future. You'd be on the run, the full weight of the United States law enforcement apparatus hunting you down. Let me tell you something: it ain't that easy to hide within our borders anymore when everyone's looking for you, not for long. You could try running to another country, but there aren't that many without extradition treaties that'd harbor you. Plus, you'd still have Century after you. If you want to fight them," he took a step toward me, looking down, arms still folded, "your best chance is with us."

I looked up at him and the staring contest recommenced. He was right, of course. Even if I broke out, the FBI would have a task force sniffing after me within hours. Air travel would become a virtual impossibility, which meant I'd be down to stealing cars and driving cross country like ... I paused, and thought of Mom, who had done something similar not that long ago. I put the thought out of my mind and focused back on Foreman. "If I do this, I walk free at the end?"

"If you help us stop Century from carrying out their plot, you will get your pardon, you have my word," Foreman said.

I wasn't much for trusting the word of a stranger at this point, but what choice did I have? I was bound hand and foot by metal cuffs, unable to move or walk effectively. Hell, I could just barely shake his hand if he were to offer it to me right now, and this was how it was going to be from now on. I looked from side to side, weighing my other options, which were laughable. My other option—and there was only one—was to say no. "What happens if I say no?"

He didn't show much emotion at that. "It doesn't pay to dwell too deeply on that, but I'll tell you the U.S. government has this new piece of property out in the desert in Arizona that we just seized from the previous owner. It's an underground prison. We had to do a bit of restaffing since Omega's assault on the place, but it's fully operational once more and there's plenty of room for another guest to stay there." He raised an eyebrow. "If need be."

I thought about it. "Someone told me once that you had your own prison."

He shook his head. "Never needed one. We handed over our captives to the Directorate."

I pictured Zack in my mind. "Why would someone lie about that?"

"They probably thought it was true," Foreman said. "If we wanted people to know we were in bed with the Directorate, we wouldn't have worked so hard to hide all the links." He was watching me carefully. "You're not asking the question."

I shrugged. "What question?"

"The obvious one," Foreman said. "The one that new senators and congressmen ask within minutes of being briefed on the existence of metahumans and our history policing them." Foreman leaned over to look me in the eyes, just a foot from my face. "You haven't asked why we didn't get back in that business after the Agency was destroyed."

I shrugged again. "I already know the answer." I waited for a reaction from him, but I got none. Recalling what I'd read in the file on the way over here, I kept going. "You don't have a direct meta policing Agency because Sovereign made it clear to you that if the United States Government ever opened one again, he'd scorch it to the ground along with whatever city it was standing in."

Foreman gave me a sad smile. "He did indeed. Everyone says he has the juice to carry through with that threat, too. But you have to admit, in light of everything that's going on right now, with his Boys and Girls Club so close to wiping out the rest of the meta species ... that just doesn't seem to matter all that much anymore."

Chapter 5

Foreman unlocked my hands and led me out of the confinement room. I was massaging my wrists the whole time but was so glad to be standing and walking that I ignored the feeling of pins and needles running down my legs which had partially fallen asleep from sitting in the same position for so long. I didn't much care for the feeling, but it passed quickly enough. Foreman led me into a dimly lit concrete hall. He beckoned me to follow him and I did, stopping outside the next door.

"What?" I was so fatigued I hadn't even asked him where we were going before we left the room. Not that I really needed a destination; I was sick enough of the confinement room that he could have told me he was leading me off to dump my body in a nearby swamp and I'd likely have gone along willingly.

"Go in," Foreman said, scanning a key card from his pocket against the panel next to the door.

I waited for him to open it, but I'm sure a quizzical expression crossed my features. "And do what?"

"The first part of your job for us," Foreman said, straitlaced and quiet now.

I tried to think it out, but was just too tired. "Unless Sovereign is standing behind that door and you want me to beat him to death, I'm going to need more direction."

"You'll see," Foreman said, and there was a squeal of the door handle as he started to open it. "You're not just the tip of the spear for us, not just here to get in fights and get your knuckles bloody. We need more from you than that."

I let out an exhausted sigh. "You've got me over a barrel here, and I'm friggin' exhausted, so if you could just please spit out what you want me to do and be specific, that'd be great."

"You'll need a team," Foreman said, annoying the hell out of me with his wise man routine. He opened the door the rest of the way and then indicated I should enter. "Start here. I'll wait outside. Knock on the door when you're done."

I wanted to glare at him but I didn't have the energy, so I just stepped into the room. It was a cell not unlike the one I'd just been in. There was a man sitting in middle of it, though he was on the floor, his chair already a shattered mess, broken into pieces just underneath the one-way window. I recognized him instantly by his curly blond locks and his ruddy complexion, and he jolted upright at the sight of me, rising to his feet.

"I see you went with the rebellious option," I said to Scott Byerly as Foreman closed the door behind me, locking me in with my friend in the otherwise empty cell.

He gave me a dismissive incline of the head, a half-shrug. "Like I know any other way."

I felt the tension bleed out of me in a half-laugh. I closed the distance to him in two steps and threw my arms around his neck and pulled close, taking care not to knock him off balance. For metas, with our super strength, this is a very real concern. I felt him reciprocate, his strong arms crossing my back, and I let out a little laugh that was halfway between a choked cry and a sob of joy. "I'm so glad to see you, Scott."

"It's only been a couple weeks," he said as we pulled back from each other.

"I know," I said, "but it feels like ... months."

He nodded. "It's been a long couple of weeks. Since ..." His face fell. "Since Kat. Since the Directorate." He looked around. "Looks like it could be a lot longer. What false charge did they drum up to bring you in on?"

I felt my excitement at seeing him fade. "Murder." He seemed to freeze, stuck in place, trying to control his surprise. "Clary,

Parks, Kappler, Bastian." I forced a fake smile. "So ... they didn't have to do much making up in that department."

"Geez," he almost whispered and looked around his small cell. "Okay, wow. Well, that's, um ..." He rested a hand on my shoulder and for some reason I felt great reassurance from it. "I take it they broke the news to you that you wouldn't be seeing a lawyer anytime soon?"

I smiled. "I don't think we're gonna need one."

He almost did a double take at me then did a slow nod of understanding. "You're here because you cut a deal."

"I'm here because they offered me a 'Get Out of Jail Free' card."

He let a low sigh then jammed his hands in the pockets of his navy pullover, which was tight on his muscular frame. "There's no such thing as a 'Get Out of Jail Free' card."

I gave him a wan smile. "What, you've never played Monopoly?"

"You know what I mean, Sienna," he said, and I could tell he was cross, getting more irritable by the moment. "They want something in exchange."

"Yeah," I agreed, "but it's something I was gonna do anyway, so I'm fine with the exchange rate on this one."

He gave me a wary glance. "Really? You think the U.S. government is just going to let you skate on four murders because you run some errands for them?"

I let my head drift sideways as I looked up, pondering it. "When the errand involves beating Century to save the whole human race, I think it might justify my price."

He frowned. "What's Century?"

I felt myself pause, as if the gears in my head had seized up. How could he not know? "They're the ones who are trying to wipe out metakind. Didn't we talk about this last time we met?"

"I was drunk, right?" His face contorted into disbelief.

"'Metakind'? That's a thing now? And Century? Really? That's their name?" He forced a tight smile that showed me all his even, shiny front teeth. "Whatever. After that—assuming you pull it off, you think the government is just going to let you walk free?"

"What are my alternatives, Scott?" I said, letting a little bit of my exasperation show through. He could be such a difficult horse's ass sometimes, and I wasn't in the mood for having this discussion, especially since I was fully aware that now that they had their hooks in me, I might not ever pry them out again. "Spend the rest of my life in jail, waiting for Sovereign and his Gang of One Hundred to wipe us all out to the last meta?" I shrugged. "Wait for an opening to stage a jailbreak, then try and stop Century while simultaneously on the run?"

He sighed, a low, loud one. "Jailbreak then a flight to Bora Bora, I'd say."

"That's really helpful."

He shrugged his arms expansively, and I caught a hint from his expression of just how in over our heads he thought we were. "I don't know anything about this Century group—"

"They wiped out Omega," I said. "Wiped them out to such a degree that I ended up in charge of what's left."

"What?" His face was scrunched, like he was trying to sort through what I'd just said. "You mean there's nothing left of them, right?"

"No ..." I said.

Scott frowned. "You? In charge of them? Like ... were you elected or something?"

"By the survivors, yeah," I said. "Not much group cohesion left. Janus and Kat are basically the only ones left alive from old Omega." Scott's lips puckered at the mention of Kat's name. "Anyway, these guys, Century—run all you want, they will eventually find you, even in Bora Bora." I bowed my head. "We're being offered a chance to use our training to stop this threat. For me, it's a chance to start over." I felt a twinge of something—guilt, I was almost certain. "A clean slate."

Scott let hang a silence between us for a minute as his face went through a cavalcade of emotions, all of which seemed to be a struggle for him. "Well, I'm happy for you."

"Be happy for yourself, too," I said. "Because you get the same deal."

He let out a little scoff. "I haven't done anything wrong. These charges are bullshit and I will fight them."

"No, you won't," I said, shaking my head slowly. "Because even if you could stomach the thought of sitting on the sidelines while I'm fighting—" he started to say something in protest but stifled himself before I had to, "you know that every meta who dies between now and when you 'get out'—if you get out—is one you might have been able to help save if you'd been working with me instead of twisting around like a wild bull trying to avoid the lasso."

There was a long pause, and his frown expressed near disbelief. "A bull dodging a lasso? Really?"

I shrugged. "Zack took me to a rodeo once. It fits."

He looked utterly disgusted, but I saw the concession on his face. "Fine." He threw up his arms. "Fine, I'll help. But not to save my own ass." His look softened. "I'm doing this because you need someone who's going to watch your back while you're involved in this deal with the devil."

I gave him a weak smile. "I don't think the U.S. government is the devil."

He gave me a wary look. "They threaten to charge you with murder—"

"Which I'm guilty of."

He kept going as if I hadn't said anything, "—then offer you a deal overlooking said murders if you work with them." He shook his head. "Doesn't sound like the forces of good and righteousness to me."

I felt a tightness in my jaw as I walked to the door and pounded on it once, hard. "It sounds like pragmatism to me. Like they acknowledge that they're in a hard place and need help. Real help."

Scott followed me to the door, standing only a foot behind me as I waited for it to open, and his face split into a wide grin. "Then why the hell are they coming to you and me?"

I heard a lock sliding and I could have sworn a draft was sweeping in under the door because I felt a chill. While I waited for it to open, I looked at Scott and gave him a sad look, one that wiped the smile entirely off his face.

"Because we're all that's left."

Chapter 6

Foreman led us down the hall a little farther, Scott glaring at the senator with eyes like daggers. I didn't know what Foreman's power was, but I hoped it wasn't the ability to sense when someone was giving you dirty looks while your back was turned.

The hall was long and dim, and when we stopped outside the next cell, Foreman paused, holding out the FBI ID he'd thrown at my feet earlier, along with another that had Scott's picture on it. "You'll be needing these."

I took mine from his hand and gave it a once over before sliding it into the pocket of my jeans. Then I clipped the badge onto the bottom of my untucked blouse. I watched Scott look at his with utter distaste before pocketing the ID in his pullover.

"Got a couple more stops to make here," Foreman said, and rapped his dark knuckles against the metal door. "None of our people have spoken to this one yet. Been stewing since they got here—"

"Dodging gender pronouns so you can be mysterious doesn't really get you any points with me," I said. "My last boss did the vague and mysterious act a lot, too."

Foreman gave me a broad grin. "In my case, I'm doing it for my own entertainment. I love the emotion of surprise. I think most people do, actually. We love the reaction when two unexpected characters meet again after a long absence, love seeing the emotional spinout from it. We love cliffhangers where the music swells, and we're left wondering how they'll play out when we come to the scene again. People love surprise, to not know what's going to come next. It gets them through their days."

I clicked my teeth together in annoyance. "Not everybody

loves surprise."

He shrugged. "I do, and since I'm running the show ..." He threw the door open and gestured for me to enter.

I sighed and did so as he moved out of the way, revealing a woman sitting on a cot at the edge of the room.

"You," Ariadne said with a hint of surprise, her red hair ratty and knotted as if it hadn't been washed in a couple days. "I should have known you were behind this." Her eyes were wild, her face in near disbelief. "It wasn't enough that you had to kill her, now you get your revenge on me, too? Having me locked away—"

"Don't get your panties in a twist," I said, cutting her off. "I didn't have anything to do with you being imprisoned." I looked back at Foreman, who was standing at the door, still holding it open, unconcerned about Ariadne taking flight. "What's this about?"

Foreman raised an eyebrow at me. "We're effectively picking up the pieces of the Directorate. We need an administrator who can run things—with appropriate legislative oversight, of course." He smiled disingenuously.

I looked back at Ariadne and avoided saying something untoward. "She's certainly capable of that."

"Oh, really?" Ariadne said and stood up from the edge of the cot. Her pants were smudged, and she had an odor about her that told me it had indeed been a few days since she'd had human contact. There was a toilet and a sink in the corner of the room and that was about it. The room was set up for longer-term stays than the interrogation room I'd been in. "I guess that's high praise coming from you." Her eyes darted from me to Foreman. "Senator."

"Miss Fraser," Foreman replied deferentially.

"What are you doing here?" Ariadne said, looking pointedly at me, "if you're not responsible for this?"

"That's a funny answer," Scott said under his breath.

Foreman made a slight noise that sounded like a cross between a cough and a laugh.

"Apparently, I'm here to recruit you because the senator thinks you'll listen to me," I said, and felt a sudden sense of discomfort.

Ariadne stared at me, and I caught a flicker of her distaste for me. "I guess he doesn't know us very well, then."

"I guess not."

There was a moment of silence as we all tried to adjust to the atmosphere in the room, and Ariadne looked past me to Foreman, now pensive. "Recruit me for what? To run a new Directorate?"

"Yes," Foreman said. "Under the direct supervision of the U.S. government."

Ariadne played it cool. "Because last time it worked out so well."

Foreman shrugged. "The guy who destroyed the Agency seems hell bent on wiping out the whole meta race, so why refrain from pissing him off now? Seems like his ire is already directed at us as it is."

I thought about speaking up, about telling them that it wasn't really Sovereign running the extinction program, but Weissman— that oily, nasty bastard who was Sovereign's number two in charge of Century. Something stopped me, though, as if I would be speaking out of turn, so I kept it to myself.

"Yeah, well," Ariadne said and sat back down on her cot, the edge of a threadbare blanket crumpling as she moved it to sit, "I've already worked for a metahuman policing outfit once. I think I'd like to take my career in some different directions."

Scott and I exchanged a look, then I cast my gaze to Senator Foreman. He appeared to give it a moment's thought. "Fair enough. How about making license plates for the State of Minnesota?"

I'd seen Ariadne cowed before; she was made of relatively

stern stuff but she was still human. The threat of jail time took any starch out of her as quickly as anything I'd ever seen. She opened her mouth then closed it quickly, as though she were stammering without any sound coming out. "I ..." she said finally, "I ... don't think that's quite the career opportunity I had in mind."

Foreman shrugged. "You've had involvement in running an organization that hasn't paid taxes for its entire existence and has run an insider trading outfit based on stealing government secrets." He didn't smile at her, even though he knew he had her. "I used to be a U.S. Attorney, did you know that? By my reckoning that makes for racketeering charges, tax evasion, fraud, espionage, insider trading ... need I go on?"

Ariadne looked faint and shifted her gaze to me. "And you? You're part of this?"

I felt a swell of pity for her. "For me, the charges were murder times four, but yeah. I'm motivated to work for the senator to make those go bye bye, same as you."

She shifted her gaze weakly back to Foreman. "That's some powerful coercive influence you're wielding, sir."

Foreman stared back at her, impassive. "I'm a politician. Coercion is part of the job, though I usually don't have to apply it quite so bluntly."

Ariadne stood again quietly and stared down at the bare concrete floor, as though trying to make up her mind. "What do you want me to do?" she asked finally, her voice reflective of how broken she truly was.

"Congratulations," Foreman said, "you are now the chief administrator of the Metahuman Policing and Threat Response Task Force. You'll be running the entire administrative apparatus—finance, intelligence gathering, liaising with the Department of Homeland Security, everything except ops—but you'll work directly with the head of operations to support them as they run response during this crisis."

Ariadne stared blankly at him and then tried to muster her dignity by straightening her worn and dirty clothing. "All right. I'll need to assemble my department. When do I meet the head of operations?"

"Oh, you already know her quite well," Foreman said casually, and I felt his heavy hand land on my shoulder. I looked up at him in alarm and saw the smile on his face. "What? I told you I love surprises."

Chapter 7

"I have to work for her?" Ariadne's voice was strained, bitter disbelief seeping into it.

"You don't *have* to," Foreman said seriously. "The women's correctional unit at Shakopee is always an alternative."

I saw the slightest hint of irritation from Ariadne at his threat; the skin around her jaw got tight and her brow creased. "Fine. I'll work with her." She trembled slightly, her lips becoming a thin, straight line. "If you can make her work with me."

Foreman gave me a sidelong glance, and just beyond him I caught sight of Scott watching the whole thing with a barely disguised look of shock. "I have faith that she'll gladly work with you," Foreman said to Ariadne then gripped my shoulder more tightly, "because she's very motivated to make this partnership work, in order to avoid the consequences of failure. Isn't that right, Ms. Nealon?"

I couldn't decide if he was referring to the extinction of the metahuman species or the fact that I could potentially spend the rest of my very long life in a cell in the Arizona desert. Neither of those was very appealing, actually. "Oh, yes," I said, with only a little sarcasm. "Very motivated."

"Good," Foreman said, and stepped out the door, gesturing for the three of us to follow him out into the hallway. Once we did, he pointed at a far distant door at the end of the hall, something that seemed like it was a mile away. "Mr. Byerly, Ms. Fraser, if you'd make your way through that door, one of my aides is waiting with Mr. Li and they'll start making arrangements for you to put together what you need." He whipped his gaze to me. "You and I have one last stop."

"Oh, good," I said, feigning breathless anticipation. "Is this going to be another one of your surprises?" I shot Scott a supportive look as he broke off to head down the hallway toward the door that Foreman had indicated. He gave me one back, something in the vein of *Be careful*, though it was mixed with some other emotions that I couldn't figure out immediately.

"Of course," Foreman said in his deep timbre. We stopped outside a door that had a number twelve on a placard above it. "What's life without a little surprise? Boring, right? I mean, if you just have the same thing over and over again, totally expected, it's kind of like only having one season."

"The irony being that this is Minnesota," I said. "The only place where the winters are longer than here is Westeros."

"It's the change," Foreman said, not losing his enthusiasm as he went on. "The same season on and on and on is boring, just the same as one note dragging along isn't music. Surprise is when the change comes and you don't expect it." He clicked the lock and nodded, preparing to open the door. "So ... are you ready for your next surprise?"

"Sure," I said without any of his enthusiasm and stepped in as he opened the door for me.

The fist hit me squarely in the side of the head as I walked in, blindsided by a sucker punch that had a lot of power behind it. I hit the wall with my shoulder, and there was a flashing of lights in my vision that couldn't be accounted for by the single, spare light source in the room. Something like dancing multicolored fireflies sprinkled all around my vision. I knew enough to throw my left arm up and it blocked the next hit, knocking it aside as I tried to recover and turn my head to catch a glimpse of my would-be attacker.

Foreman beat me to the punch. The senator unleashed an uppercut that knocked my assailant back, catching her - and it took me a moment to process that it was a her - on the chin and causing long brown hair to flash between the fireflies in my vision. I couldn't help but feel that if I could have seen the person who'd attacked me, I might have known her. I watched her roll back from Foreman's blow, springing to her feet in a move that was all too familiar—something I did all the time when I got knocked down.

I had my hands up in a defensive posture, ready for another attack, my head clearing as I looked at my assailant while Foreman stood just slightly to my left, helping me form a defensive line between our opponent and the door. I wanted to be shocked at the realization of who it was, but I was still clearing the cobwebs out of my head from nearly getting my skull caved in.

"Oh, God," came her voice, annoyingly familiar, staring back at me over raised fists, defensively placed in almost a mirror image of my own. Which was unsurprising, considering that she'd taught me almost everything I knew about fighting. "They got you too?"

"Hi, Mom," I said, still feeling the unpleasant sharpness of her punch to the side of my head.

I turned my head just slightly to look at Foreman, and he gave me a sympathetic shrug. "Surprise?" he offered weakly.

"Your surprises suck," I said.

Chapter 8

"I'm not really interested in working for the government again," my mother said a few minutes later, after Foreman had explained what he had in mind. I had stood quiet the entire time, next to the door, ready to bail. "I've trod that path before. I left and got into radiology so I could do something safer."

"While training your daughter to be a street brawler on your nights and weekends," Foreman added.

My mother's already severe expression became more stern. "It's dangerous out there, Senator. Surely a man as worldly as yourself must realize that by now."

"Indeed it is," Foreman replied. "Which is why I'm looking for some help to make it less dangerous."

My mother laughed lightly. "Good luck with that."

"I'll take luck," Foreman said, reminding me of how he'd gotten reserved every time before he'd sprung an unpleasant threat on me. "But I could use some more help."

My mother rolled her eyes. "I don't know what kind of help you think you're going to need, but it isn't enough. Whoever your enemy is, they've got a Hades-type at their disposal."

"No, they don't," I said. "Your Uncle Raymond is dead."

She looked at me like I'd grown a second head. "My uncle who?"

"Their Hades-type was your uncle," I said. "Your mother's brother, Raymond. He died in London a couple days ago."

My mother actually looked a little dumbstruck for once, like I'd caught her off-balance. "Wait ... their Hades was my uncle? How do you know this?"

"I was there when he died," I said. "He told me he'd met you once, a long time ago, when you were a kid."

My mother frowned. "I think ... maybe I vaguely remember him. Kind of a big guy?" She frowned, as though trying to recall. "When I met him, he had this pompadour hairdo, though of course that's long ago out of style—" She stopped at my pained expression. "Still had it, huh?" I nodded. "Sorry, Uncle Raymond," she muttered under her breath.

"As lovely as this familial introspectionis," Foreman said, sounding more patient than he probably was, "I have a specific purpose for this conversation and sharing can wait until later." He looked back at my mother. "You have a variety of criminal charges leveled against you, and there's a hell of a threat coming our way from a man named Sovereign." Foreman looked at my mother, whose eyes became very wide, very suddenly. "I believe you might be passingly familiar with him."

She hissed like a snake, mad as I'd ever seen her. "I'm familiar with him, yes. What the hell does he want? Other than hearing rumors about a Hades making its way through Europe, I'm a bit ... out in the cold." She looked a little chagrined, and I caught her gaze and it revealed something I had rarely seen from her—a kind of desperation that made her willing to ask questions that revealed her weakness, her ignorance.

"He's formed an organization called Century that's dedicated to wiping out every meta on the planet," Foreman said.

She frowned then looked at me. "No, really. What's he up to?"

I waited just a second for it to sink in and spoke. "Really. That's what he's up to. He's making a pretty good show of it, too, down to just North and South America."

Her nostrils flared. "This is a little more ambitious than I would have given him credit for."

I stared back at her. "He wiped out the Agency, didn't he?" I waited for my mother to answer, but she said nothing, steel-eyed and sullen.

"Yes, well," Foreman said, "past history aside, you have a decision to make. Are you in or are you out? If you're in, I'll cut you loose right now." He narrowed his eyes and leaned forward, pointing at her with one finger. "But if you betray me, I will send everything I have at you with an order to bring you in dead. Not alive, just dead."

My mother gave me a look out of the corner of her eye. "Did he offer you this same charming deal?"

Foreman leaned back and folded his arms. "I didn't have to. She's not as much of a flight risk as you are and doesn't have connections everywhere in the country that would allow her to go underground for months or years."

She wavered just a little. I saw it in the shape of her mouth as she came close to chewing her bottom lip, a dead giveaway that she was experiencing a moment of doubt. I saw it on those precious few occasions when she had started to punish me, to put me in the box, but I managed to talk her out of it. They were few indeed. "Did they offer you the same deal?" she asked me.

I looked to Foreman, who nodded at me as if to give me the go-ahead to talk about it. I cleared my throat. "I dunno. What crimes did they threaten to charge you with?"

A brief look of surprise crossed her face. "Crimes? I got thrown in here without any idea of who I was even dealing with, though I guessed government after I saw the place. Too big to be a private concern. So ... what 'crimes' did he get you on?"

"I bet the surprise is going to be good on this one," Foreman murmured quietly.

"Murder," I'd had to admit to being accused of murder on three separate occasions in the last half hour, and as I watched my mother's face deteriorate into shock, I realized that she was the only one of the three of us who even seemed surprised by it.

"Who did you kill?" she asked when she found her voice

again. "Erich Winter?"

I looked to Foreman before I spoke. "We've got you dead to rights," he said, as if he sensed my hesitation. "Fingerprints, physical evidence, traffic camera photos. It'd be a slam dunk to convict you, so you might as well tell her, because you've already incriminated yourself enough for me."

I tried to be cool. "No, I didn't kill Erich Winter. That would fall under attempted murder, though. I was accused," I said, putting the emphasis on the word, "of killing the four members of M-Squad." I smiled sarcastically at Foreman, and he nodded his head at me.

"Did you now?" Mother didn't seem impressed. "M-Squad was that group of metas who were Erich Winter's personal lapdogs, weren't they?"

"Yes," I said quietly.

"Uh huh," she said, and I could see the wheels turning. She looked up at Foreman. "Your terms are acceptable. I give you my word that I won't run, for a variety of reasons, not the least of which is that Sovereign is the most dangerous son of a bitch I've ever met in my life and if he's plotting something involving wiping out our species ... he'll probably succeed unless you have someone with some brains and skill to stop him."

"Well, we have your daughter," Foreman said.

"I said brains and skill, Senator," my mother said, "not a girl who follows her genitals in whatever direction they lead like a bitch in heat."

"Oh, screw you," I said and turned to Foreman. "Can we just leave her in here?"

"She's a valuable resource, having seen your enemy face to face," Foreman said. He wagged a finger at my mother. "You'll be answering to your daughter as she's running the operations side of our new agency."

"*What?*" Her shock was palpable. "Who have you got running

the finance department? An infant with a sliding abacus in their crib?"

"I considered an aging radiologist I know for that job," I said. "But I'm not sure she could hack it, since I overtook her level of learning in math when I turned thirteen."

My mother seethed a little then tried to put on a polite face. "Fine. I will ... deal with you placing my daughter in a superior position in order to secure my freedom. That doesn't seem to be totally unreasonable. You have to suffer to get what you want, after all."

I bit back an angry reply that was ringing in my head, something about suffering and not getting what I wanted for years and years. It was pointless, though, bickering with her. The tables had turned in title, if not in fact, and somehow I was now in charge of her. That boggled the mind. "That's very mature of you," I said, without even bothering to throw some emphasis on the word mature. She caught it anyway and gave me a narrowing of her eyes in response.

"All right," Foreman said, and gestured toward the open door. "Now we've got a basic working group, so we can start hammering out everything we know and everything we need to start doing."

I walked out of the cell first, warily, keeping one eye on my mother as I edged out the door. She caught me looking and nodded subtly. I knew what she was thinking; she was pleased as punch that she'd suckered me on the way in the door. It was her way of reminding me to always be vigilant. Tempted as I was to repay the favor by bludgeoning her with something heavy the first time she turned her back, I promised myself I would resist the temptation. Probably.

"We need to set up fast," Foreman said. I walked on the left side of the hallway; my mother was an arm's length away at my right, and the two of us only had eyes for each other, watching as though each of us was a heartbeat away from striking the other. "Our latest intel suggests that Weissman—Century's leading man, second in command next to Sovereign—is in Rio de Janeiro. He's got a net of telepaths working the streets, tracking down the metas." He stopped just outside the door that he'd sent Ariadne and Scott through earlier, and indicated for me to run my ID badge across a metal strip nearby, which I did. The door buzzed and opened, and we walked through a guardroom where we were greeted by two men with AR-15s pointed at us. "Sentinel," Foreman announced, and the men lowered their weapons. He glanced back at us. "Prearranged code word. If I hadn't given it within five seconds of walking through the door, they would have opened fire."

"Clever," Mother said, unimpressed. "We used to do something similar at the Agency."

We walked on, and I suppressed my desire to make another joke about her age, something about being on the cutting edge back in the 1890s. I tried to remind myself I was a better person, and I caught a vague whiff of disagreement from the souls I'd thrown in their own little boxes in my mind. It may have been me arguing with myself, for all I knew.

We passed the door behind the guards and found ourselves in a more open space. Foreman led us down a carpeted hall and knocked on the door of a room labeled "Conference 4." He entered without bothering to wait for a response.

It was tense inside, with three people spaced around a long, rectangular conference table. I took one look at Ariadne, seated near one end of the table, Scott, across from her, and Agent Li, sitting in the middle, and wondered what the hell had happened in this room to make my mother and I walking in together actually lower the tension level. I started to voice that thought, but Senator Foreman took a seat at the end of the table and waved for us to do the same. I made my way over to Scott and sat down, across from

Agent Li and just a couple seats from where Foreman had sat. My mother made her way to the opposite end from Foreman and took it, staring down the long table at him with Ariadne directly to her right.

"Let's get this discussion under way," Foreman said, surveying all of us. "Welcome to the first advisory council meeting of the Metahuman Policing and—"

"Whatever," my mother said, interrupting. "Let's just call this what it is to spare us an unwieldy acronym—Agency 2.0."

Foreman appeared ready to argue for just a beat, then he seemed to pause. "Fair enough. For the sake of expediency." He looked around the table. "To start with, let me state that Ariadne Fraser will handle the administrative side of this new venture— which is strictly off the books, in spite of sharing intelligence developed by the CIA, NSA, Homeland Security and other departments. She will be reporting to Congress and the Executive Branch. Sienna Nealon will be our head of operations, and Agent Li will be your liaison and oversight for the foreseeable future." Foreman looked from Li to us. "He'll be here to make certain you stay within the boundaries and guidelines wherever possible, since he has experience with FBI procedures already."

"Lovely," my mother opined from the end of the table. "It's always nice to have a professional on the team. Maybe it'll help make up for the amateur in charge of operations."

"You know what?" I asked. "I bet I've bagged more wildfire metas in the last year than you have."

"I think we can agree you've probably bagged more men in the last year than I have," she said acidly.

"If we're talking body bags, I bet it's neck and neck," I shot back. "Though I probably haven't smacked around nearly as many unsuspecting convenience store clerks, if we're keeping count of those—"

"No mother/daughter cat fights on company time, ladies,"

Foreman said, unamused.

"I could host one later, if you want," Scott said, drawing a glare from Foreman. "Sorry."

"So tell me about this 'Century.'" My mother looked attentively down the table, waiting expectantly.

Foreman looked at me, and it took me a minute to realize this was my department. "Uhm," I said, and listened to my mother cough quietly. "Let me start with the basics. By the accounts I've heard, there are one hundred of them—one hundred of the strongest metas on the planet. Their immediate goal is to wipe out the competition, at which point we've speculated there's some unknown 'Phase Two' that relates to subjugating humanity." I cleared my throat. "As for what we know specifically about them, it's very little. Sovereign is at their head, though I haven't run across anyone able to give me a description of him—"

"He looks to be in his early forties, olive skin, dark, curly hair," my mother said pointedly. She looked over at me and I could see Li across the table, scribbling furiously on a notepad. "Talks in a deep voice, with a thousand years of accumulated confidence that says, 'Don't mess with me because I never lose a fight.'" She folded her hands on the table. "He's powerful. More powerful than any meta I've ever come across. He can do things I've never seen, and since I hunted wildfire metas for several years and accumulated the best record in the Agency for capturing them," she looked at me pointedly, "that says something."

"I can get some sketch artists working on his face," Li said, looking up at Foreman.

"Don't waste too much of your time," I said. "One of Sovereign's powers is to change his appearance."

There was a moment's quiet. "How do you know that?" Foreman asked.

I tried to remember; I thought I had heard it in a flashback involving Adelaide, a mysterious Omega operative who'd apparently killed my Grandfather, but it was vague, fuzzy. I couldn't be sure, so I lied for the sake of convenience. "It was in a record I retrieved from Omega."

"Speaking of Omega," my mother said, "I don't care for them, but they could be useful in a threat situation like this. It sounds like we have a common enemy."

Foreman looked at me. "We might as well ask the Primus of Omega what she thinks." There was an uneasy silence as I realized that he and I might have been the only ones at the table that knew what he was hinting at.

My mother's sigh was loud enough to fill the room. "Yes, that was my suggestion, to parlay with Omega's Primus, though—and I admit my information could be out of date—when last I heard, it was a man named Gerasimos and had been for several hundred years."

"There's a new one now," Foreman said dryly.

"Oh?" My mother's impatience was her undoing here; she was walking right into the rake that Foreman set out for her. "How soon can you make contact? They have a lot more resources to draw on than you might expect."

"I'd say we can make contact very quickly." Foreman angled his head toward me. "What do you say? Are the resources of Omega at our disposal?"

"Such as they are," I said. "The remaining operatives in England will need visas—"

"Oh, dear God," my mother said. "YOU?" She swore under her breath, but we all heard it. "How did you become the Primus of Omega?"

I inclined my head slightly. "There weren't many people left—"

"There would have to be nobody left," she grumbled.

"Well, it's pretty damned close to that," I said back, not keeping the heat out of my reply. She wasn't wrong, but it was still annoying.

"Give me their names and I'll make sure we don't run into any problems," Foreman said. "We're cooperating with the UK government on this, so I suspect I might even be able to expedite things on their end as well."

"That'd be good," I said. "There are a few of them whose help I'd like, especially for field operations."

Foreman nodded. "So ... what's your first order of business?"

I froze and felt my mouth go dry. There was hot air blowing directly on me from the duct above, the smell of the furnace-heated air heavy in the room. I looked around the table from Foreman's earnest mien to Li's slightly hostile stare to Ariadne, who wasn't even looking at me. My mother was staring coldly, and I came back to the empty hardwood space in front of me. "Um, well—"

"Our fearless leader," my mother sighed.

Something snapped in my head and I felt rage flood me, a kind of cold anger that fueled my thoughts and made them race faster. "First priority is identifying the metas presently in the U.S."

Foreman nodded. "Then what?"

My mind raced back to the preliminary thinking I'd done while I was on the flight back from London, hashing over ideas with Reed and the others before I'd left. "Two parts to that—one is to start bringing whoever we can under our protective aegis—"

"Brilliant," my mother said, "round them all up strategically in one location. I'm just now realizing that's what happened in China and India. It wasn't an accident of fate at all, not some random hostilities or regional conflict." She wore a look of calculated ill ease—which is to say she was pissed and trying not to show it. "That was the opening salvos in this campaign to wipe out metahumans. They clustered them together and made them the low-hanging fruit of the equation. Now the first part of your plan is to re-enact it?"

"We have to do something to try and protect them," I said.

"Rounding them up like you're suggesting just makes them easier to kill," she replied. "If you want to protect them, disperse them further."

"Century will wipe them out a cloister at a time," I said, "then go after the spares with mercenaries or some of their other members."

"Let's table this part of the discussion for now," Foreman said. "You mentioned a second reason to start sniffing out the metas in the U.S. What is it?"

I felt myself blush a little. My idea was starting to sound stupid, and my first instinct was to get flustered, just like I always had when mother called me out on something I was doing wrong. "Well, uh ..."

"'Well, uh,'" my mother said. "Spit it out."

I didn't look at her. "We speculate that Century is tracking down uncloistered metas by using telepaths. So if we can find those telepaths first—"

"You can take them out and seriously hamper Century's tracking efforts," Foreman said shrewdly and shot a look at Li. "Any idea how to do that?" His gaze came back to me and I could see he was giving it serious thought.

"They only have the capability to sweep a few cities at a time," I said. "I'm not exactly sure how telepaths work, but from what we do know, they come into a town trying to get a reading on metas, then capture a few so that they can try and use them to locate any friends or acquaintances that these individuals might have who are also metahuman."

"Like links in a chain," Scott said with a nod. "Makes sense. If you're a meta, odds are overwhelming your family is as well, that someone up the tree came from a cloister or knows others who are metas. We're all connected, except for wildfire metas and a few other loners. You just keep following that chain in both directions until you reach the end, then try and get hold of another chain and another until there are none left."

"An apt metaphor," I said. "And they're cutting more links out all the time. If Weissman's in Rio, they'll be putting all their attention there for the time being. Except for Sovereign."

"Oh?" My mother gave me a questioning look. "You know something else about him?"

"I guess I'm a priority for him," I said, feeling myself flush. "Not sure why, but Weissman said I'm the only meta outside Century that he's categorically forbidden to kill."

Scott gave me a funny look. "How'd you make the list?"

"If I knew, I'd tell you," I said. "There are some things going on with Century that make no sense at all. Like, remember when they tried to kill us in the woods, when they shot Andromeda? But now they're not allowed to kill me? Weissman said that was direct from Sovereign. Same with this whole extinction protocol: Weissman said it's his program, that Sovereign doesn't really care about it. Meanwhile, Raymond told me that Sovereign and Century are going to make the world a better place by removing the old order of metas and putting a new one in power." I shrugged. "I don't know. It's like we're in the middle of this giant puzzle, and there just aren't enough pieces in place for us to see the entire thing yet."

A pall hung over the conference room. "Who would have the answers?" Li asked, watching me with a measured gaze.

"Sovereign," I said. "Weissman. The other members of the one hundred." I sighed. "But I don't know who any of the others are."

"So we have two problems that need solving," Li said. "One, we need to gather intelligence to ascertain where metas are located in the U.S. regardless of what we decide to do with them. Second, we need to discover any Century operatives within our borders, and—obviously this would be much worse—any operating within the government or even our new agency. Counterintelligence," he finished, "in order to fend off their efforts against us."

I leaned my head back against the worn leather headrest of the chair. "That's a tall order, and we can't even do it by traditional means."

"Because of telepaths?" Li asked after a moment's hesitation.

"Yes," I said.

"There aren't that many telepaths in the world," my mother spoke up from her end of the table. "If there are only a hundred metas in Century, I can almost promise you that they can't have gathered more than ten telepaths at most to be part of their number."

Foreman placed fingers on his chin, contemplative. "How do you know that?"

My mother smiled. "With the Agency, we started to track the basic disposition of metas by type. Pure telepaths are rare. If Century got their hands on ten, it'd be probably half of the current supply worldwide. More now, I suppose."

Scott leaned forward. "Is it possible they could be tracking metas through other means?"

"Cloisters," I said. "They're a good starting point, since they're essentially communities where almost everyone is a meta. I don't know how well a telepath can sift a brain, but my impression would seem to suggest that they can go through it like—"

"Like you or I would with our touch," my mother said. "They just don't have the touch requirement, and can do it without anyone but a very well-trained person knowing that they've done it."

"So a telepath could sit at the edge of a cloister," Scott said, talking it out, "and just dig through the inhabitants one by one, pulling out their memories of every meta they've ever had contact with?"

My mother nodded slowly. "Yep. Depending on the strength of the telepath, they could be as close as a few hundred feet away or as far as hundreds of miles."

I chewed my lip. "Or more. Some can do more." Everyone looked at me. "I'm pretty sure Zollers touched my mind from a lot farther away, unless he followed me to England."

"Maybe he was in England?" Scott asked.

"He touched my mind only a few days earlier when I was still here in Minneapolis," I said. "So unless he traveled in the intervening time, I think we can safely assume that the range might be longer in certain circumstances."

I looked around and saw my mother contemplating that, deep in thought. "Maybe because he'd touched your mind before? That could have had something to do with it, helped him find you, the lone grain of sand in the middle of a beach."

I played her statement back in my mind again, searching for the sarcasm, the barb. I didn't hear it. "Maybe."

"So, for agenda," Foreman said, and I looked over to find him writing on a small, pocket-sized notepad, "so far, I've got inventorying the metas presently in the U.S., gathering intelligence, and setting up counterintelligence in preparation for Century's first moves ... what else?"

"We should track down the remains of Omega here in the U.S.," I said. "They had a presence here, complete with operatives and facilities. They may have lost their European operations, but I suspect they've still got some people in place here." I looked at Foreman. "Karthik—one of my people in the UK—could help with that."

"Expediting visas," Foreman said, writing on his notepad. He looked up. "What else?"

"We had a lot of kids in school at the Directorate," Ariadne said at last, drawing everyone's attention to her. She sat, red hair limp and lifeless around her pale face. "Someone should check on them to be sure they're all right."

I felt a surge of concern, like I'd forgotten something. "Joshua Harding," I said quietly.

"Who?" Scott said, looking over at me.

"This kid," I said. "He helped me evacuate the dorms on the night the Directorate was destroyed. He promised me he'd help get the kids to the nearest cloister." I looked to Ariadne. "That's definitely something we need to look in on."

"The nearest cloister is up on the North Shore of Lake Superior," Scott said, frowning.

"Should be easy enough to take a look at," Foreman said, looking up from his pad. "Anything else?"

I shook my head, my mind completely blank. I honestly didn't know what else I could think of that we'd need to deal with right now. Nothing pressing, anyway.

"Money," Ariadne said quietly, pulling everyone's attention back to her. "We'll need a payroll if you want me to pull the old Directorate back together."

"Ah, yes," Foreman said, and I could see the chagrin on his face. "For that, I'll need you to put together the old trading unit again so you can make it self-sustaining because we don't have any budgetary help from Washington. At all."

That just sort of lay there like a bomb had gone off in the middle of the table until my mother finally broke the silence. "Let me clarify this, just so I can be certain I have it all straight." She put her hand up and started ticking off points on her gloved fingers one by one. "We're forming a new agency to replace the Directorate. We're reporting directly to the government, but they're not paying us. Our job is to stop the extinction of our entire subspecies of the human race from a threat we know almost nothing about save for that it's headed by probably the most dangerous man in the world—"

"His second-in-command is probably one of the most sadistic

I've ever met," I added helpfully. "And can freeze time, making him near invincible."

"Yes, thank you," my mother said. "We have no real plan, no idea what's coming, no resources to draw on save for the intelligence that you can filter to us. So we can see parts of the threat as it's coming to wipe us out, but really the only thing standing between us and the one hundred most powerful metas in the world is me, my shut-in daughter, her teeny-bopper friends, and whatever castoffs from Omega have survived the extermination of our kind." She sat back and let the silence consume the table. "Yes. This is going to be marvelous. I've saved myself from prison just so I can be killed by Sovereign."

No one said anything for a long time after that, not even Foreman. His face was so grey it was almost ashen. I felt more than a little annoyed and tried to figure out the most creative way to bring our morale back from the brink that my mother had just pushed it toward. "Look on the bright side," I said, looking directly at her, "at least you didn't get locked in a box by one of your loved ones who then disappeared on you for months and months."

Nope. That wasn't it.

Chapter 9

Norway
1635

His breath frosted in the air, the chill of the Norse morning sensual on his bare skin. It was almost like a lover's touch to him, something with its own appeal, something that gave him a thrill of pleasure. Bjorn walked down the path that had become familiar to him over the last year, a trail between the new halls of his family and a village just down the way. The place where he stayed with his father and brother and other family members was good enough, pleasant enough, but it lacked mortal company. Female mortal company. And so Bjorn walked this path at least twice per week, sometimes more, to partake of the girls of the local village. They were accommodating enough, having seen an example of the folly of resistance, and made him welcome in their own way. He took a breath of the frigid air as the partially snow-covered ground crunched under his feet. *Even if they weren't as willing as they are, I've dealt with that before.* He smiled at the thought. *And it carries its own pleasure and rewards.*

The trees were bare, brown, with branches standing out from the trunks like fingers stretched out to each other. It reminded him of the skin of the men he had met in the years he had gone south, across the wide sea below Rome, and onto the shores of a much hotter land. He walked stark nude, his clothing clutched in his hand out of sheer enjoyment of the cold weather. When he had done so in that hot, dry land, he had not been nearly as comfortable.

The winter is in my blood, he thought, and luxuriated in the

ROBERT J. CRANE   55

chill prickling at his flesh. He touched one of the rough trees as he passed, letting his palm cross the gnarled bark and caress a knot where a limb had been lost a century earlier. He leaned his shoulder into it and felt its rough touch. Everything was blissful this morning. He'd been well fed the night before, well satiated by a village girl. Now he looked forward to a day of lounging around the fires of home. Perhaps later, if he felt the need, he'd walk this path again. *Two nights in a row. I might end up spoiling these village girls, getting them too used to what it feels like to have their wombs blessed by a god.*

His nose caught the scent of something in the wind as it shifted direction from ahead of him. It was sharp, heavy. It was smoke, a fire, but stronger than the simple fires that kept their stronghold warm and the houses heated. This was more pungent. He cast off from the tree and regained his balance, standing there in the chill morning, hesitating as he took another deep breath. The smoke was heavy with the smell of roasting flesh.

Bjorn felt his feet move underneath him without giving it thought. They carried him onward, running under the canopy of bare and empty branches that only allowed the orange of the rising sun to peek down on him every now and again. It was a short enough run, a mile or two, and the smoke smell grew heavier and heavier until he caught sight of a black cloud where the village should be.

He burst out onto a clearing at the edge of the field before his village and his eyes beheld a sight of purest horror. Everything was in flames, a thick, orange conflagration rising from the angular frames of the wooden homes, burning bright and roaring with great fury. The semi-circle of buildings was completely enflamed, the heights of the fire reaching above the trees.

Bodies were stacked on the outside edges of the fire, just starting to be consumed. They were still a few hundred feet off but his eyes could see them from here. There were only a dozen who lived there, all grown men and women, and few enough women at that. Most prominent among the bodies was his brother, his golden hair visible at even this distance. His father was there, too, his grey beard stretching halfway down his chest, easy to pick out from the small mass of corpses.

"You must be Bjorn," came a voice from behind him. He turned and saw a man standing there, dark of hair and eyes, watching him coldly, arms folded.

Bjorn did not answer, but an answer of sorts flashed across his mind. *It was him. He did this.* Bjorn felt a roar of fury bellow from his throat and the war-mind blew from him automatically, sending the image of darkness, of ravens, through his thoughts and blasting his enemy's mind with it. The man did not stagger, though, like others he'd fought, did not even react. Bjorn came at him in fury, expecting him to hold his head and duck away like all his other foes always had—

But the man did none of those things. He stayed still, and just as Bjorn was about to strike him down with a mighty fist, the man reached calmly across and gripped Bjorn by the neck, interrupting his charge and slamming him to his back on the cold soil. Bjorn's head hit the ground, the wind rushed out of him and he grunted. He lay there for a moment before realizing that the man had done this to him, this interloper, this killer, this—

"That's enough," the man said, still watching him coldly. "If you get up again, I will break your knees."

Bjorn roared and started to stand, but before he had fully reached his feet the man was moving, and there was a searing pain in his knees. He sunk to the ground once more in exquisite agony, cheek hitting the packed tundra as a glob of saliva ran down his chin.

"Be a good lad and stay down," the man said, and Bjorn looked up to see he'd shifted positions and was now standing between him and the burning village. "I have something to tell you, as you are the only survivor of this monstrosity."

"What do ... you want?" Bjorn choked out, trying to ignore the pain in his legs, anguish as he moved one and felt the grind of bones where there had only been sweet, unnoticeable movement before.

"I don't want anything," the man said. "I've done all I intended to do here. I had hoped for a witness, though, but I failed to keep one alive over there, in spite of my best efforts," the man swept an arm behind him to indicate the fires blazing behind him. "They made me a little too angry for that."

"Wh ... Why?" Bjorn asked, feeling the agony from his legs as he rolled to his side, shifting, looking for a more comfortable position. He didn't find it.

"Because you and your people were a mass of ticks, burrowing your way under the skin of this land," the man said, staring down at him. "You took from their harvests what you would, took from their daughters everything you wanted, and left nothing behind but your blighted seed." He leaned down, slightly but not enough to seem like he was by any stretch of the imagination on Bjorn's level. "Your day is over in this land, do you hear me? Your time as a leech, sucking the blood of people whom you do no good for is at an end. Be on about your business elsewhere. Tell your friends, the ones like you, still playing at the illusion that you are gods, that if I catch them running this deception, I will reveal them for the weak, pathetic deceivers that they are, and if they do not move on ..." He looked back at the fires. "I think you get the idea." The man stood.

"Who are you?" Bjorn croaked, looking back at the blaze, and saw it starting to consume the pile. He could see the smoke beginning to rise from the clothing of his father, his brother. "Who are you to do such a thing?"

"I am Sovereign," the man said and stood stiffly, looking down at him without emotion. "That ... and this," he gestured at the destruction behind him as his feet lifted off the ground, floating into the air as if a bird's wings had lifted him up, "is all you need know. Harken to my words, Odin-son." With that, the man called Sovereign flew into the air, straight up and out of sight.

Bjorn lay there on the dirt for a long time after that, the smell of smoke thick in the air around him, the pleasant chill turned bitter on his skin. He lay there until the next morning when his agony subsided and his bones had knit back together. When he got up and left, though, he took care to go a different path than the one he had trod the morning before.

Chapter 10

Sienna Nealon
Now

"Is this going to be a problem?" Foreman asked me after the conference room emptied. "You and your mother?"

I held a hand on my chin, trying to think it over. "I don't know. My instinct says yes."

Foreman studied me through smoky, inscrutable eyes. I'd heard the stereotype that politicians were supposed to be charmers; that they would tell you sweet things to your face and then say different things behind your back. I saw none of this as he leaned closer to me and started to speak. "Listen to me very carefully. The life of every single metahuman in the entire country is now in your hands. That includes my life," he said, eyes narrowed, "that of my wife and my children. Our survival hinges on what you're able to do. Your mother is a resource. She has more experience running down metahumans than anyone else you have available to help you."

I felt something unsaid, and it took me a moment to realize that the subtext was that I'd killed the four people who might have been able to bring as much to the party as my mother did.

"You're in charge. Find a way to get this done." With that, he stood without ceremony and headed for the door.

I felt my mouth dry. "Wait. That's it?"

He looked back from where he stood at the doorframe. "That's it. No fancy speeches, no last minute warnings. Your life is on the line. If you fail, we all die, and you get to live with that." He smiled, but it was grim.

I looked at him with more certainty than I felt. "I've killed quite a few people now; how do you know that would even bother me?"

He looked at me through those smoky eyes. "Because I know."

I almost fell out of my chair with shock. "You're a telepath?"

He gave a light shrug. "An empath. Like your friend Janus. I can detect the emotions, even stir them when necessary. It comes in handy when you're trying to get a read on people."

I rapped my knuckles against the wooden table, felt the sting of the hard wood against my skin and bones. "What does your power tell you about me?"

He didn't answer for a moment, looking down at the carpeting, then he sighed. "That you're the only one that's a hundred percent committed to stopping this calamity." He waved out into the hallway. "I've visited cloisters, seen the people there who have gotten faint warnings from Europe about what's coming; they don't have a clue. Most of them aren't taking it seriously yet; they think it's an 'old world' thing." He waved toward the wall behind me. "But they're coming. This ... Sovereign ... his minions ... they'll come for us." He let a faint smile creep out, a worried one. "See, we know what happened now in the European Union. How it happened. The authorities have found enough of the bodies, sniffed around the edges enough that it's obvious that there's been a genocide that almost no one has noticed. There were just too few of us, y'know? There are five hundred metahumans in North America by our guess, three hundred in South America, and once we're gone, it'll be down to ... dozens, maybe. Outside of what Century's got, I mean. The very few who have managed to hide at the corners of the world. Three thousand people now down to nine hundred or less," he snapped his fingers, "just like that. And no one else has the power to stop it."

"What about the government agencies here?" I asked, feeling the creep of terror coming back, that same feeling that had been haunting me since England.

He shook his head. "Our people—metahumans, I mean—have done too good a job hiding themselves, finding ways to subvert the system and keep underground. We had all these secretive organizations to cover for us, to keep us out of the spotlight, but it turns out that when no one knows you exist, they don't care when you're being killed off."

"But *you* know," I said. "A sitting U.S. Senator, you've gotta have some high-powered friends—"

"I do," he cut me off, "and I'm trying. My colleagues are not unsympathetic. But this secret is burying us. It may end up being the death of us. Think about it—even if we had the full support of the U.S. government, even if all this were out in the open, what do you think it would really lead to? It's not like we can deploy the U.S. Army against Century." He laughed mirthlessly. "It's not as though I know where to send the Marines to give Sovereign a good ass-kicking. Assuming anyone could kick his ass."

"Metas can be killed by armies, you know that," I said, feeling the thoughts tumble through my head. "Based on what I've heard, Weissman has plans for the armies of the world. He's just got it in his mind to deal with the metas first."

Foreman nodded. "Like I said, it's down to you. This whole thing is a lot to put on your shoulders, but there's no one else clamoring for the responsibility. Your mom would run given half a chance. Your friend Scott is quite content to retire to the nearest bar and continue putting away rum and cokes until Century comes through the door to spill his drink. And your friend Ariadne—"

"I don't think we could really be called friends at this point," I said. "Since I killed her girlfriend."

Foreman gave me a nod of concession. "Ariadne's powerless on her own. But she could be of tremendous aid to you. Once you get past your ... personal problems," he said it with an air of distaste, "she'll probably turn out invaluable."

"Great," I said, rubbing my hands over my face. "So all I have to do is make up with a woman who's got a deep personal grudge against me, fight off a superior army, and—oh, yeah—try and make some sort of peace with my mother." I rubbed my face harder, focusing on the bridge of my nose. "By the time this is finished, I may wish I'd taken the jail option."

Foreman did not speak for a long minute, and when he did, it was filled with a sort of quiet authority that I would forever associate with Old Man Winter, when he was a mentor to me and not a murderer. "You've left a trail of bodies behind you. A series of bad decisions, heated emotions, and broken laws. You've made mistakes," he said, his eyes meeting mine, and I could feel his words resonate in me. To his credit, I never once believed he was using his powers to stir me. "You are awash on a sea of blood you've let, paddling against the tides of fate to keep from being swept up in an even greater wash. By all rights and under normal circumstances, you would be in jail. You would be in jail for hundreds, maybe thousands of years, depending on how long you lived. You deprived people of life in the name of your own self-satisfying vengeance, and that's not the sort of thing that the soul just calluses over and forgets about.

"But these are not normal times," he said, and I listened to every word as the guilt crept through me in time with his almost lyrical delivery. "You have an opportunity to save yourself, and it comes in the guise of saving others. You can't just pay for a life with a life. You're going to have to save a hell of a lot more than one life to balance the scales for what you've done. Every day you wake, until this crisis is resolved, I want you to remember that you are doing the impossible. The penance for your crimes is to do what no one else has done before, to beat a man who is hell-bent on destroying our people to the very last. It is ... impossible." His voice was filled with quiet strength, and not a whiff of desperation was present in the way he said it. "But these are not ordinary times, and you are not an ordinary person. There is something about you that is Sovereign's weakness, something about you that no one else in all the meta world has." He straightened, and his spellbinding words drew me in just a little further as I hung on, waiting to see what he would say next. "Find it. Find out what makes you special, find out what it is that makes you unique. Find the strength to do the impossible." He turned and opened the door, and took his first step out. "You do that, and you'll actually earn your redemption." With one more step, he was carried out of view, but I still heard the last words he said, echoing down the hall.

"Save us, Sienna Nealon. Save us all, and you might just save yourself in the process."

Chapter 11

The flight came in from England a little over a day later, a Gulfstream IV that had been modified for the seventeen of them who were left plus a hospital bed in the back for Janus. I watched them disembark as the cold winter wind of Minneapolis greeted them. It was beyond brisk, a late November kiss that I could tell from Karthik's reaction as he stepped off the plane's stairs was more than he was used to dealing with in London.

"Not exactly a balmy day now, is it?" Breandan said with a grin as he crossed the snowy tarmac to reach me. The Irishman's mustache was still waxed in the oddest affectation I could remember seeing ... well, ever. He bent and gave me a hug that lifted me off the ground and I let him. He was wearing a fedora, and I patted him on the back as he set me down.

"Welcome to Minneapolis," I said and was promptly picked up again by the next man in line. Reed's embrace was firmer than Breandan's and just as appreciated. He gave me a peck on the cheek as I gave him one in return, albeit brief. He pulled back from me and smiled. "It's good to see you."

"Yeah, it didn't take as long as we thought it would," Reed said, watching me cannily then looking past me to the waiting vans. "Looks like you made some new friends in the last couple days."

I smiled. "I'm a friendly person. People are just drawn to me. They want to help me."

"Which affirmation book did you get that out of?" Reed deadpanned.

"Sienna!" A blond streak cut through the crowd and hit me with a surprisingly firm hug.

"Kat," I said, giving her a light squeeze in return. I would have asked her to stop, but I had a feeling it wouldn't have done any good. No matter how many times I tried to bat her away, Kat Forrest ... or Klementina Gavrikov ... or whoever she was this week ... just couldn't seem to stop being nice to me. It annoyed me for reasons I can't even fully describe.

I finally pulled back from the skinny blond cheerleader. Karthik gave me a polite nod and I gave him the same in return. Karthik was my type of person: all business, no affection. This I understood. However, I was willing to make exceptions for people like Breandan and Reed who had saved my ass a few times. And Kat, because truthfully she was still like a little kitten that I couldn't bring myself to strangle the life out of. Not that I would strangle a kitten.

I saw a few other familiar faces; the crew that was with me in the last attack on Omega's headquarters and a girl named Athena that I'd helped recruit to Omega's protection. She gave me a faint smile even as she looked desperately lost on the cold airport tarmac. "We've got hotel rooms booked for you," I announced to the small crowd. "These vans will take you to there. We'll all meet soon to talk over what the next step is, but first I have to speak with this lot," I gestured toward Karthik, Reed and Breandan, "to figure a few things out. This way," I said, leading them toward the vans.

I'd had Ariadne handle the arrangements. She still had access to all the Directorate accounts, and we were already up and running. Omega may have blown up the buildings, but they weren't able to damage the banking apparatus. The Directorate still had millions on deposit, ready to be used by us. Which was fortunate because we needed it. Ariadne was looking for temporary office space for us even now. I hadn't ever given much thought into exactly how convenient our setup was at the Directorate. Helicopters were available to shuttle us around, along with an extensive motor pool. Now we had nothing, and Li had to fight with the FBI as it was for use of the vans we were now sitting in.

I got into the lead van and Karthik, Breandan and Reed followed me. I watched Kat help load Janus into a converted ambulance at the rear of the motorcade. He was on a gurney, a stretcher designed just for transport, his figure looking even more shriveled than I remembered.

"So," Karthik said, breaking the silence as the van started into motion, "would you care to bring us up to speed with what has happened since we parted?"

"Yeah," I said, slowly nodding, "I probably should give you a heads up, shouldn't I? Well, the good news is that our fight just got a little easier ..."

By the time we pulled into the rear loop of the FBI offices, I had them up to speed. There was some disbelief (Reed), some angst at my initial arrest (Breandan), and some minor excitement at the idea that we were no longer in this completely over our heads and by ourselves (Karthik).

"So we have your government's blessing to do what needs to be done to fight Sovereign?" Karthik asked, listening attentively.

"Indeed we do," I said with a smile as I opened the van door to step out. "I hope you're prepared to be deputized."

Breandan frowned. "Deputized? What the hell is that?"

"It's where they make you a lawman," Reed answered.

"I can't join the law!" Breandan protested. "I have a reputation to uphold! What would my friends think?"

Reed shared a knowing look with me. "That you're afraid you're going to be wiped out like the rest of your kind if you don't get on the side of the only people who are fighting against Century?"

Breandan looked ready to argue then shrugged. "Ah, who am I kidding? I can see which way the wind is blowing, and I do not like the present direction. I'm in."

"Never doubted for a minute you would be," I said as we entered the FBI offices. We filed down the hallway in silence until we hit the conference room where Scott was waiting with Li, Ariadne and my mother. Foreman was conspicuous by his absence; it felt like there was a power vacuum in the room. Part of me wondered who would be running this particular meeting, until I realized it was going to be me. I took my place at the head of the table opposite my mother, while Karthik, Reed and Breandan took seats all in a line. Reed exchanged a nod with Scott, a slightly less friendly one with Ariadne, and sent a glare at my mother, who gave him an "eff off" look right back.

"Um," I said, "I call this meeting to order. Or whatever." My mother rolled her eyes. Ariadne had moved halfway up the table and sat between Reed and Li. My mother was all the way down at the end by herself. She was quite content with that, I was sure. Breandan had his hand up before I got a chance to say another word. "Yes?"

"Introductions," he said.

"Right," I replied. "This is Scott Byerly, he's a Poseidon-type and a damned good field agent," I said, nodding at the blond-haired man to my immediate left, "Agent Li of the FBI is our government liaison, Ariadne Fraser, head of our administrative division, then there's—" I skipped over my mother, "Karthik, head of Omega's field operations, Reed Treston, my brother and head of Alpha's field operations, and finally, Breandan Duffy." I paused with my hand extended at the Irishman, who waited expectantly. I searched for something to say. "Um ... he's Irish."

Breandan frowned. "Is that all? I've saved your life."

"So has everyone else at the table," my mother said. "It's like a big, giant 'We've Saved Sienna's Ass' club. She'll forget that at some point, though, mark my words, and probably forget you—"

"If you had my mother, you'd try to forget her, too," I

muttered under my breath. "That is Sierra Nealon."

Breandan and Karthik looked down the table at my mother and Breandan looked back with a quizzical expression. "Is that your mum?"

"Tragically, yes," I said before my mother could beat me to the punch. "She'll be working with us on this."

Breandan looked back at her again. "Wait, so your name is Sierra, and you named her Sienna? That's a bit vain. Just a couple degrees off of naming her Sierra, Jr., isn't it?"

My mother let out that hissing exhale that announced her patience was strained, and I took it as a cue to get us back on track. "We have a couple things to discuss now that we're all gathered. First on the agenda—Karthik, can you help us locate the remnants of Omega in the United States so we can try and pull their resources together, maybe help us make a better stand?"

"I can try," Karthik replied. "I likely won't be much help."

Reed leaned forward. "Because I've been watching Omega operations here in the U.S. for a few years, I have a lot of knowledge about the suspected locations of their facilities. When Karthik and I started comparing notes, it didn't add up at all."

"Because you were really lousy at your job?" my mother offered helpfully.

"Ha ha," Reed said, faking a laugh. "No. I'm actually really good at my job, thank you. It's because Karthik's security clearance with Omega is so low he doesn't have access to anything more than a very basic list of some of their oldest safehouses and facilities." He looked over at me. "For example, the safehouse in Eau Claire that we visited a few months ago wasn't on the list. Neither was the Andromeda facility in Eagle River."

"Site Epsilon," my mother said. "That's what they would have called it in their files. Like every super-secret organization, they had ridiculous code-names for everything."

"I can search for Site Epsilon in the Omega database," Karthik said. "We left the servers on and connected, so I can access them from here so long as they remain intact. I tried to copy everything we could, but there were so many files, stretching back such a long time ..."

"That should be fine," I said. "Hopefully Century has better things to do than destroy Omega's empty headquarters."

"Even that wouldn't necessarily put them offline," Karthik said. "We moved the servers down into the basement before we left, and it has its own power supply and independent data connections. So long as that sub-basement isn't destroyed, we have whatever limited access I can manage to Omega's entire library." A troubled look made it's way over his swarthy face. "Unfortunately it isn't much for now, but I can continue to try and work on it."

"We may be able to help with that," I said, glancing at Ariadne. "We're looking to bring on some high-powered IT support, someone who might be able to help you break into Omega's databases."

"J.J.?" Reed asked, watching me. "Did you find him?"

"We never lost him," Ariadne explained. "He was furloughed with the rest of the Directorate staff just before the destruction. I sent him an email last night and he responded. He'll be in tomorrow."

"Speaking of old Directorate problems," Li said, "we need to talk about facilities. We're running into the end of the FBI's good graces, taking up all the space we currently are. Your new arrivals will probably push the special agent in charge of this field office over the edge."

I looked over at Ariadne, who made a little noise as she placed a palm flat against the table. She was back in her normal work attire, looking much more like the Ariadne I knew, her hair straightened and her suit looking appropriately drab. "I've looked at a few spaces, but ..." she let her voice trail off, then looked over at me for just a second before shifting her gaze back to the table, "... we need something of suitable size, with a motor pool, preferably a helicopter landing pad—"

"Do you anticipate landing a helicopter on it?" Breandan said, a little glib.

"The Directorate's Black Hawk is sitting at the airport in Bloomington," Ariadne said, taking no note of Breandan's sarcasm. "I've already spoken with the pilots; they're ready to work for us."

"Are there no facilities available that meet our criteria?" I asked. "Or are there none we can afford?"

Ariadne looked grudgingly at me before she chose her next words. "Money is not an issue. Foreman has assured me that we can make big moves with the trading unit in order to gin up cash and he'll be able to keep the SEC from nailing us to the wall. We used to keep it small so it would glide under the radar, but he's given us permission to do a few things that will quadruple our money in the next six months, which will give us enough to construct a facility that will meet our needs." She grimaced. "But I don't think you're going to like the idea I have for it."

I looked at her pained expression and felt my internal temperature drop. "You want to rebuild the Directorate campus."

She was calm and cool when she answered. "We own the land outright, it's well located. It does need some serious attention from a demolition company, but I have contacts in the construction industry that could get a primary building up in three months or less, assuming Senator Foreman could help with the permitting process. We'd be up and running in a facility that was designed for us in no time. The only downside—"

"Is that it was the scene of a rather spectacularly heinous murder," I whispered, almost too low for the rest of the room to hear it. Almost.

"Who?" my mother asked. "Those four meta thugs you killed?"

"It makes sense to use what we've got," I said, letting pragmatism drown out the screaming of my own voice in the back of my head. "Priority goes to a headquarters and a dorm—"

Ariadne nodded slowly. "I've got those marked down. A parking garage and training facility are secondary priorities. That will pretty much cover us for now, though, for what we need."

"Do it," I said. "Can you get us temporary office space while—"

"I signed a lease agreement this morning on eight thousand square feet in Eden Prairie," Ariadne said. "Not far from the airport in case we need to land a chopper, and there'll be enough space for admin with some room for your operations teams to at least plan and train in the place."

I nodded. "And for housing—"

"There's a motel across the parking lot," she said. "Decent enough and convenient. We'll be able to cover the expenses for your new charges without any trouble, though if you could hand me any who aren't fighters, it'd certainly help us cover some of the jobs that aren't presently filled—secretarial staff, all that."

I nodded. "I think we have more than a few that can fulfill that function. Okay, so headquarters is covered for now. We'll get Reed and Karthik working on Omega's tattered remains here in the States. The next priority is expanding our footprint and recruiting new talent." I looked at each of them. "If we're going to fight the most powerful army in the world, we need an army of our own to do it with."

"What's your plan on that?" Breandan asked.

"I need to visit cloisters," I said and turned to look at Scott. "I could use some help from someone who's grown up in the meta culture."

"Sure," Scott said with a nod, his usual grin sadly missing. "I can help with that; my parents grew up in the North Shore cloister before the family decided to get out and move to the big city. Used to go back every summer for reunions."

"What kind of army are you looking to build?" my mother asked, her fingers interlaced in front of her. "Are you just looking to throw together anyone with a meta power, regardless of how much they've got?"

I didn't know exactly what to say to that. "I'm just looking for some fighters. Some people who are willing to stand between Century and the rest of our kind with me."

"So, basically anybody with more guts than brains." She leaned back in her chair and made that damned hissing sound again. "You know there's a power scale for a reason. You put a bunch of level ones against Sovereign and he's going to wipe them out in about five seconds, not sparing a thought as he walks over their corpses to get to you."

"I'm just trying to find a way to fight him—"

Her voice rose. "Everything you're talking about so far is just going to make it easier for him to kill us all."

"That's enough for now," I said, controlling my voice. "You," I said to mother, "I need to talk with. Outside."

"I guess I'm in trouble now," she quipped as she stood and started to follow me to the door.

"Not quite 'Getting locked in a metal box' trouble," I said before leading her out the door, "but close."

As I made my way down the hallway, I could hear her behind me, stalking along, keeping pace. The beige carpeting and white walls were uniform and boring with only a few wall-hung decorations to break the monotony. I took a left and opened the rear door where a suited agent nodded at me before I stepped outside into the cold. I wasn't wearing my coat because I'd left it inside without thinking.

My mother followed behind me a few steps, sauntering into

the chill air and taking a deep breath, which frosted in front of her as she exhaled. "Well, here we are."

"Here we are," I said. "Again."

We stared at each other in tense silence for a minute until she spoke. "So ... are we going to fight?"

I nodded. "I think so. Unless you want to stop challenging my authority at every turn."

"If your ideas weren't the product of an eighteen-year-old's idiotic idealistic notions, maybe I wouldn't have to challenge them constantly." She kept her hands out, evenly spaced. She didn't look tense, but I knew she was wary, prepared for me to attack her. I wasn't going to make it that easy on her, though, when the moment came.

"First of all, none of them are final, just brainstorms—"

"Your brainstorms aren't exactly getting me wet, if you'll pardon the—"

"Gross," I said. "I have a job to do, one I'm taking seriously. I understand you don't want to be here—"

"That's an understatement," she said, cutting me off. "If I weren't presently being blackmailed by the U.S. government into helping you try and teach a pig how to fly, I'd be so deep underground that one poorly-placed shovel from a Chinese farmer would unearth me."

"So go," I said, throwing my arms wide. "I know Foreman says he'll come after you, but I'm the one in charge of metahuman policing and you know what? I don't have the manpower to waste on your old ass right now." I threw the 'old ass' part in as a dig just to piss her off. It's what I do.

She hesitated and I caught her looking slightly down as if she could see her own ass. She caught me watching her, and I'm pretty sure I had at least a slightly satisfied smile. "He'll alert every border crossing, warn every department. They snagged me this time without meta help; I'm standing in a train station in New

Mexico and bam! Fifteen men with guns surround me in a half moon: no escape without a ton of bullets perforating me. Probably would have killed me."

"Aren't you the one who told me to avoid confining spaces?" I said with a grin. "You know, when you weren't throwing me into them to prove your superiority?"

"Very clever," she sniffed. "How did they catch you?"

"Pretty much how they caught you. Ambushed me in customs coming back from England."

"Where you took over Omega," she said, and this time it was an icy glare. "Do you have any idea what that organization has done to our family?"

"You mean other than killing your father?" I sniped back, almost gloating.

She looked like she'd had the wind knocked out of her. "They ... what?"

"Simon Nealon," I said and started to slowly circle her. She looked stunned, stunned enough that she didn't move to counter me and maintain equidistance as she would have normally. "They sent an assassin after him because he knew about Wolfe, about some of their deep dark secrets."

She looked flabbergasted, absolutely uncertain. "I ... didn't know they did that. My mother ... she spent her last days with an Omega operative—"

"Oh?" I gave her a disinterested look. "Why?"

"Because he was incubus and he could touch her," she snapped.

"Oh, God!" I said, something snapping into place. "Fries? She slept with Fries?"

My mother gave me a nasty smile. "Looks like you have something in common, doesn't it? It's why I didn't bludgeon him to death when last we met. He didn't kill her, and he did make her last days a little easier. His payment was that she spilled the beans about me and Charlie, told him all about us, our upbringings, everything."

"Meanwhile, they killed your dad," I said.

"They gave me a fair amount of hell in my Agency days, too," she said. "I ran across Wolfe a couple times, and it wasn't much fun for me either round." She looked down. "But that was nothing compared to the last time, the time that you—"

"You know what?" I said, and felt my annoyance burn to a new high at how much she'd held back from me, how much she'd kept secret. Her casual reference to the time she locked me in a box and just left made my fists clench so tightly I thought my knuckles were going to break. "I think you had the right idea before. Let's just fight."

I didn't do anything as prosaic as jump at her, striking before she was ready. No, I stood there and raised my hands defensively. A sneak attack now was just as likely to go wrong for me as right, and I had faith I could break through her defenses without having to resort to cheap tactics. I didn't bother bowing, though, as we would have back when she was training me, just situated myself for offense and defense and waited for her to do the same.

She didn't disappoint, lowering herself into a defensive stance. "So it comes down to this."

"Again," I said. "You trained me. You helped make me what I am, even though I didn't ask for this."

"You think you can ... what?" She had her hands up, looking at me over balled fists. "You think beating me will avenge all the wrongs of your childhood?"

"I think beating you is going to feel damned good," I said. "Beyond that, I don't much care."

"Well, you're all about feeling good in the moment, aren't you?" she sneered. "Everything I tried to teach you was about long-term planning, keeping your eye on the bigger picture, the long game."

I shrugged. "Probably got lost under the fact that you were so busy planning for the long game that you never actually lived your life, or let me live mine."

Her expression changed, and suddenly her face looked haggard in the day's dim light. "The world changed, sweetheart. Changed from when I was a kid, changed in a heartbeat. This Sovereign guy? He didn't need to be planning anything as grandiose as the end of our kind to scare the living shit out of me. He's simply the most frightening man in the meta world, which is saying something if you know some of the other candidates who have vied for that title. Metahuman life is dangerous, especially for exiles like us."

I eased a little closer to her, and she to me. We both stood, waiting to see who would throw the first punch, make the first move. "You've met Sovereign. Fought him?"

"If you could call it that." She swiped at me with a jab and that was all it took. I dodged and came back at her with another one that she evaded. "He beat my ass flat in about ten seconds." I flung a high kick at her and she went inside and hit me in the stomach as I hammered her on the top of the head, causing her to stagger back as I tightened my gut from the extreme pain. "What he did ..." she breathed, her head bobbing like I'd caused it to swim. "You have no idea."

"It'd be tough for me to have any idea since we were never allowed to talk about what happened outside our house." I came at her again and this time landed a punch that she couldn't block, slamming into the side of her head. She hit me in the jaw in return, but the fact that I'd struck first weakened the blow a little since she was rocking back from the impact of my punch. Only a little, though; it still hurt like hell.

"There was a reason for that!" she said and came up again, her eyes aflame with anger. "I had to protect you! From Omega, from Sovereign. How else was I going to keep you out of the spotlight? Didn't you notice I only ever left the house to go to work? That was it. That was all. The rest of the time I bought groceries, bought necessities, and came directly home. I didn't leave you alone any longer than I had to. I was right there with you in confinement."

"Except for your work furlough," I said and came at her again, this time with a round kick that was far too slow. She turned it aside and popped me in the nose with a counterpunch that she tried to follow with a kick of her own. I raised a knee and ran her into it as I sidestepped, though. "I never realized how much I missed of living in the outside world until I was in it. It was always the little things, too. Cake on my birthday, friends to share my life with—"

"You don't think you're actually gonna win this, do you?" she said and came at me sideways. I blocked her and threw her back with a volley of punches.

"I did last time," I said. "I'm still convinced part of the reason you ran out on me is because after all those years of training when I couldn't touch you, I started to manifest and land some hits. Then you disappear. You've been slumming it all these years, fighting a little girl without a tenth of your speed or power, and when I started to get good enough to take you out, your ego was too big to handle it."

"Ooh," she said, taunting, and came at me with a kick to the midsection that I deflected with both hands, but not without some pain. "You talk to me about ego? Look whose head seems to have inflated about what a badass she is?"

"I have some minor accomplishments to back it up," I said and flung myself back in a flashy somersault that bought me a moment of breathing room. "I killed Wolfe—"

"Totally by accident." Three punches and a kick that I dodged followed her reply.

"I beat Odin's son, Bjorn, like a red-headed stepchild.

Twice."

"I hear he was always the dumbest of that brood." She was on the attack now. She kept coming at me, but I was parrying almost everything, letting her score only minor hits.

"I stalked and killed Glen Parks," I said and came back at her with a countering punch that caused her to move laterally into a kick I landed in her ribs, causing her to double over and retreat. "I ambushed Clyde Clary, an ironskin, trapped and killed him. I dragged down Eve Kappler, a peri, and I killed Roberto Bastian, a Quetzlcoatl-type while he was in full dragon mode." I punched her in the nose again, sneaking one through her defenses. "While I was in England, I personally beat the living hell out of all four ministers of Omega."

"Even Heimdall?" My mother dodged my next punch but got caught by the one that followed.

"Especially Heimdall," I said and launched a front kick at her that caught her under her guard and caused her to grunt in pain. "I beat him to within an inch of his life." I pressed the attack, causing her to fall back.

"Did that make you number three?" she asked, deflecting my next attack. "Third to beat him, ever?"

I hesitated. "Yeah. How did you—?"

She launched a counterattack that broke through my defense and landed a punch on the side of my head that caused me to see a flash of light even as I whirled away, trying to protect myself. "Nice to meet you, number three. I was number two."

I looked up at her, the pain all over my body fueling my rage. "Figures you'd be number two; you were shitty mother."

"I was what I had to be," she said coldly, "to keep you alive until you were ready for the deep end of the pool, darling girl. Before you criticize me too harshly, just remember that everything I put you through has made you what you are today."

"I didn't ask for this!" I screamed the words and flung myself at her, clumsy, awkward, an attack that should have been easy to deflect for a calm, cool operator like my mother. She didn't deflect it, though; she committed the cardinal sin of wavering, hesitant, and I slammed into her midsection with my shoulder, taking her down to the snowy pavement. I heard her hit and the air went out of her. "I didn't ask to be what you made me!" I brought a hand back and hit her in the face, hard, rocking her skull against the concrete. "I didn't want to be a killer! I didn't want to get involved in Old Man Winter's games!" I punched her again and she took it, ineffectually trying to block me with her hands. "I didn't want to watch my boyfriend die at his hand!" I hit her again, and this time she managed to get up enough strength and momentum to buck me off of her into the air by arching her back and pushing my weight up with her hips.

I flew into the air and took a standing position as she rolled away and got to her feet. There were already dark bruises and cuts on her cheeks, trickles of deep crimson running down her face from where I'd battered her. She looked woozy, like she was going to fall over at any moment. "I didn't ask for it either," she said, and spat a gob of blood onto the snow at my feet. "But it got handed to me just the same as it did for you, and no one prepared me for it. I did everything I could to make you ready for it. I'm sorry if I failed you," she said, and I could hear the remorse. It actually slowed me up, kept me from launching at her again. "But I will not apologize for coarsening you, for overprotecting you, for exposing you to ridiculous levels of hardship to prepare you for monsters like Wolfe and Omega and Sovereign. I knew they'd be after you from day one. I knew it."

"Why?" I asked, and I felt my hands drop to my side. "Why ... won't they leave me alone?"

I watched her hands fall to her sides, wary, weary, and I saw a single tear run down her cheek. "I don't know. I wish like hell I did, but I just ... don't know."

Chapter 12

The two of us brushed our way back inside at a wary truce, exchanging glances but nothing more, and with a lot less hostility than had been in them previously. I didn't really know what to say, so after staring at each other for a couple minutes she just turned and started walking back to the rear door of the offices and I followed. This round was over. The bigger part of me hoped there wouldn't be another, ever.

As we walked past the guard at the rear door, he gave us both the once-over real good, as though questioning what the hell was wrong with us to come back in looking like we'd been through a war. He didn't say anything, though, and that counted for a lot with me.

We walked down the long hallway back to the conference room, my mother limping slightly. I was probably doing the same, since I was matching her pace in a way that felt natural given the state of my body. As we approached Conference Room 4, the door opened and Scott Byerly appeared, Agent Li in tow.

"I can maybe get you a car," Li said as the door closed behind them with a faint squeak. "A towncar, that's about it."

"I have a car," Scott said. "It'll be easier if I just drive myself. Save your favors for when we really need to call them in."

"What's up?" I asked as we got closer. Scott took one look at me and his eyes widened. Li actually gawked, showing the most emotion I'd seen from him thus far.

"Get it all out of your system?" Scott asked after he recovered.

"For now," my mother said, continuing past him without a look back. She slapped Scott on the ass as she passed, causing him to jump and glance back at her. She let a small smile of satisfaction show on her bruised and bloodied face as she disappeared into the conference room.

"Was that my mom or my aunt Charlie?" I asked under my breath.

"I got a line on the Directorate students that you escorted off campus," Scott said when he turned back to me. "My folks talked to a relation at the nearest cloister, the one up on the North Shore near Little Marais? I guess they turned up there a couple weeks ago."

I frowned. "Did they have relatives up there?"

He shook his head. "No, they were all the ones without meta relations, ones that we'd identified by various means, orphans, that sort. Only about ten or so, but the cloister took them all in."

I nodded. "We should go talk to them and speak with the folks in charge of the cloister."

Scott gave a self-satisfied smile to Li. "That's what I was just saying. We can take my car."

"Do you want to take anyone else with you?" Li asked, back to serious.

"No," I said. "Get the England group settled in. This should be simple, and we might need room to bring back a passenger or two if we can find anyone willing to fight."

Li nodded. "Little Marais is almost four hours from here. Better get a move on if you don't want to stay the night."

"It's probably going to snow anyway," Scott said, giving me a careful look. "Might want to pack something just in case." He looked me over. "And maybe change before you leave."

I looked down at my dirty clothing, flecked with blood. "What? Are you saying I don't look my best after I've been in a fight?" I gave him a grin.

He inclined his head a little like he was considering me. "It does put a certain flush into your cheeks. But really ... when since

I've known you, have you not just been in a fight?"

"You have a point." I couldn't really argue with that.

I said a quick goodbye to everyone in the conference room and implored Reed, Breandan and Karthik to keep a close watch on things and help the new kids get settled while we were gone. Ariadne didn't give me much expression, and I realized I didn't know what to say to her.

"We'll be at the temporary offices tomorrow," she said to me, preempting any efforts I might have made. "I'll send the address to Scott so he'll know where to find us. Your British imports are already there."

"Thank you," I said, trying to keep things cool between us. She gave me a slight nod and walked away before I could say anything else.

"Is it cold in here?" Breandan asked after Ariadne had shut the door. "Or is that a draft from outside?"

I retrieved my bag from where I'd left it in an empty office and went to the bathroom, where I quickly cleaned up the excess mess and changed into an unsullied pair of jeans and a blouse. I slipped on my wool coat as I started to apply just the slightest amount of makeup to make myself presentable for my meeting with those who ran the cloister. I was just finishing with the eyeliner when the door behind me opened and my mother swept in, still looking tattered. She gave me a quick once over then shook her head. "You ..." She just stopped speaking, shook her head again, and started toward one of the stalls.

"I what?" I asked.

"You look ..." She hesitated. "All grown up. Be careful on your trip. I'll work with Reed while you're gone, see if we can fill in the map on Omega so we have some places to look when you get back."

I stared at her in the mirror. "You taught me almost everything I know. You made me what I am."

She shook her head. "Not really. I may have hurt you a lot, but Reed just explained in detail what Winter did to you—to Zack. I may have made a prisoner of your body to try and keep you safe, but he made a mess of your soul."

"It's all right," I said, looking back at my face in the mirror. "I've got a few of those to spare now."

She seemed to deflate. "Be safe," she whispered and disappeared into the stall.

Chapter 13

The roads were snowy as we drove north out of the cities on Interstate 35. The snow wasn't coming down terribly hard, just flurries caught in the beams of the headlights like little dots of white against the black of the night sky. Winter meant it got dark early, around six p.m., and we rode north in silence in Scott's SUV. I pushed myself back against the soft leather as the seat heater warmed my backside, still a little bruised from the fight with my mother.

"You warm enough?" Scott asked as we passed Circle Pines, Minnesota.

"I'm fine," I said. "You know, for a member of an endangered species who's just been put in charge of our whole race's survival."

"No pressure, though, right?" He cracked a grin.

"No, none at all," I said. "We're never under any pressure, ever."

His chuckles died as we pressed on into the growing dark. The smell of the heated air surrounded me, and I realized I hadn't really slept last night. The tiredness crushed in on me.

"You can sleep," Scott said, urging me on as he caught a glimpse of my fluttering eyelids. "I don't mind."

"You sure?" I could feel my eyelids fighting to close.

"It's fine. I'll wake you up when we get there."

"Okay," I yawned.

"Besides," he said as I closed my eyes and leaned my head against the side of the car, "I'll probably need you to drive back."

I drifted off into a quiet calm, warmth around me, feeling safe and secure. The steady sound of the tires on the road faded away, and the hard surface of the window against my cheek turned into something else, something soft. I opened my eyes and I was lying on my side on a couch. I sat up abruptly, looking around the room.

It was a little dim, the only light cast by ugly lamps on either side of the couch. It was all very familiar, somewhere I knew I had already been. Dim awareness pressed in on me. I had been here before, many times, but the colors were blurring in the dark and everything seemed strange. There was a man seated in a chair opposite the couch, just where he'd always sat when we were in this room in the real world, not in dreams.

"Hello, Sienna," Dr. Quinton Zollers said to me, looking up from the pad on his lap.

"What's up, Doc?" I asked calmly, not really feeling like I was in control of this.

He gave a light shrug. "It's your dream, I'm just visiting."

I thought about this for a moment. "Like a dreamwalk?"

He shook his head. "No. You can control those. I'm doing the shaping work here, but I'm not really in control, either. Your subconscious is, which means you'll probably say things that will make sense to you now but not when you wake up." He smiled. "If you even remember this when you wake up."

"The price of cranberries is two pounds," I said.

He looked at me evenly. "Thank you for proving my point."

"Why am I here?" I asked.

He smiled. "It's just a dream, Sienna. In spite of your remarkable abilities, you dream just like everyone else."

"Cranberries to that, I say."

"I came to tell you something," he said with a smile, "and I should hurry, because I don't have much time." The smile disappeared. "Sovereign will be coming for you. I don't know when it will happen, but he will. And when that time comes, you won't be able to stop him."

"The duck-billed platypus is a mammal," I replied, my brain

doing everything in its power to not be helpful.

He inclined his head like he was searching for the right thing to say. "Indeed. I'm warning you about this because you should be aware that he's coming."

"But how do you know?" I asked, and once more the world made sense for just a moment.

"Because," he said, "I—"

There was the sound of a honking horn and the sudden feeling that the world was out of control. My head hit the glass hard enough to jar me awake. I took a sharp breath and realized that we'd just swerved, that we were still driving up the interstate, that whatever had happened had wakened me at exactly the wrong moment.

"Sorry," Scott grunted. "Who goes forty miles an hour in the left lane?"

"Grandmothers," I replied, feeling a sudden sense of loss, like I'd left something very important behind in the dream, something I'd never be able to get back. "Illiterates who can't read signs that say 'Slower traffic keep right.' Assholes." I took a breath and smoothed my hair back. I had let it loose after the fight with my mother, and it was frizzed. "Sometimes they're all the same person."

I heard another chuckle from Scott. "Sorry about that. Really." He glanced over at me and must have caught the look on my face. "You all right?"

"Maybe," I said. "I was having a dream about Zollers. Except he was really there, trying to tell me something."

Scott's mien changed only a little, expressing just a faint waver of concern. "What?"

I took a breath of the warm air in the car and looked out at the snowy shoulder of the road, blurring by at well above the speed limit. "He said that Sovereign was coming for me."

Chapter 14

We arrived at the cloister just before nine p.m. We turned on an old back road into a farming area and my visions of a cloister like the quaint little village I'd seen in England were put aside. The cloister was a trailer park, a dirt road leading into it. There were about ten trailers all set out on a plot of land, trees all around it making a forested boundary. It looked much the same as other trailer communities I'd seen, with corrugated metal sides on some trailers and the fancier wood paneling on others.

I looked over at Scott and saw he wore a pained expression. I had just woken up and felt like I'd left my tact behind in the dream world. "What's wrong with you?"

He looked over at me, almost apologetic. "Oh, uh. Nothing. Sorry."

"Clearly it's something," I said. "Your face looks like that time you spilled coke all over the carpet of my dorm room and didn't want to admit to it."

"We'll talk after," he said, bringing the car to a stop outside one of the trailers. He took the keys out of the ignition and opened the door without ceremony, and I heard the crunching of the snow as he got out.

"Whatever," I said and opened my own door. I didn't really have time for any emotional issues he might be having, anyway. Not right now.

The chill air seeped through my coat; there was no breeze tonight for whatever reason. I followed him up to the three wooden steps that led to the door and waited down at the bottom while he gave a good, solid knock. "This is my Aunt Judy's place," he said, glancing back. "Like, great aunt, I think." He gave it a moment's thought. "Twice removed? Wait, no, that's cousins. It's something removed, I think."

The door opened and a woman around my height appeared, her grey hair back in a ponytail and a yellow faded t-shirt covering her upper body. "I like to think of myself as a great aunt, with nothing removed," she said, but she didn't add much humor to it, completely deadpan.

"Aunt Judy," Scott said weakly and leaned down to give her a hug.

"Come in," Judy said briskly, without any further explanation or warning. "It's too damned cold to stand outside jabbering all night." Scott gestured for me to enter first, so I did, and he followed behind and shut the door.

The trailer was immaculate, the brown and white spotted carpet looking as if it had been vacuumed every day since it had been put in. The white linoleum flooring at the far side of the room in the kitchen area was spotless, my meta-enhanched eyesight could already see from here. The walls were covered in faint, blue-striped wallpaper, which blended well. A few pictures of perfectly hung natural scenes were on each wall, evenly spaced. A television was going quietly to my right.

The trailer was warm, pleasantly so after the bitter reminder I'd had from the car to the door that it was in fact winter in Minnesota. Judy was ahead of us, her face looking tired. She gestured to the kitchen table and pulled out a chair. "Will this suffice for our talk?"

"Sure," I said, taking off my coat and hanging it on the back of the chair she gestured to.

She was eyeing Scott now, her old, faded jeans and yellow t-shirt quite the contrast to his khakis and dress shirt. I knew he'd gone home last night and changed, and it made a world of difference. Scott always tended to dress up, preppy boy that he was. I was just surprised he wasn't wearing a tie. Meanwhile, my natural tendencies made me want to dress like Judy (except for the yellow; it was not in my color wheel), but unfortunately my current job being blackmailed by the United States Government required me to look a little more professional. Or so Senator Foreman had told me. I felt in my coat pocket and found the FBI ID that rested within for reassurance. I didn't think I'd need it—or the guns that came with it—but I carried them all just the same. Always.

"The kids from your Directorate are staying with a few of the bigger families around here," Judy said, a little primly.

I looked around at her trailer, which seemed roughly the same size as all the others, but it was quiet and there was nary a sign that anyone inhabited it with her. "Any of them staying with you?"

"Heavens, no," Judy said. "I'm a terrible person to live with, especially for a child. My sense of rules and order is very clearly defined and much too strict for most people, which is why I have chosen not to inflict it upon anyone else."

I blinked at her. "I've ... uh ... never heard anyone be quite so critical of their own personality quirks before."

She shrugged. "I don't see it as a flaw, but others certainly do, and since I have no desire to annoy, I find it better to live on my own." She thumped a hand lightly on the table. "Now then. You've come about the children, but Scott mentioned on the phone that there were other circumstances propelling you up here. What are they?"

I cleared my throat as Scott took off his coat and sat next to me. "Have you heard the rumors out of Europe?"

She inclined her head slightly as if to say, "Meh." She was of a generation that probably wouldn't know what that meant, but the sentiment was definitely there. "I have a few friends in the old world who have stopped returning any phone calls or emails. The responses I do get are from their local constabularies, looking for clues to their deaths or murders."

I thought about that for a second. "But they're all murders."

"The local police in several countries do not share your rather obvious conclusion, I'm afraid," Judy said, a little primly. "Of course there are some ways in which a meta can die that, by their nature, look like natural causes. Incubi and succubi, naturally—" Scott cleared his throat rather abruptly and Judy looked at him, annoyed, before speaking again. "In any case, the truths are percolating their way out to even us, here at the edge of the wilderness. Something is destroying our kind."

"But you're not concerned?" I asked.

"Of course I'm concerned. What kind of a foolish question is that?" Judy's lips were pressed together tightly, stealing all the color from them.

I realized suddenly that I hadn't had much to drink in the last few hours. "But you're not doing anything about it."

She watched me with a clear sense of annoyance. "Oh, be assured, we'll do *something* about it. It's just that we're still deciding on what that something will be."

"There is a man called Sovereign," I said, just launching into it, "and he's leading a group called Century that is planning to wipe out all of us to the last meta."

Judy's face was already ruddy compared to her yellow shirt. "That son of a bitch," she said under her breath.

Scott's eyes widened. "Umm ... Great Aunt Judy? You know him?"

She looked him over like he was an idiot. "Of course I know him. Anyone who's been around these parts for a few hundred years knows him. He's been through before, that ass. Used to take pride in breaking metas who'd run local protection rackets, which was a pretty common thing even a hundred years ago. You had these metas who would watch out for a town or county in exchange for money. Sometimes they'd even take the sheriff's job. Some were honorable about it," her expression tightened, "some weren't. Anyhow, Sovereign passed through a few times, and it seemed like every other time he'd break some damned fool who tried to shake him down. The man didn't say shit to anyone when he'd come through, he'd just walk along, buy food or eat in a restaurant without saying more than a required word to anyone, and be on about his way when he was done."

"So he was like a good guy, back then?" Scott asked. "Breaking up protection rackets?"

Judy snorted. "Hardly. Sometimes it was warranted, sometimes I think he was just spoiling for a chance to bust someone up. Didn't kill 'em most of the time, though, and that's to his credit because he certainly could have. Just warned them off, told them to find an honest job. A lot of them learned to steer out of his way when he came to town. They'd give him a wide berth and he'd given them no trouble."

"He seems to have changed his mode of operation," Scott said.

"Yes," Judy said pensively, a frown on her face. "He didn't truck with anyone else that I knew of. Damned sure not anyone with as dumb a name as 'Century.'" She looked over at Scott. "What does it mean?"

Scott almost gulped. "Like, a hundred years—"

"I know that, you dunce," Judy said, and I almost thought she was going to reach across the table to take a swipe at him. "Why did he name his group Century?"

Scott looked at me, I looked back at him. "We don't know," I answered.

She frowned at me. "Might be something you ought to look into."

"I'll add it to the list of things to discuss when I meet him," I said, trying not to let my voice carry too much sarcasm.

"So why are you here?" Judy asked, looking at me now. "Really. Because you didn't know I knew Sovereign from before, did you?" She leaned in closer. "You know why he calls himself that? Sovereign, I mean?"

"Because he's a man unto himself," I said. "Like an island all on his own. Says he doesn't need anything, or anybody."

She gave me a curt, perfunctory and satisfied nod. "That's what he always said."

I watched her carefully. "You don't believe him?"

She shrugged again. "Everybody needs something."

I looked at her, she looked back. "Do you know what he wants? Or what he needs?"

She breathed in and out, thinking about it. "He needs food and water, I know that. Needs to sleep from time to time, because they say he'd find shelter in an inn for the night sometimes, and woe betide anyone who was dumb enough to wake him in the night for any reason. Just like the rest of us in that regard. But other than that ... no, I don't suppose I know of anything else he needed or wanted. He never really talked to anyone, never visited a whorehouse while around here or showed any interest in any of the women in the area." She got a glint of amusement in her eyes. "And I recall one even threw herself at him, stupid trollop."

"What did he do?" I asked.

"Not a damned thing," Judy said. "Just walked right around her like she was nothing more than a stone in the road he was stepping out of the way to keep from tripping on."

I filed that away for later. If he wasn't interested in women, maybe men were more his cup of tea. I was desperate for a vulnerability. After all, what could make a man as long-lived as that apparently not interested in anything or anyone? "You asked us why we're here," I said.

Judy didn't blink, just gave me the flint-hard look back. "Yes?"

"We're here to check up on the kids that fled the Directorate, for one," I said. "But the other reason we're here is because I'm trying to organize a fight against Sovereign. Against Century."

Judy leaned back in her chair. "Well, that'll be an interesting sort of slaughter, I suppose."

I hesitated. "You don't think there's a way to beat him?"

She laughed but it sounded more like a cackle, completely bereft of any amusement. "Sweetie," she said, but there was nothing sweet about her pronunciation of the word, "if he's got a hundred metas at his disposal and they've already rolled through the cloisters of Europe, he will not have any trouble making you and anyone dumb enough to line up with you into a flat smear on the pavement wherever you're standing when you meet him." She turned to Scott. "You too, numbnuts. Might want to think this one through with your head, for once, instead of your crotch."

Scott bristled. "You think I'm going into this fight because I'm running on testosterone? Like I've got some need to prove the size of my manhood?"

Judy didn't back down, but now she was amused. "Oh, no, I'm sure that's still as insubstantial as it was when you were a kid taking baths with your cousins." She waved a hand in my direction. "No, I mean that you're going into a battle that's going to get you killed to impress your girlfriend here."

"Oh, me?" I said after a moment's pause allowed that to sink in. "I'm not his girlfriend. His girlfriend—well, ex, now—she's ..." I looked down at myself. "She's blond and leggy, and I'm ... so not." She looked at me like I was an idiot. "No, really," I said. "We're not! I can't even—" I halted myself and saw a flicker on her face. "Well, anyway, we're not, in spite of whatever you might think. I mean, we couldn't, even, because ... well, anyway." I stopped myself short of explaining how my last boyfriend had died only a couple weeks earlier.

She had an even more suspicious look now and glanced down at my hands, my leather gloves tight around them. "It's kinda warm in here, isn't it?"

"Yeah," I said absently.

"Why do you still have your gloves on?" Judy asked, and she cocked her head at me with her eyes narrowed.

"It's for—"

"She just forgot to take them off," Scott interrupted me.

"—your protection," I said, looking over my shoulder at Scott like he was a moron for answering for me.

I turned back to see Judy glaring at me, then she turned back to Scott, all hostility now. "Did you bring a soul eater into my house?"

Scott shook his head swiftly. "Nooooo …" He stretched out the word to make it even more obvious he was lying.

"You're as bad a liar now as you were as a kid," Judy said, stating the obvious. Her face was flushed a bright red and I started to get an inkling that this was not the place to be. The image of a raven flashed in my mind and there was a stir in the back of my consciousness, a screaming from the place where I was keeping my hitchiking souls.

She is an Odin-type, Bjorn shouted once I let him out. *Her ire is raised.*

Tell me something I don't know, I shot back at him.

"Maybe I did," Scott said, trying to cover for himself now. "But she's a good person—"

"You got a death wish?" Judy said, and came to her feet. "You are as dumb as a box of rocks, boy. You got the hots for a succubus? Let me spell how this is gonna end for you—she'll either get you killed in a fight with Sovereign or she'll eat your whole entire soul before she realizes how much it would burden her to be weighed down with an idiot like you for all the rest of the days of her life! *Do you know how long these things live?*"

Her last words came out as a scream and I stood from my place at the table, not sure whether I should be offended or not. "I am not a *thing*, I'll have you know, and the only souls I've ever willingly absorbed are the people who have tried to kill me."

Judy's eyes got wide and the raven flashed in my head again. "Get out of my house," she said as the blood drained out of her face.

"I'm not going to make a snack of your consciousness—"

"You're not eating my damned soul," she snapped back.

"You got that right," I said, and started for the door, "I don't want you shrewing in my head—"

"Get out!" she screamed. "OUT!"

I held up my hands to try and be peaceable and went for the door. She was a few steps behind me, giving me my distance. "I didn't come here for a fight," I tossed back over my shoulder.

Scott was trailing behind and started to say something. "She's not—"

"I don't want to hear it," Judy said, following us across the carpet. "Bringing a soul eater into my house. I oughta—"

"What you oughta do is watch your mouth," I said, stopping before I turned the handle. "I've eaten Odin-types before." I fixed her with a sweet smile and turned on my heel. Scott just missed getting the door slammed on him as we stepped out into the cold of winter.

Chapter 15

"I'm so sorry she treated you that way," Scott said as we pulled out of the driveway. I was in the driver's seat this time, and he didn't say a word as we started back down the road.

"I'd heard metas hated succubi and incubi," I said. "I hadn't really ever experienced it until now."

"Yeah," Scott said as the car went slowly down the drive toward the edge of the trailer park, "it's not subtle. You see it a lot in cloisters. Incubi and succubi are kind of like the bogeyman for meta kids."

"Nice," I said, not really feeling all that pleased about it. I reached up and put the tip of my right-hand glove's middle finger in my mouth, and started to pull it off with my teeth, one finger at a time.

"Don't take it too hard," Scott said, and I could see the tentativeness in his posture toward me. "It's a backward view, and it's fading."

"Not like there are a ton of my kind still out there, even," I said, looking at the windshield wipers as they squeaked, sweeping powdered accumulation from the glass. I started on the second glove, biting on the leather as I removed it and then tossed it on the center console.

"No," he said. "There really aren't." He waited just a minute. "Is there a reason you're taking your gloves off? Are you about to off me?" There wasn't a trace of fear in his words anywhere.

"Off you?" I asked, and sent him a sidelong glance. "According to your aunt, it's more like I'd be getting you off—without the gloves, I guess, because you're super dumb and want to die for a kinky thrill. No, I'm not about to 'off' you, I just don't like driving with gloves on." I looked back out the windshield and hit the brakes, hard, as a shadowy figure dashed out into the road from behind the last trailer in the line. The figure was small and wearing a black hoodie. The car went into a subtle fishtail, the back end going left about forty-five degrees before I managed to bring it to a stop. "Way to almost get yourself killed, kid," I muttered, my hands white-knuckling the steering wheel. The headlights illuminated a boy, around twelve or thirteen, peering out at us, hands buried deep in his pockets.

"Hey, I know him," Scott said. "That's Rajeev."

"He looks familiar," I said, squinting out into the dark. "He's from the Directorate, I assume?"

"Yeah," Scott said, already reaching for his door handle and stepping out. "Rajeev! How you doing?"

I followed a moment behind, stepping out into the dark of the night, the snowfall lit by my headlights and the front porch lights of the nearby trailer. I got a look at Rajeev and he looked a little familiar, dark hair, the faintest beginnings of what would probably be a mustache in about five years lining his upper lip.

"Scott," Rajeev said, and when they got close they shared one of those bro-hugs where their right hands met in the middle and pulled close, like a shoulder bump, but slightly more masculine. I didn't roll my eyes, exactly, but it was only through epic self-restraint.

"Glad to see you made it okay," Scott said.

"I'm glad to see I made it okay, too," Rajeev said. "You were gone long before it happened, right?"

"Yeah," Scott said, a little hushed. "I was far away when the Directorate went boom." He shifted a little uncomfortably in his shoes. "Listen, we came up here—"

"I know why you came," Rajeev said, nodding. "They had a meeting about it this afternoon, about this threat that's coming." He made a gesture to encompass the cloister. "They're talking about leaving. Pulling up stakes, going to Canada."

"Yeah," Scott said with some discomfort. "I bet they end up doing it tomorrow, too, now that they know what's coming." He clapped Rajeev on the shoulder. "Listen, we could use some help. We're going to take on this thing that's destroying the metas. You should come with us."

I gave Scott a searing look. "He's like twelve."

Rajeev looked offended. "I'm thirteen."

I tilted my head at him. "Have you even manifested yet?"

He shook his head. "Well, no."

"How old is the oldest of the kids who came with you?" I asked.

"Sixteen," Rajeev said.

"Yeah, we're not recruiting any of them," I told Scott with great finality.

"Their lives are in just as much danger as ours," Scott said.

"Still no," I said. "I'm not taking a bunch of teeny-boppers into battle, unless I find out that Sovereign's secret weakness is high levels of angst or a deep affinity for Justin Bieber."

"Hey!" Rajeev said, "just because I'm young doesn't mean I like Justin Bieber. Besides, we all want to stay with the cloister anyway," he said, stopping Scott from what was looking like a really burgeoning argument. His face was red and everything. "We took a vote."

"Smart kids," I said.

"What?" Scott said, turning his red face to Rajeev. "The entire species is being wiped out, do you realize that?"

Rajeev gave a nod. "Yeah, and that's tragic, but we're not that old, and none of us want to die. This thing is killing metas thousands of years older than us and more powerful, and besides, we already had one brush with them outside Brainerd and barely got away."

"What?" I asked, honing in on Rajeev again. "What do you

mean you had a brush with them?" Scott turned his attention on the boy as well, fully attentive.

Rajeev hesitated, thrusting his hands deeper in his pockets. "We stole some cars to get up here. We were on the road and a helicopter dropped down on us, caused one of our cars to flip on the icy road."

"Rajeev," I spoke quietly, my mouth dry, "was everyone else all right?"

"Mostly," Rajeev said. "We were lucky, none of them were metas. They shot up the cars, almost killed me. They would have, if not for—" His face bore a subtle hint of anguish. "We managed to get in the other car and speed away while—"

I felt a flash of fear. "Who was it? Who died?"

"They saved our lives, the three of them," Rajeev said. "It was unbelievable. He took out all the men that were after us, I think."

"Who?" I asked, more insistent. "Who died?" I had a sickening sense I already knew.

"Jeremiah Stevenson," Rajeev said, hushed, the snow falling around him as he cast his eyes downward in the reflected light of the headlamps. "They shot him first, right through the head. He didn't stand a chance. Sara Astley did much better, managed to take a few rounds in the body and still kill one of them with her strength." Rajeev wore a ghostly smile. "And Joshua, he—"

"Joshua," I whispered. "Joshua Harding?"

"He died in a blaze of glory," Rajeev said. "Broke the necks of two of them himself that I saw and managed to work a grenade off one of their belts and blow it up in the chopper, before the last of them put him down as we were driving out of view." He put his head down. "We threw all our cell phones out the window after that, got rid of everything they could trace and just ran for it."

I felt a stir of emotion at the thought of a kid I'd met only once, who probably—no, almost certainly—had a little schoolboy crush on me. I tried to picture him, but all I could see clearly was the glasses. "Damn," I whispered.

"He saved our lives. They all did," Rajeev said. "But what we were up against wasn't even metas and they nearly killed us." He cast a beseeching look at Scott. "Please forgive me for not being excited about stepping up to go toe-to-toe with this group's A-team when their B-team already nearly wiped us out."

"I don't blame you," I said quietly. "You should stay here, with the cloister. They'll be able to better protect you than we will."

"They will?" Scott asked, giving me the sidelong.

"They will," I said. "Because we're not going to be about defense, we're about offense. Our job is to take the fight to Sovereign and Century, not circle the wagons and stay carefully cocooned until the threat is over. Tell them to run," I said to Rajeev, and he nodded. "Tell them to keep running. Run as far as you think is safe and then run farther, because nowhere is safe. Nowhere is safe from this man." I felt a burning deep in my gut. "And nowhere is going to be safe for him to run from me."

Chapter 16

The cranberry bogs were full to the brimming, flooded with water to bring the berries to the top. There were patches of red filling swampy little square ponds on either side of the road. It all looked quite magnificent from above, which was how Aleksandr Gavrikov saw almost everything. It was an early fall day with just a hint of a blustery wind, though he couldn't truly feel it within the fire that covered his skin; he was aware of it, though, dimly, as though it was blowing in the face of someone else. He flew a little lower than he normally would have, taking in the majesty of the view. "I barely notice it anymore," he said aloud, the mild wind whipping him in the face. "And it is such a shame."

He took a breath and smelled something a little different. More of the slightly sulfuric smell that he had long since grown accustomed to. It was heavier somehow, though, more fragrant. He paused in his flight, idly curious. *Nowhere to go, no great hurry. Several days until I'm to rendezvous with Janus in Chicago ...*

He took another whiff and caught it again, stronger this time. He stopped his flight, ceased the forward momentum and extended his hands out. The winds were always warm around him, the heat from the flames that wrapped his body doing their level best to warm the air. Something was different, though, something ... more.

"Hello, Aleksandr," came a voice from just behind him. He spun in the air, twisting, his jaw slack as he looked up. *HOW?* The sight sent waves of shock through his body. Another figure was hovering just behind him, wreathed in flames that glowed blue, a slightly off-color mirror image of himself, staring back at him, an odd, fiery grin set upon non-existent lips. With a black hole as the only sign of a mouth, it was really more of a leer.

"Who are you?" Aleksandr asked and felt himself bob in the air from a sudden lack of control over his flight. He steadied himself, trying to push aside the shock of seeing a doppelganger hanging just outside his reach, staring back.

"Sovereign," the other figure said casually. "But that's just a name."

"What do you want?" Aleksandr spat with a hiss and a crackle of flame. He could feel his non-existent skin burning.

"Nothing," the other figure said with something approaching a shrug. "I just sensed you flying over and thought I'd introduce myself, let you know that you're not the only one in the neighborhood right now."

"The only what?" Aleksandr said, looking the flaming body up and down. "The only fire-covered freak?"

The figure gave another slight incline of the head and the flames dissipated as they'd been snuffed. A man remained behind, a figure a little taller than himself, clad in khaki pants, dress shoes, and a dress shirt. "Now I'm not fire-covered, at least." He smiled. "Though one could argue that every meta-human, by dint of being so comparatively rare, is a freak."

"What do you want?" Aleksandr asked again, his brain running along the same grooves repetitively, his mind still reeling from the shock of seeing someone like him hovering just a few feet away.

"I told you, nothing," the man said, his amusement gone. "Like I said, I saw you flying by and just thought I'd say hello." He gave a semi-formal salute with two fingers. "That done, I'll leave you to your business. I wouldn't want to impose upon you, after all." He tilted in the other direction and began to float slowly downward, toward a state highway a few hundred feet off in the distance.

"Where are you going?" Aleksandr asked, struggling for a word, for a question, something beyond the rote instincts that were throwing absurd question after question at him. He was vaguely aware that he should be asking something different, something more ... intelligent, yet he could not seem to find it in himself to do so.

"Wherever I want," the man called Sovereign said, not bothering to turn back as he sank toward the road below, drifting as casually as a leaf on the wind and no more concern about his direction, it seemed. "Just like always." The man turned and gave Aleksandr a little smile. "Take care of yourself. As far as I know, you and I are the only fire-covered freaks left in the world."

Aleksandr watched him go, silent, unsure what he should say or if he should say anything. The man reached the pavement and began to walk—to stroll, really—along the blacktop, slowly, seemingly unconcerned with anything.

For a time, Aleksandr watched him, trying to think of something to say, something to ask. After a few minutes, the man disappeared behind the trees lining the road, and Aleksandr flew on toward Chicago, his head now swimming with all the questions he wished he had asked.

Chapter 17

Sienna Nealon
Now

Six months passed quickly in a fever of activity. They all started to run together, really, and the only differentiation until we moved into our new headquarters building (it took them only five months to build it) was what the weather was like outside my window on any given day, and whether or not Senator Foreman was in the building. He was with us at least once a week, popping in to make sure we weren't slacking off while the world was burning, I supposed.

And burning it was.

"Estimated casualty reports say it's all over but the crying," Agent Li said from his place at the head of the conference room. We did things a little more formally in the new Agency. Li was standing in front of a map of Mexico City, which was the last place in the entire country of Mexico to feel the tentacles of Century snake their way through.

"The Mexican authorities weren't able to muster an effective counter to their efforts?" Karthik asked from side of the table to my left, closer to Li.

"No," Li said. "We extended another offer the week before last to assist, but they felt it was their ..." his face soured, "sovereign business to deal with. Mexico didn't have a huge meta population, but they had some very good cloisters that are now smoking craters, including one in a neighborhood in Mexico City that's being attributed to drug war violence."

"And Canada?" Scott asked, seated just to my right, which

was fitting. He, Karthik and Reed had become my lieutenants, helping me keep the crazy fevered pace of operations running. Well, with a little help.

"They infiltrated telepaths into the major metro areas weeks ago," my mother said, putting her elbows on the table, "after they were done nailing down Mexico. They're finishing up a clean sweep now."

"She's right," Li said with a curt nod. "Hawaii and Alaska are similarly already stitched up, Century's work already done. We didn't get much warning on either of those, of course."

"Why is Sovereign saving the United States for last?" This one came from Senator Foreman; it was one of his days with us, and his deep, resonant voice echoed in the conference room.

Li paused. "We've speculated quite a bit about that, but the truth is we don't have a solid answer."

"Because of me," I said, drawing Foreman's attention my way.

"Pure conjecture," Li said.

"But probably good conjecture," I said. "We still have no idea what he's planning beyond the extermination. I leaned back in my chair, barely noticing the leather padding. It had been a long six months, a frustrating six months. Most of the countries of South America hadn't even wanted to acknowledge they had metas, let alone that they were being hunted to extinction by some unknown, shadowy force. Even having Foreman on our side hadn't allowed us to intervene in any but the smallest cases. We'd managed to save five metas in Ecuador, to move them to a cloister here in the U.S. I'd also killed eight submachine-gun toting mercenaries and a meta who didn't even get a chance to show me her power before I shot her dead. She'd been about a half an inch from breaking Scott's neck, and so she had to go, no choice.

"I love how the phrase 'conjecture' is really just replacing the word 'guessing' with something more sophisticated-sounding,"

Breandan added, watching the whole conference unfold with his hand cautiously over his mouth.

Breandan, he was here for the comic relief. And oh, how desperately we needed it.

"We've got action on the border crossings near Seattle," Li said, and the slide on his presentation changed. "Unfortunately we didn't connect them in time, because they were using new passports, but some things developed after that that steered us in that direction." He clicked his remote again and five passport photos showed up, three women and two men. "If they'd been using the same passports, we might have been able to track them from country to country, at least among the ones who have electronic records. As it is, we flagged them because they were all caught on a security camera in downtown Seattle in a shootout with unidentified operatives."

"Of Omega," I said.

Li cast me a withering glare. It was a regular thing between him and me, so I ignored it. "We haven't been able to substantiate that."

I pointed at the blurry, black-and-white images on the screen, which showed the very vague and only slightly enhanced faces of the quintet of Century operatives whom he'd just shown us being shot at by a woman and three men. I reached into a thin file sitting on my desk and tossed out three photos on the center of the conference table, one at a time. "I'm telling you, these are the same people." The woman was a blond, looked to be in her late thirties, severe, with a worn look around her eyes. "Katheryn Hildegarde, an Omega field officer." I stood, because that was how I did things whenever I was about to butt heads with Li. "Last known posting was Seattle, along with a few of Omega's field operations people."

"You haven't had any luck chasing down Omega's remnants?" Foreman said in a way that was just a little shy of accusing me of failing at my job. He wasn't wrong, though. I'd also spent the last six months chasing Omega's ghosts with little success.

"No," I said. "Their headquarters is essentially fallen, remember? These people aren't dumb. They know if HQ is gone, it'd be smart if they were in the wind."

"They've been highly trained," Karthik put in. "They were in charge of helping expand and run Omega's illicit businesses here in America with very little oversight. These are seasoned people, experienced thugs, and usually quite savvy. They're also used to going well under the radar since Omega's political connections in the States were significantly weaker than back home in Europe." He looked down at Hildegarde's picture. "They're resourceful, mean, tough fighters. We have yet to get a reasonable line on what Hildegarde is planning to do, other than potentially disrupt Century's plans."

"What type is she?" Foreman said, staring down at her picture.

"Medusa," I replied, and he looked at her hair questioningly. "No snakes," I answered before he could ask, "but she does have the ability to control her hair, lengthen it, use it as a solid appendage to beat and flail at an enemy, even entrap them within it."

"She doesn't really look like she'd turn you to stone with a gaze," Breandan said, looking at the picture on the table. "She's actually quite fetching, you know, might be she'd turn parts of you to the same consistency as stone—" He stopped, as if he was remembering where he was. "Sorry," he said as he flushed.

I ignored it. "Whatever she's doing, I'd like to talk to Hildegarde. She's already put a thorn in Century's eye, and I can't pretend I don't like it." I pointed at Li's backdrop photo. "Three of Century's agents were killed in the exchange, along with two of hers."

"Type?" Foreman asked, his jaw level.

"Impossible to say for sure," Li said, his voice clipped, "but we suspect at least some of Century's losses were telepaths, coming down to start the reconnoitering."

Foreman leaned back. "So this is very good news."

"If it's true," I said cautiously, "yes. Which is why I'd like to find a way to make contact with Hildegarde. Maybe make her an offer."

"You think she's going to be interested in any offer that you have to make?" Foreman asked.

"I think she's killed Century agents, and that puts us on the same side for now," I replied. I caught my mother's worried look out of the corner of my eye.

"You don't expect some sort of Omega power struggle between the two of you?" Foreman asked, fingers stroking his chin.

I glanced at Karthik. "Omega is dead. She's welcome to whatever's left, absent the people who have chosen to side with us. We've visited a few safehouses in the last few months, and everyone has pretty much flown the coop, except for that one Siren-type we ran into down in Chicago." That hadn't been pretty. Breandan, Scott, Karthik and Reed had almost been wiped out before I had ended her allure by breaking her jaw. Now she was stuffed in a cell in Arizona and fed three times per day by female guards.

"You might not want to assume she's fighting the same fight as you," Foreman said.

"I don't," I replied. "But she's going to be forced to by Sovereign, eventually. All of us are. It'd be nice to have some more fighters on our side."

"All right," Foreman said warily. "Next moves?"

"We need to keep watch on the border," I said, cutting off Li, who was about to start talking before I halted him. "We need to comb the records of who's crossing and flag as many people as we can. As soon as we figure out where the next target is, I'll move a team into position to start doing some hammering back."

Foreman gave me one quick nod. "And here on the home front?"

I looked around the conference room. It was expansive, with glass windows overlooking a grassy campus that was deeply familiar, for obvious reasons. I'd spent most of the time I'd been outside my house here on these grounds. We had three buildings now, the construction companies doing wonders with what we were paying them. We now had a dorm, a headquarters building, and a training center with a gym, and they were working on a parking garage. They were also reinforced against easy demolition such as Omega had managed. "Not much we can do," I said. "We'll protect the people we've got as best we can, but—"

"But the minute you've got a line on something more interesting than sitting around here, you'll be off chasing it and leaving everyone unprotected," Li said, drawing a few shocked looks and a deathly silence.

I turned to look at him. "Playing defensive given what's at stake seems like a really good formula for losing everything."

Li smiled, but his face was haughty and smug. "Trite fortune cookie wisdom is not a sound strategy for fighting this war."

"Given it's my people at the sharp end of the blade, I think I know what's at stake here," I said. "Fortune cookie wisdom or not, it's true. Standing here and waiting for the entirety of Century's one hundred metas to descend upon us using their "overwhelming force" strategy is a pretty sure way to die messily."

"She's got a point," Foreman said, looking over at Li. "I don't care how good these people are, everything we've got on Century says that they're top of the food chain for meta powers. Sienna could assemble a team of veritable badasses from what we've got in the files, but they're going to be outnumbered."

I put my hands over my face and buried them for a minute. This had been a constant topic of discussion over the last few months, hashing and rehashing how we'd fight Century. So far the answer was the same as how I'd go about eating an elephant: One small bite at a time. "We need a line on them. We can't turn the tables until we know which table they're sitting at, and right now we're not even in the same restaurant."

"Looks like this Katheryn Hildegarde got a pretty good line on them," Breandan said. "Maybe you should ask her how she did it?"

I pulled my hands away from my face and looked up. My mother caught my gaze and I knew I was wearing the same expression she was.

Foreman caught the look and I could see the caution plant itself all over his dark features. "I know that look. That's the look my wife and daughters share when they're about to tell me something they know I won't like."

"What if we could approach Hildegarde?" I asked. "Now we've got two motives—find out if she's on the same side, and failing that, find out how she got a piece of those Century operatives."

"She probably just waited for them," Karthik said, the voice of reason. "They're coming for all of us metas, sooner or later. She probably laid a trap where they wouldn't suspect and blindsided them."

"So how do we find the telepaths?" I asked. "How do we ambush people who can read minds?"

"Send someone who doesn't have a mind to read," Scott suggested, waving a hand at Breandan.

"Hey!"

I thought about it for a moment. "Is there anyone who can block a telepath's abilities?"

"Sure," Foreman said cautiously. "An empath can do it. We

can even use our powers to push a little gap in their abilities. Drives telepaths nuts because unless they're really paying attention, they don't see us coming. The converse is we can't use our powers of persuasion on them, either."

I felt a little surge of glee. "But can you tell when there's a telepath about?"

He shook his head. "Only by noticing there's no empathic presence to correspond with the person I'm seeing with my eyes. Obviously," he said, holding up a hand, "it only works in plain distance. If I can't see them ..." He let his voice trail off. "Same goes for me with them, I'm told."

"Well, that is some helpful information," Scott said acidly. "It might have been even more helpful to know this six months ago, since that's how long we've been trying to figure out how to dog these bastards."

Foreman shrugged. "There's a limited application for it, and you'd need to know where the telepaths were going to be. I've kept apprised of everything going on, it's not like I would have held it back from you if something had come up before now wherein that information had to be disclosed."

"Playing the wise man card in this group is not the smartest strategy," Reed said, but he was more calm than malicious. "You might consider being more open."

"About everything else, I am," Foreman said, tight-lipped. "About my own personal life and abilities, forgive me for being somewhat reticent." He folded his hands in front of him.

"This is all a distraction," I said. "The revelation is what's important, not the circumstances. Now that we know this, I have an idea." I smiled. "Okay, a couple ideas."

There was an uncomfortable silence finally broken by Scott. "Please stop smiling." He looked uneasy. "It makes me nervous in a meeting when you get that look, because what inevitably follows is something that makes our previous plans look sane by comparison."

"Oh, I think you'll like this one," I said, but I'm pretty sure my smile got wider. "Because it involves finally scoring a point on Century."

Chapter 18

Orlando's McCoy International Airport had a massive open courtyard outside the terminal arrival area. A fountain in the center spewed water under a glass-paneled ceiling hundreds of feet above, giving the whole place a certain majesty. Concrete planters a couple feet high were arrayed around the fountain with wooden benches stationed in front of them for seating. There was a hotel above, balconies around the edges of the courtyard and extending a few stories up toward the glass ceiling. The whole thing was bright and totally appropriate, I thought, for the Sunshine State.

I was getting very accustomed to sitting there, a mocha in hand while we waited outside the security checkpoints, watching the lines peak and subside throughout the day as new arrivals flooded by as their flights came in. Right after the meeting wherein Foreman had let slip what an empath could do, I got us a flight down to Orlando. It was pretty easy because it turns out that our little Agency was doing so well in the markets that we were able to charter a private Gulfstream. The U.S. senator who sat across from me for the whole flight didn't seem to like it very much, but Scott, Reed, Breandan, Karthik, my mother and I luxuriated in the travel arrangements as we flew down with only a brief stopover in Nashville to pick up a passenger. That was days ago, though, and sitting around the courtyard in Orlando's airport at odd hours for the last few days had already caused me to forget what it was like living to live in luxury for once.

Reed was standing next to me, munching on a burrito that he'd gotten from somewhere down the concourse. Ahead of us was the security checkpoint blocking entry to the courtyard. His eyes were fixed, watching a stream of people come out of the customs line. Breandan was completely bored, just zoned out with his head back, resting against the bench he was lounging on. "How much longer?" he asked, his Irish accent affecting a high whine.

"Until we get the word they've all cleared customs," I said, annoyed.

"This is getting repetitive," Breandan said, splayed out on his seat. I expected more nerves from him, but all he did was occasionally fiddle with the waxed ends of his mustache, like a man with all the time in the world and nothing to fill it with.

"You forgot the charger for your phone, didn't you?" Reed asked between bites of the burrito.

"I was doing so well on Candy Crush, too," Breandan moaned.

"This isn't my idea of the greatest way to spend my time, either," Foreman said from just down the row. "But this plan is sound." The fountain was a continuous roar behind us; not loud enough to bother me, but enough to add some white noise to the buzz of conversation already going in the courtyard.

"The plan was sound days ago, when it was originated, when it was fresh, and when my bum didn't have four days' worth of hard benches underneath it and wake-ups at all hours of the night and day to wear it out," Breandan replied.

My earpiece buzzed with a burst of static. "Last of the passengers from Flight 1834 from Mexico City are now through customs."

"Last of them coming through now," I said, parroting the missive I'd just overheard.

"Using the DEA to do spotting for us was pretty smart," Reed said. "They can watch like they normally would, thinking they're looking for drug mules." He gave me an amused glance. "I wonder how pissed they'd be if they knew we were just using them to keep an eye on passengers moving through customs?"

"I don't know," I said, "and I don't care much, either. Maybe they'll turn up something for themselves in the bargain, but it's fairly irrelevant. I just need to know when each flight is finished offloading so we can take a break every now and again." I looked down at Foreman. "Anything?"

He was looking at the customs gate with intense concentration. "Maybe." He seemed to focus, to stare harder at the portal where arrivals were streaming through. "I think ..." He stood and started to walk toward the portal, where a few TSA employees waited around a podium to block anyone's attempt to enter. "Oh, yeah." He straightened instantly. "Four of them." He pulled his cell phone out and pointed it in the general direction of the customs gate as he took a picture that I knew was immediately uploaded to J.J. back at the Agency in Minneapolis for flagging in case they got past us. "They look like businessmen—and a woman. Suits, ties, roller suitcases—"

"I got 'em," I said, taking the lead. Reed moved to my left side, just a little off my shoulder. Foreman fell in behind with Breandan just next to him. We tried to avoid looking ridiculously conspicuous, but it was kind of hard. Subconsciously, I knew Foreman's ability to keep us blocked from the telepaths' power was limited by distance, and so I hung close by him, not wanting to tip our hand, especially now that we had a line on them.

It turned out not to matter.

It was the woman who screwed it up. The men were oblivious, talking, laughing, enjoying their cover assignment. It was the woman, a strawberry blond with a deeply serious expression, who looked back. Her lips were too wide for her face, her most prominent feature, I noted as she caught my eye. At least until her eyes went wide like she'd just been stabbed in the ass with a knife.

"We're made," Reed said, stating the ridiculously obvious.

"Made of what?" Breandan asked.

For my part, I was already running, any thought of casual

behavior tossed aside. I vaulted onto the top of the planter that was between me and the group of them just as she said something to the rest of her party, prompting them all to immediately turn to look rather than run, which was what they should have been doing.

I leapt through the air and descended into their midst after screaming, "HOMELAND SECURITY! You are under arrest!" There was a brief moment of shock that rippled through the courtyard while I came down, and panic broke loose as people scrambled to get away in the moments following. For my part, I angled my landing at the blond who'd fouled up my ambush. I hit her hard enough to knock her out when I came down. I swept the next guy in line, and he cracked his head against the burnt-orange tile floor. The next tried to run, but I picked up the woman's discarded roller suitcase and flung it into his back, dropping him like an empty bottle of Snapple—of which I'd had more than a few over the course of our stakeout.

I turned to face the last of them, but as I did, his suit swelled, muscles bulging underneath like a tent billowing in a gust of wind. He looked so diesel after about five seconds that even an MMA champion might think twice before starting a fight with him. His dark, short-cropped hair framed a face highlighted by a cruel expression—sneering lips, squinty eyes, and a definite sense that he thought he was about to come out of our altercation on top.

"Heya, Hercules," I said, keeping my distance. "I guess you're the brawn of this operation."

He almost snarled. "I was their escort, yes."

"Ooh," I said, "you sure you don't mean 'bodyguard'? Because 'escort' kinda makes you sound like you were their hooker."

He didn't bother to respond, just came at me in an attack, leading with a hard punch. I'd seen a Hercules type before, in a dream. They grew muscle mass on command, getting insanely strong. I dodged back, only narrowly avoiding his punch. He was fast, too, less out of shape than the Hercules I'd seen in my dream a few months earlier. My gloves were on, and that wasn't going to help my cause because putting my skin against his was the fastest way to make sure he went down.

A blast of wind shot by me, stirring the Hercules back a step but not lifting him. He smiled at Reed, whom I saw just over my shoulder. "Mass increase," he said smugly. "Your little gusts aren't gonna do squat to me, Windkeeper."

He came at me again, and this time I vaulted back over a planter, clipping a palm tree as I rolled back over the edge and back to the blue, thinly carpeted floor on the other side. He hit the sculpted concrete edge of the planter with his fist and it shattered, slinging dirt, plants and pieces of tile and stone in a shotgun blast pattern toward me. I was already low to the ground from having rolled over the planter, but I ducked down and avoided all but a little dirt that hit my right eye over the edge. It hurt, though, and I felt tears spring to my eyes. I kept my left eye squinted open and tried to open my right as well, my cheek pressed against the planter's uneven, graveled surface and the floor.

I sprung up to my feet in a quick move that looked like an overpowered pushup, which it was. The Hercules was still across from me, looking smug, the wreckage of the planter separating us. "Tough luck," he said.

It took me a second to realize what he meant. I glanced back and saw Reed on the ground, blood and shards of the planter scattered around him, his shirt soaked with red and dirt stains. Breandan was a little farther back, clutching his midsection and rolling like someone had kicked him in the gut. I saw Foreman off a little farther, apparently uninjured, but keeping his distance from the fight. He didn't look like a man who was well versed in the martial arts, so it was probably better that way.

The blood around Reed and on Breandan chilled me, like the air conditioner had just kicked on in my soul. I felt my pulse slow as I looked back at the Hercules, who was grinning like he was enjoying a particularly hilarious joke. "Look at you kids, playing at being big boys and girls. What are you? Twelve?" He laughed, sneering derisively. "The kid gloves are off, little girl. Now run home and wait for us. We'll be back for you later."

I pulled my hands up, slowly, showing them to him. "My gloves are still on, actually." I ripped the leather, tearing them from my hands. "Now the gloves are off." I clenched my fists open and closed.

He watched me, a wary caution creeping over his face. "I know what you are, and if you think you'll even be able to lay a hand on me—"

I threw myself at him, but I went low, rolling over the remains of the planter and throwing a sharp kick upward from the roll. It connected with his thigh and he grunted, balling up slightly. When I came out of the roll, his face was right there from his instinctive turtle maneuver and I punched it, hard, in the nose and heard the cartilage break. I followed with another and his head snapped back, sending him staggering a step. His hands came up to defend his face but it was too late; I was on to other things.

I went low, grabbing him on the back of the neck, and swept his feet from underneath him. He tried to grab at me, but my free hand slapped his aside and he had no leverage for all his strength. His back and shoulders hit the hard floor and I stomped on his face, twice, then kicked him in the ribs with so much force that he flew in a low roll through the air and into another, smaller planter, roughly the size of a vase. It broke open, sending a cascade of dirt down his prone body.

I jumped through the air to follow him, landing both feet on him with all my force. I hit his belly, causing him to gasp with the shock of my impact, all forced through the toes of my boots. I didn't stop there, though, savagely assaulting his fallen body with a series of devastating kicks as he tried to get to his feet. I broke his face, shattering it with a volley of attacks that stopped only when his head slumped and he sagged to the ground, his overmuscled frame beginning to deflate. His body was limp, and I reached down and grabbed him around the neck, holding my hand there until I heard the screaming in my head, the sound of his soul starting to pull away from his body. In the moment before it left, I slammed the back of his head to the hard tile floor and let myself sag to my hands, down on all fours. I stared at the fountain, roaring just in front of me. I hadn't even realized I'd gotten this close to it.

"You didn't drain him?" Foreman's voice shook me out of my weariness, my body chastising me for not finishing the job, for not giving it a sweet, just reward for the fight.

"No," I said. "I've got enough trash in my head without inviting in more. I got his memories, though, the ones about Century."

"Oh?" He offered me a hand up, but I shook my head and gestured at my bare palm.

"Yeah," I said, getting to my feet only with great effort. I looked back toward the destroyed planter just across the courtyard. "Reed and Breandan—"

"They'll be fine," Foreman said. "Looks worse than it is." I heard a trilling from his pocket and he took out his phone, staring at the screen. "Looks like the team in Miami got a result of their own."

"Oh?" I asked, my legs unsteady as I made my way slowly over to Reed, who was still clutching his midsection in silence. Breandan was making no attempt at bravery, moaning and wailing softly. "Was it sheer luck that you married an empath or—"

"No," Foreman said. "She and I got a sense for each other immediately, were drawn to each other." He smiled. "Been married twenty-eight years."

"Lucky you," I said as I slumped down next to Reed. "Lucky

us, actually, since it sounds like having her along helped out our Miami group." I tilted my head down to look at my brother. "How are you doing?"

"Took some slivers in the gut," Reed said, moving his hands away from his shirt to reveal shredded cloth all around his abdomen. "They'll get pushed out as I heal, but ... damn, if you know what I mean."

"Yeah," I said. "Gut wounds are never fun." I looked over at Breandan, who had settled down a little. "What about you, Irish?"

"Oh, don't mind me," came Breandan's voice, a little weak. "I'm just bleeding to death over here."

"Come off it," Foreman said. "You pretty much have to take the heart out of a meta to get them to bleed to death, and your heart looks fine from here."

Breandan moved his hands away from his abdomen and a single red spot, only about the size of a dime, darkened his silky green shirt. "You don't think this looks serious?"

"It looks like you accidentally peed yourself," I said.

"No, that was lower."

I chuckled and nodded to Foreman. "You have the briefcase?"

He nodded and ran a few steps back to where we'd been sitting, retrieving a black leather case and opening it just as the TSA officers were starting to make their way over to us. I had met them all before, when we'd first arrived, and they knew to give us a wide berth. Foreman opened the case with a couple clicks but fumbled it, hand and leg cuffs spilling out onto the floor in front of me. "Sorry," he said.

"It's fine." I stroked Reed's hair idly before I stood, walking over to Foreman and helping him retrieve the cuffs from the ground. Let's get 'em bound for transport." I looked at the fallen telepaths and the Hercules bleeding over near the planter, a host of TSA officers standing around him. I smiled at the carnage, dimly aware that I was feeling a lot happier than someone ought to feel at the scene of so much destruction. "We struck our first blow against Century today." The happiness faded then, my smile lingering but without feeling behind it as I wondered how long it would be until they struck back.

Chapter 19

The flight back to campus was longer somehow and filled with the swearing of the prisoners until we had enough and gagged them. Foreman started to raise the point of constitutional rights, but tossing out the phrase "indefinite detention" shut him up pretty fast.

We dropped Foreman's wife off in Nashville in a quick stopover then got back into the air for the flight to Minneapolis. We were set for a landing at Eden Prairie's Flying Cloud airport, but it was still hours off. The prisoners had their own seats, and Scott was loud and jubilant, the minibar clouding his ability to think straight. Reed suffered in silence, his body doing the hard work of healing the injury he'd suffered. Breandan, meanwhile, didn't shut up and moaned all the way back.

"All I'm saying is you're suited to this sort of thing," he said, using illustrative hand gestures more appropriate for an Italian than an Irishman. "You're a fighter. Me, I just sort of do my thing, stick to the shadows, keep myself out of trouble. Getting life-threatening wounds is just so far out of the—"

"I wouldn't worry about life-threatening wounds," I said, not looking at him. "You still haven't had one of those yet."

He was quieted for a moment, one in which I heard Scott shout from the back of the plane, near where the prisoners were trussed up, "We need a par-tay! When we get back."

"You all right?" Breandan asked.

"Fine," I said. "Would you go check on Scott? Make sure he's not too overdone?"

"Sure," Breandan said, unfastening his seatbelt. "But when I come back, maybe we could discuss hazard pay for this danger you keep thrusting me into—"

"Take it up with Ariadne," I said, sinking into my seat, a padded one, with a sigh. I thought about pushing the seat rest back, maybe trying to nap, but I wanted to be awake in case I had to pound the stuffing out of a prisoner. I'd considered starting the interrogation right then and there, but the interior space of the plane was too small to start working them over one by one, and I really wanted to get them on an individual basis. I wasn't entirely sure I'd even have to use my power to sift their memories in order to get what they knew.

I sighed and stood, as I looked back at Scott, gyrating to music only he could hear, a bottle of open champagne in his hand. The prisoners were behind him, strapped to their seats, most of them looking fearful. As telepaths, I suspected they conversed to each other largely through speaking with their minds. Now that they were gagged and Foreman was shutting down their ability to communicate mentally, the six of them were frantic, eyes wide. The Hercules was still out cold, his face a mess. Blood crusted his cheeks below his eyes, and his head was tilted to the side, right-angling his neck. He would definitely have a crick in it tomorrow, and that bothered me none.

"You did well on the Hercules," came my mother's voice from my right. She eased into the seat across the aisle that Breandan had just vacated. "I didn't even get to find out what type my escort was; he came at Karthik a little too hard and I had to put him down."

"Yeah, well, I knew what to expect," I said. "Thanks to Adelaide." I thought about it. "Thanks to Zollers, I guess."

"What do you mean?" Her face was a little scrunched. She and I hadn't talked much over the past few months outside of work. If she was interested in more of a relationship with me, time didn't allow for it. We worked a lot of hours, and almost always it broke down with her leading one team, me leading another. She was good; I couldn't deny it. It's why I had left her in charge of the second team rather than letting Karthik lead. She had experience, and it showed.

"I had these visions while I was in London," I said. "Zollers gave them to me. They were of a succubus named Adelaide who worked for Omega." I stroked the leather arm of my seat. "She was the one who killed your father." I looked up at her and saw her surprise. "She drained him in an alley in London on the orders of the Primus."

My mother's reaction wouldn't have been obvious to anyone but me. Her emotion just cut out and she got cold. "When was this?"

"I don't know. Late eighties sometime, maybe early nineties by then," I said. "I didn't get the full story, just a quick shot of the fight."

"He left on a business trip," she said slowly, "and never came back."

I didn't say anything for a minute. "I have some passing familiarity with how that feels." I didn't add any judgment or spite to it, but my mother blanched almost imperceptibly nonetheless.

"Wolfe got me," she said. "Captured me. I was coming out of the hospital from work one day and saw him, he saw me, and I had a quarter second to run before he was on me. He beat me down, knocked me unconscious. I thought I was dead for sure. I woke up in a warehouse, hanging from the ceiling by a chain. I only barely got out, had to break my own bones to do it." She smiled bitterly. "I crawled outside and managed to get to a convenience store. A good Samaritan picked me up. I knocked him out by draining him, took his phone and called the Directorate. I was useless, arms broken, couldn't drive, couldn't fight, even. I tried to move the car but couldn't. I just passed out. When I woke up, I knew it had been too long. I was healed. When I got back to the house, you were gone." The bitter smile faded. "I saw you on the Directorate campus. Once I knew you were safe, I headed for Gillette, Wyoming, where I had a safehouse. Dug a hole in the earth and pulled it in after me." She leaned her head back against the headrest. "Didn't come out until someone sent me an email from an anonymous account spilling some of the details of the Andromeda project."

"I don't understand," I said, leaning toward her. "What was so important about Andromeda?" I stopped her before she answered. "Wait, you came out of hiding for an anonymous email detailing some mysterious Omega project? What the hell were you thinking?" I felt hot irritation flood me. "What about all those times you told me that 'Motion reveals the prey; hold still and go unnoticed'?"

She looked deeply uncomfortable. "I think the moral of the story there is that after six months of not leaving a house, even I get a little antsy. Maybe too antsy to think things through logically."

I just stared at her for a moment, then burst out laughing.

"What?" She frowned, and I caught a hint of irritation.

"Come on," I said, "Surely you can't possibly miss the irony in that statement." She stared at me blankly, so I leaned toward her, as though my proximity might wake her up. "You went stir crazy after being confined to a house for six months without being able to go outside ..."

"Oh," she said with a subtle hiss of impatience. "I get it now, yes, very funny. There's a big difference between being locked in a house and not even being able to see the light of day because you're underground."

"What?" I laughed. "Rule #3 was that I wasn't allowed to look outside, remember?"

"Oh, please, you looked out the back window all the time," she dismissed me.

I stared at her, a little shocked. "You knew about that?"

She slanted her head, everything about her expression asking me how dumb I thought she was. "Of course I knew. You weren't that good at putting the curtain right after trying to peek out past the armoire I covered it with." She straightened in her seat. "But that was fine. I wanted you to have at least one open channel to quietly defy me, so I left it that way."

"Why?" I asked, a little befuddled.

"Because," she said, "expecting you to perfectly obey me in all things would be an exercise in futility. Everything I did, I did with an eye toward practicality. I had to keep you away from the world, away from the threats outside. Getting you to buy into those threats at age six was impossible. So I worked you like a dog, trained you in martial arts, fighting—"

"I thought that was so I could defend myself," I interjected.

"Dual purpose," she said. "It did that, which was obviously most important, but it also gave you an outlet for your frustrations and physicality, wore you out so you didn't have as much energy to expend trying to find ways to escape or subvert me. Same with your studies. Admit it," she said and smiled a little. "You may have been confined to the house for ten years, but you were never bored."

"No," I conceded. "Not when I was in the house at large. I always had studies to work on, or something else." I glanced down at the bulkhead in front of me. "Still wouldn't have been the way I'd have chosen to spend my childhood, though."

There was a quiet from her seat for a long moment. "It wouldn't have been the way I'd have chosen for you to spend it, either."

I started to say something else but a hideous, groaning screech came from behind me and I stood. Mom matched my motion and we both looked back to the rear of the plane. The Hercules who had been unconscious was most definitely not unconscious now; he was on his feet, the chair he had been resting in ripped from the floor of the plane.

"Oh, hell," I breathed, but I was already running down the aisle. I could hear Mother two steps behind me.

Scott was blocking my passage and I hipchecked him out of the way. Breandan was quick enough to move on his own, just behind Scott, tripping onto Reed, who screamed in pain as the Irishman landed on his stomach. The narrow cabin forced me to slow my run so I didn't bounce up and hit the low ceiling. I didn't make it back in time to keep the enraged Hercules from doing something stupid.

He was still well secured to the seat, but it was ripped free of the cabin floor, hanging off his back. I saw him stress it, trying to break the handcuffs, but the sound of the seat resisting and the metallic grind from stress in the chair itself were the only noises.

The Hercules viewed my approach with a wild-eyed demeanor. He knew he was stuck: his hands and feet still bound, he was unable to fight me. I saw the options roll through his mind and the desperation set in, eyes darting. Finally, something clicked as he looked back toward the wall of the cabin, and I didn't even have a chance to scream, "NO!" before he launched himself into it full force, leading with the seat.

The sound of the explosive decompression of the cabin was, in fact, explosive. It felt like my eardrums blew up with the sudden change in air pressure, and I only just got a hand on the chair next to me before the wind ripped me toward the back of the cabin where the Hercules had made a hole in the fuselage. I couldn't hear the straining of his muscles over the horrendous noise of the wind, but I watched as he broke the seat into three pieces with his strength; one hung by the handcuff chain from each of his massive paws; the last clung to his feet in one great chunk.

I held on as the hole in the cabin widened, the fractures the Hercules had created shearing as the wind tore at them. Someone screamed over the speaker above me about an emergency landing. My total focus was on the Hercules, though, as he stood, unmoved by the wind, his feet planted and one hand on the chair of the telepath who had been chained next to him. He flashed that smug, nasty smile at me as he turned loose his free hand in a long wind up and swipe. I knew what was about to happen but I couldn't stop it.

The telepath who had been seated next to him got hit by the remnant of the seat chained to his hand; the results were like a watermelon getting splattered by a sledgehammer. I held on, my fingers clutching Foreman's chair as the Hercules wound up for his next swipe, moving back in the line and taking the head off the next telepath, this one the woman from Orlando. Her scream was lost in the sound of the roaring gusts around me as air rushed out of the plane through the hole.

He got one more swipe in unchecked before the tempest began to die down. I was holding my breath, something we metas could do for longer than a human without passing out, but I reached out and grabbed the nearest oxygen mask and took three hits in rapid succession. Then I tossed aside the mask and launched myself at the Hercules as he took a long step toward the back of the plane and brought down the chair pieces on two more screaming telepaths.

I hit him in the center of his mass as he tried for the last telepath. My shoulder hit his ribs and I couldn't tell whether I broke something of his or he broke something of mine, or both. It hurt like hell, though, and stunned me long enough to prevent me from following up in a timely manner. It gave him just enough time to throw an arm at the last telepath, though, and he buried the remnants of his seat in the man's chest, destroying his heart, lungs, and anything else in his upper chest. The man's head lolled forward, and I knew I'd lost.

"You failed!" the Hercules said with a wide grin. "You won't learn anything from them," he said over the howling of the wind.

"They're not the only ones I can learn from," I said, matching his grin with one of my own, one I didn't remotely feel. I threw my ungloved hands at him and he tried to bring his hands together, to catch my head between the two chair pieces. It would likely have killed me if I hadn't dragged him down before he could complete the maneuver.

I saw his eyes widen as my power began to work, the cumulative drain restarting at virtually the same point I'd left off. I could hear his howls over those of the wind, and he fell atop me, jerking with great muscle spasms as I started to pull the last of him free of his body. He screamed in my head and through his mouth and I heard both, combining with the blast of air that thundered around me, and the sound of blood rushing and pounding in my head from my exertion and what I was about to get, to reach—the climax.

He swung his arm wildly one last time as I felt the finale build. It was so close, within the touch of my fingers. It was almost mine, that sweet release, when something exploded and he flew from my grasp. It took the split second before I flew out of the plane to realize that he'd struck the hole in the side of the cabin with one of his cudgels and broken it wide, wide open. The wind reached out and plucked him from atop me, ripping him from my grasp before I could take the last of his soul. I had not even a moment to think about it before I felt the deck of the cabin that had been so tight on my back disappear from beneath me as I, too, went flying out of the side of the plane and found myself falling, freely, my jacket whipping as I saw the ground, tens of thousands of feet below, but rushing up so very, very fast.

Chapter 20

Free-falling without a parachute was without a doubt the most frightening sensation I had ever felt. The wind blasted at my face, drying my eyes even as I tried to keep them open. Why? I don't know. It was like I wanted to look death in the face or something as I plummeted through the rapidly diminishing space between me and the ground. The chill wind caused my jacket to flap wildly around me. I wasn't screaming, but it was only because I was still too stunned to realize that I'd fallen out of a plane. I quelled my panic with a thought, reaching inside for desperate answers. My skin had gone numb from the cold, and I couldn't force my brain to think, no matter how much I wanted it to. I could see the Hercules a few hundred feet below me, his hands pinwheeling wildly, and I wondered if I was doing the same.

I hoped in flash for Reed to come save me. Then I remembered his stomach wound, how he coughed and blood came out, his semi-conscious state, and knew that if he came after me, we would both die instead of just me. My breathing was wild, my lungs trying to sift oxygen out of the thin air so high up. I tried to remember a lesson, long ago, from Glen Parks about combat drops. I moved my body into a more wind-resistant position, my arms and legs extended, my body flat against the upward pressure of the wind. I had no idea why I bothered, but I was desperate enough to try anything to prolong my life by even a few seconds.

My metahuman abilities wouldn't solve this problem, and I doubted there'd be enough left of me to heal after impact. I remembered reading something once about how someone had survived a skydive gone wrong, landing in a swamp after a parachute failure, but that had to be a one in a million shot. There was no hope of that for me; I saw nothing but flat green fields in every direction.

I was about to reach in and beg for help, for anything, when something hit me in the back, hard, and I felt arms wrap around my midsection. The little oxygen in my lungs was knocked out, and I gasped for breath even harder. I threw up my head to look at who had struck me, hoping against all hope and logic that it was Reed.

It wasn't.

"You idiot!" I gasped between frantic breaths. "You've killed yourself, too!"

Scott Byerly's face was redder than normal, and I could tell he was trying hard not to pass out. He was holding his breath, and a quick look down confirmed that we were not going to be in the air much longer. "Hold on to me!" he shouted, then took another long breath, a look of deep concentration on his face.

What else could I do? I turned in his grasp, pushing around so that my chest was against his, my arms wrapped around his neck. Once I had a good hold, he unlocked his hands from around my midsection and extended them. His eyes closed and his face got deep with concentration. I wasn't sure if I should say anything or not, and I waited, in silence, for what felt like minutes before I finally spoke. "What are you doing?"

He opened one eye and grinned. "Just enjoying the feel of a woman pressed against me before I die."

"You ass!" I screamed, and looked down again. It wasn't far now, a thousand feet at most, and it was coming up ridiculously fast.

"HOLD ON!" he shouted and I felt something rush past my legs, something strong and powerful, something that stirred the air around us. Scott's face went red again in spite of the fact that we were now low enough to breathe without difficulty. I clenched my arms around his neck as if he were a life vest and I was a drowning woman. I thought about kissing him on the lips for the hell of it and decided against it, but only because his face was veiled in utter and complete concentration.

The jets of water coming out of his hands were so intense that I could feel the power of them. My arms snugged tight around him, I could feel us start to fight back against gravity's pull, a little at a time. We began to slow and I held on, the centrifugal force on my brain causing me to see spots. Just when I thought I couldn't handle another moment of the force, my feet hit the ground, hard enough that I knew I'd dropped but not hard enough to break anything. I didn't let go of him, though, and we ended up in a tangle in the middle of a cornfield, the foot-high stalks and a puddle of mud cushioning my landing. Scott's chest thudded against mine, knocking the wind out of me. I felt his arms take up his weight for only a second before he collapsed on me, his head buried on my breastbone, the smell of wet dirt filling my nose. It was warm against my back, oozing into my clothing, seeping down my neck.

I looked left, then right, and all I saw was spring corn, barely out of the ground. I was breathing slowly but steadily, long breaths reassuring me that I hadn't died and entered some afterlife that began with endless fields.

"Are we dead?" Scott asked, his voice muffled from where his head lay buried in my chest. "Is this Elysium or something?"

"I think it's Iowa," I said, "which means we're probably closer to hell." I glanced down and realized his head was pretty much right between my breasts. "You ... uh ... you can get up anytime now."

"Huh?" His head came up and his chin rested right on my sternum, his face completely drained of color. His brow was coated in sweat, his eyes almost closed, and he looked like he'd just run a five-hundred mile race.

I felt a little stiff, my back feeling the corn stalks underneath it. It was a little awkward because he was right between my legs, too. I had a very embarrassed flash as I remembered the last time I'd been in this position. It had been about six months. "You should probably get up," I said, feeling the flush of red on my cheeks.

"I don't know if I can move right now," he said, and his head bobbed to the side, his blond, curly head lying against my chest. "I may actually fall asleep like this."

"Um." I clumsily rolled him to the side, as gently as I could, pitching him off me. "Sorry," I said when he looked at me reproachfully. "I don't like to feel trapped."

"How about splattered?" he said as his head lolled back into the muddy field. "How does squished work for you?"

I pulled myself to my feet and looked around us. Warm mud rolled down my hands in beads and dripped to the puddle beneath me with a plop. The field was a wide expanse of open ground. The only thing disturbing the perfect flatness of the scene before me was a road in the distance, at least a mile away, and, a couple hundred feet away, an impact crater caused by something hitting the ground. "Hercules," I said. "Guess you weren't so damned invincible after all." I twitched my fingers, one after another, as though I could somehow compel the last of his soul to come to me, to finish what we had started.

I looked over the fields, found the road again in the distance. It was getting close to summer and the days were longer, but I could see the sun hanging low in the sky. We could be at the road in a few minutes at normal speed. I looked back down at Scott lying in the mud and knew we'd be going far slower than normal speed. I took a deep breath, sighing once more. Scott was spent, I was sure of that. I lifted him up onto my back with as much gentleness as I could manage and started carrying him, fireman-style, across the field toward the distant road. Every pain and ache from my fights and the landing seemed to shout at me every step of the way, but that was all right. I was alive. And in Iowa. That part of creation where even God got bored enough to nod off for a while.

I surveyed the flat ground around me, judged the distance to the road, and wondered how long I'd have to walk down it before I found any sign of civilization. I sighed. Could be a while.

"Iowa," I said, breathing the word like a curse. Because it kind of was.

Chapter 21

Scott and I managed to get a ride from a trucker who was passing through on the way to Decorah, a mid-sized town in northwest Iowa. I should say I managed to get a ride from the trucker. Scott remained passed out and still reeked of mud and champagne, like a pig farmer who'd had a good night, I guess. Probably not out of place in Iowa.

I took a shower and bought some new clothes at a truck stop then rented a car in Decorah. We pulled into the Directorate campus a few hours later, long after nightfall. Ariadne was waiting outside HQ with my mother, her face dark and sullen. I pulled up and got out of the car, stretching my legs as I did so, tilting my arms up in the air. "Hey, guys," I said from where I'd stopped on the loop just in front of our HQ building, a square, modern-looking structure that rose about four stories above us and two below the ground.

My mother wore a small smile. "I was a little worried until we got your call."

"A little worried?" Ariadne's arms were folded and she shot an astounded look at my mother. "She fell out of an airplane."

My mother's face didn't change much, but I saw a hint of something more. "Okay. Maybe more than a little."

"Senator Foreman caught a flight back to D.C.," Ariadne said without preamble as I crossed behind the car and opened the passenger door. Scott was still passed out and I hefted him onto my shoulder. He didn't stir. "He didn't seem too happy about the outcome of the mission."

"Did you have to make an emergency landing?" I asked my mother as I walked by her, toting Scott on my shoulder as I headed toward the dorm building. I heard Ariadne's heels clopping behind us to keep up.

"In Des Moines," she said. "We caught the next flight back. What about you?"

"Splashed down in a cornfield," I said. "Managed to hitch to a city where we caught the car rental place just before closing."

"You lost every single one of the telepaths," Ariadne said, her voice strained.

"We did," I agreed. "And the two escorts."

Her face was grim. "How is this in any way not a catastrophe?"

I kept walking, Scott's body bobbing lightly on my shoulder. It had been a long day, but he still didn't seem too heavy. I stopped, realizing we were about halfway across the lawn to the dormitory building. "I should probably take him to medical to be checked out, huh?"

I turned and saw Ariadne looking at me with cool disbelief. "Seeing as you don't care that your captives were killed in a glorious bloodbath that culminated in you being thrown out of a plane in flight, I might recommend you get yourself examined as well."

"I'm fine," I said. "And I suspect he's just hungover and worn out." I altered course and started heading back to medical.

"About the telepaths—" Ariadne started.

"No use crying over splattered pawns," I said, "especially when they didn't know much."

"They were mind-readers," Ariadne said dully. "They had access to Century. You can't tell me they didn't—"

"Oh, they knew some stuff," I agreed as we reached the front of the HQ building and my mother opened the outer door for me. I nodded at her and slipped inside before opening the inner door myself and stepping into the lobby. It wasn't as grand as the last one, but close, with tile floors leading up to the entry desk, and an open second-floor atrium that had a balcony around it. The concierge desk had only one person manning it, but I knew there were armed security waiting just behind the doors to my left, watching the monitors and paid to fire first and ask questions later if someone who seemed even the least bit hostile came in. "The Hercules I drained nearly to empty was their escort, and he was in on all their briefings, saw what they saw, and had even asked a couple of them individually if they knew what was going on, what the endgame of the bigger plan was."

"They didn't, I assume by your tone," Ariadne said as we navigated into a hallway, the white plaster walls looking a little plain in the low light. Decoration wasn't high on the priorities list at the moment.

"They knew only the basics," I said. "That Century was going to overturn the old order, was going to kick over the secretive hierarchy of meta organizations, that the members doing the work would get wealthy or whatever else they wanted in the process." I suspected my eyes gleamed. "They did know one thing that's a little more than what we've gotten before, though not much."

"And it is?" Ariadne asked.

"That what we suspected about phase two is true," I said. "The plan was always to subjugate humanity somehow. Eliminating the metas who could oppose them is stage one, but the rest is being kept really close to the vest. The telepaths—and this Hercules—were motivated by two things. The first was the promise of gain, which is to say that they thought they were going to be on the top of the pyramid once everything shook out."

"And the second?" my mother chimed in, listening intently.

"Intimidation," I said. "They got visits from more powerful metas and were each promised—well, threatened—that should they fail or betray Century, they were going to be entering a world of pain. Sort of how Zollers was warned, it sounds like." I shrugged. "I've got a face for the guy who paid the visit to the

Hercules. It was Weissman."

Ariadne started to ask me something but stopped as we passed through a set of double doors that opened automatically with an electronic hiss. A row of hospital beds lay along the far wall, empty save for two of them, and the lights started to snap on automatically as we came in. One of the occupants of a bed stirred; the other didn't.

"Can I just say I'm a little surprised to see you alive?" Reed asked weakly from the bed nearest the door. "Most people don't survive jumping out of a plane without a parachute."

"You could have survived it," I said as I put Scott into a bed. He made a slight snoring noise but otherwise seemed to take no note of his change in position.

"As a Windkeeper, I'm a little different than the average meta," Reed said, turning onto his side to look at me. His color had returned, and he grimaced only a little as he moved, the white sheet pulled up to mid-chest. He looked like he had a bandage wrapped around his abdomen, and his long hair was loose against the pillows that were stacked behind him.

"You calling me average?" I asked with faux outrage, turning back to face him, "I wasn't going to be outdone by big brother. Call it sibling rivalry." I flashed him a grin. "Anything you can do, I can do better."

He smiled weakly. "Try peeing standing up."

"What a touching scene of reunion," came a harsh voice from behind me that sounded more than a little haggard. I turned to see Dr. Isabella Perugini standing at the door to her office, her dark hair frizzed and her eyes bearing dark circles underneath them. "I had thought that you might have actually—finally—perished, ending my long suffering from the damage you do."

"You're not that lucky, Doc," I replied, smiling sweetly. "Like a cat, I just keep landing on my feet."

"Burying your claws into some new poor soul that doesn't

know better than to get close to a cat that's trying to find a soft place to land," she said, coming to a stop at Scott's bedside. She looked him over once, then took her stethoscope from around her neck and put it on, listening to his chest. "He's hungover and tired," she pronounced with a yawn as she finished. "Give him a good night's sleep and he'll be fine." She gave me the evil eye again. "You, on the other hand—"

I sighed. "I don't know why you're upset with me. I never locked you in the trunk of a car; Kat did." I gestured vaguely to where Janus was lying in the corner of the room, a feeding tube down his throat and a respirator quietly hissing, breathing for him. "I bet she's in here all the time, you should take it out on her. Besides, that was months ago."

"But who led the mission where she lost her mind?" Perugini said, still giving me a fiery look. "Hm? See? Everything is your fault. Always." She turned on her heel and went back into her office, the automatic door hissing shut behind her.

"She's really warming to you," Ariadne said.

"Yeah, I know," I replied. "Another couple months and it'll almost be like having a conversation with you." I regretted it after I said it. Ariadne had been mostly indifferent to me of late, but that lit a fire behind her eyes. I didn't grimace but close.

"The telepaths?" she prompted.

"Right," I said, trying to remember where I had left off in our earlier conversation. "It's actually a good thing they're dead, because they didn't know anything and now we don't have to worry about guarding them. That would have been a headache in and of itself since we don't have an empath on staff to block them out." I shrugged. "Plus now Century can't storm our headquarters and recover them, thus applying them to their nefarious purposes once more. Because you know we would have been damned near powerless to stop them."

She looked like she wanted to argue, but she didn't. "They

still could have had valuable intel. Something. Anything to get us closer to Century, to their plans."

"Their plans are getting more and more screwed by the day," I said. "They just lost at least half of their telepaths, which is going to slow down their extinction agenda by a lot. A hell of a lot." I let out a long exhalation and took a deep breath of the medical unit's cool, sterile air. "As far as victories go, I'll take it." I looked around for a wall to lean against but finding nothing, I placed a bare palm on the cold surface of Scott's bed rail. "I need some sleep." I looked from my mom to Ariadne. "If there's nothing else that can't wait until morning, ladies?" I looked over at Reed, and he frowned. "I'm not calling you a lady."

"Damned right," he said. "Again, back to the peeing standing up thing."

"There is one other thing," Ariadne said, and I saw a little nervous tension between her and my mom.

"Okay," I said with a sigh. "Out with it."

She hesitated. "Well. We got a flag from customs in Los Angeles."

"Oh?" I shifted, and found myself suddenly a little more awake. I didn't relish the thought of rumbling with a Century team in my present condition, but I could sleep on a plane on the way there, and a Red Bull or twelve would have me in fighting shape by the time we landed.

"Flagged at LAX," Ariadne went on, and everything about the way she said it was dull. "Customs didn't act on it because they had orders not to engage without sufficient backup, which they didn't have—"

"Spit it out, Ariadne," I said. "What are we dealing with here? Mercenaries? Metas? More telepaths? Because if we could mop those up, we'd really put a dent in Century's efforts—"

"No," my mother interrupted, and I saw the look she traded with Ariadne. "Potentially more problematic than that."

I'm sure I looked mystified. What could be more problematic than any of those things? A slow, damning thought came to mind. "Weissman."

"No," Ariadne said, dispelling my rising discomfort. "No, I'm afraid it's not Century related, exactly—"

"If someone doesn't give me an answer," I said, looking from Ariadne to my mother, "I'm going to start accusing you people of playing the role of Old Man Winter—"

I stopped speaking mid-sentence. My mother's face exhibited a fairly obvious twitch at the mere mention of the name, and Ariadne looked away so quickly it was obvious. "Winter," I said softly. "He's back."

Chapter 22

The wind was a low, chill whip around Erich Winter's face. It hurt, numbly though, and paled in comparison to the other pains that filled his body. *It was not supposed to be like this,* he thought, looking at the scorched flesh on his right arm as he dragged a faltering leg behind him. He limped, the pain in his right thigh a searing, continuous agony as he stumbled forward, the flesh blackened down that side of his body. He had run as far as he could, keeping low across the grain field, toward the town of Peshtigo. It wasn't logical and he knew it, but the instinct was there nonetheless, the need to run toward people when in danger. *Not that any of them could save me. Not from that. Not from him.*

He fell, gasping, to his knees, dodging the long, dried grass that had curled up, near dead from the summer's drought. It couldn't hurt him, not really, but every stroke against his burnt flesh added to the pain. *This will take time to heal. Time I hope I have.*

He had lived for thousands of years and had not done so by stupidly engaging in fights with his own kind. He crawled now, the sand sticking to his exposed, burnt flesh, and it felt like every grain was a knife, picking at him. *I have never even seen a meta capable of doing what was just done to me. It is simply impossible. No one can have that kind of power ...*

His fingers clenched at a weed that had survived the dry summer and he stopped his desperate crawl. *Will I be like this weed? If he comes for me ... I cannot endure, cannot fight ...*

Winter began to crawl again, the smell of his charred skin filling his nostrils, his strength fading as he pulled himself along, hand over hand. He tried to spark the power to encase himself in ice. *Protection. I need protection.* There was little humidity in the air to work with, but still he struggled on. *Concentrate. Feel the freeze. Look for the faint strands of moisture, pull them to you, make them yours. Bring on the ice.* They dangled before him like little strings but far off in the distance, and his reach was not long enough to gather them to him. The pain blotted them out, pushed them away, and his eyes fluttered shut as he tried to will the screaming agony out of his mind. He tried again and failed, collapsing in the dirt, his cracked lips feeling and tasting the dry soil. *I have failed. Perhaps if I wait here, he will not find me—*

"This is really quite sad," came the voice, dispelling his hopes. "I've been sitting up here watching you." The voice carried a hint of an English accent, and as Winter rolled over, he looked up at a man hanging ten feet in the sky above him, wearing trousers and a cloak that wouldn't have been out of place in metropolitan Chicago.

"You have defeated me," Winter said quietly, as he felt blood run out of his nose and settle on his lip. It didn't freeze, which was cause for alarm in and of itself. *How can I be so weak? Admitting defeat like a coward.* He paused and realized the truth. *I would admit worse and beg for my life if it would cause him to spare it.*

"Oh, I know that," the man said, continuing to hover, floating in the air. "You really shouldn't try and shake down visitors to your little town, especially when you don't know who they are."

Winter felt the lack of cold, and his teeth chattered from it. "I am the patron of these towns. Their people—"

"Are your people, yes, I heard you say it when we met on the road," the man said, staring at his hand with bored disinterest. "I've seen this sort of thing before, where you old gods stake a claim to an area where descendants of your original worshippers settled and run a protection racket on any metahuman who tries to cross it." He smiled. "Didn't work out so well for the last folks that tried it on me, either." He shrugged. "Of course, that was in Mongolia, so I doubt anyone will hear about it for a good long time, but this ..." He looked around, into the fields off in the distance, and Winter saw his eyes alight on the smoke in the distance. "Brushfires?" he asked, as though his train of thought had been halted.

Winter nodded. "It has been a dry summer, bereft of rain."

"And here comes autumn, settling in," the man said, still hovering, eyes fixed on the smoke. He looked down at Winter. "I'm going to have to teach you a further lesson. Not necessarily because you need it—though all you old gods need it—but because I have a reputation to maintain. Or restore, I suppose, in this case. I've been gone for a long time from western civilization, from the world of our kind, and I think everyone's just about forgotten me." He chuckled. "You wouldn't think so, as long-lived as we are, but it happens. Events fade into the near distance, and we're left living our lives as day-to-day as any of these short-lived humans."

The man set down, his feet gently crushing the dry grass as they settled. He took a step toward Winter and the seeds of panic took full root in the older man. Winter tried to scurry back, his long arms and legs brushing against the dried vegetation, sparking more pain from his burns and finding futile purchase in the dirt and plants as he tried to retreat—

The man grabbed him in one motion, seizing him by the burnt remains of his shirt, a lapel in each hand, and pulled him close. Winter felt the heat now. A blazing fire lit in the man's eyes, a literal one, flames crackling as if he were a fire djinn of old. Smoke poured from his eyes like eyebrows of black that wafted toward the heavens. "I'm going to make an example of you. I need them to remember that I am a man apart from the rest of you. I don't care what you do, what Omega does, what happens in the world around me. I need nothing from any of you, and I want no part in your foolish chess games or territorial pissing matches. I am nothing like you ..." His eyes flared, the fire blazing as if kerosene had been poured on the flames within. " ... I'm better."

There was something stirring now, a howling roar in Erich Winter's ears that was louder than a train, those monstrosities that seemed to be taking over everywhere, showing up all over the map, knitting the world closer together. Winter felt his feet start to leave the ground, but the roar did not abate, it grew louder, and he looked away from the man. They flew high into the air, the cold wind whipping Winter's cheeks as they ascended. A fire blazed below them, consuming the land. It was a wall of sheerest flame, a hundred feet high, and Winter could see it roaring, burning, snaking like a living thing as it thundered across the ground toward Peshtigo in the distance like a high wave crashing on the shore.

"The people ..." Winter whispered.

"Are going to die," the man said, watching coldly. "It's a shame; I didn't mean for it to get quite that out of control. I let my anger get away from me. I had intended to scorch the ground around us, leave you in the middle of a smoking crater, but when people interfere with me, when they try to shake me down, take what's mine, it makes me ... so angry." Winter watched the scorched ground as the black smoke started to rise. The man shook him, diverting Winter's attention back to him. "Listen to me."

The man started to smoke, the clouds rising from below them. There was a blinding glow where the man had been only a moment before, and it took Winter only a second to realize the man was turning to flames now, his skin covered in the fire, and his hands burned through Winter's shirt and caught him under the arms, like a baby. Winter could feel the inferno surrounding the man beginning to burn his flesh. He screamed, a long, agonized burst that drowned out the wind that was growing hot around him.

"You will tell them," the man said, "you will tell them who did this to you. You will tell them that the mighty Erich Winter was brought low, was broken, was defeated, and you will tell them who did it if they ask. You will be my herald, to spread the word that any who interfere with my passage, who challenge me will end up as broken as you. Warn them not to defy me. I want no part of your world, but I will not hesitate to destroy any of you who interfere with mine."

Winter screamed. "I will! I will tell them!" He felt the fire scorching his skin. "I will tell them whatever you want!"

"I know you will," the man in flames said quietly, his voice just audible over the roar of the firestorm below. "There's only one thing you need to remember when you land," he said, and Winter felt his personal gravity shift, as if he was being lifted sideways. The pain was agonizing, taking away his breath as if his flesh was burning off an inch at a time. Even still, he could feel the world move, as though he was about to be thrown like a ball. "Remember my name. Remember ..."

The last word came out as a whisper and the man threw him, casting him through the air with ferocious speed. Winter did not remember the landing, just a vague sense of his flesh burning, of his own screaming, of incredible distances passing underneath him in a blur.

Three days later he crawled out of the scorched wreckage of a field of ashes in Chicago, his skin still scarred around his arms and chest from the burns that the man had given him. They remained with him as he trudged across the blackened earth, naked, still burned, and so did the name he'd heard whispered in the moment before he'd been released to fly some two hundred and fifty miles through the air.

Sovereign.

Chapter 23

Sienna Nealon
Now

Winter. The name chilled and burned all in one. I stood in the medical unit, just staring at my mother, then Ariadne, one after another, not saying anything.

"What do you want to do about him?" My mother spoke first, breaking a brief silence that had felt like years.

"Nothing," I said after a pause. "We let him be; we have other things to worry about."

I saw a flash of red on Ariadne's cheeks. "Really?"

I felt a searing embarrassment inside at the thought of what Ariadne had to be thinking: *If only you'd come to that conclusion before you killed my girlfriend.* I didn't flinch from her unspoken rebuke, but only because I tried to make my face into stone, unmoving. "We have bigger problems. Saving our race from extinction is more important to me than settling any grudge I might have with him."

"He might know something important about Sovereign," my mother said.

"He's on the wanted list," Ariadne said. "Foreman's pissed at him for failing to live up to his agreement to run the Directorate as it was supposed to be run to keep metas in line."

"He probably does know something," I agreed, "and he's certainly done his share of wrong, but tracking him down and catching him is going to take a lot of resources, none of which we have available to spend at present." It sounded logical in my head when I said it. In truth, I could picture myself pressing my fingers against his throat while the frigid life drained out of his blue eyes. I would have savored every moment of his agony, even now, months after he had wronged me so. "I can't justify it. If he was as imminent a threat as Sovereign and Century, I'd be all over it." I clenched my arms tighter to my chest. "For now, we let him be. His day will come." I paused, and took a breath. "We need a plan, though. We've gone on the offensive, we've stung Century, but we need to draw some of them in, start to break them a piece at a time. We need to build some momentum."

"I thought you were happy about the splattered telepaths," Ariadne said, her arms folded across her.

"It's a stall, not a win," I said. "There are a hundred of them at fighting weight and eight of us. I'd like to start drawing down their numbers and doing so quickly—and preferably, quietly. That way they don't know what's happening until we're down to the very last of them."

"They're still wrapping up in Latin America and Canada, right?" My mother asked, fingers kneading her chin. "If they're still mopping up elsewhere, most of their operators probably aren't even in the country yet."

"They're finishing up, probably only getting stragglers now," Ariadne said. "According to Agent Li, anyway." She looked sideways at me. "You should probably brief him, by the way, on how this all turned out. He doesn't enjoy being left out in the cold on things like this."

"I'll think about it," I mumbled. Li was not one of my very favorite people and I avoided him as much as possible. I could tell he felt just about the same, but his duties didn't allow us to avoid each other as much as both of us would have liked.

"We've always got other things we could be dealing with," my mother said.

"More important than the twilight of our species?" I asked.

She rolled her eyes. "Why can't you be like a normal girl and be worried about boys and dances or something?"

I smiled at her sadly. "Because that's not what you made me."
I looked to Ariadne. "She has a point, though. We've got no real
line on what to do next with Century, which means we're reduced
to waiting for something to happen. We need something else to
focus on until we can go on offense again."

"Maybe focus on defense?" Ariadne said acidly. She caught
my pitying glare in reply. "Just a suggestion."

I started thinking about it, but nothing was occurring to me.
"We need to know more about Sovereign."

My mother shrugged. "Good luck with that. I met him *once*,
and it was pretty short, as far as meetings go. Other than a sense of
overpowering terror, I can't give you much of a feeling of the
man."

"I'd say you got that across," I said, rubbing the back of my
neck as I fidgeted idly. "You got anything else?"

"He hovers like an avenging angel," my mother said, "speaks
in a voice of infinite authority, and if you defy him, the response is
swift and unpleasant." She kept her reply level, but I could hear
the slightest quiver beneath it. "When it comes to terror, what else
is there?"

I sighed. "I'm exhausted. Any further thinking is going to
have to wait until tomorrow." I cast a look over to the bed in the
corner, where Janus lay, not as shriveled as I would have expected
from a man who had been in a coma for six months but still just a
shell of what he had been only months earlier. "If only he could do
my sleeping for me, I'd be all set." I winced a little inside, looking
at Janus's face, which had grown pale from the months he'd been
confined to the medical unit. What had been a swarthy, pleasant
look on him, a healthy man—a little weathered at times, but still
vital—had been reduced to deadness, quiet, the silence of a
vegetable and nothing more. "I need to sleep," I repeated.

"Go on, then," my mother said, "we'll see you in the

morning."

"Or possibly afternoon," I said and started toward the door. I barely noticed that Ariadne and my mother remained behind. I wondered if I should worry about what they were discussing and decided it ultimately didn't matter.

I dragged myself across the campus toward the dormitory. Off in the distance, a new building was being constructed, nominally at my behest. It was a research and development lab, to be populated with the best and the brightest minds that we could muster. Right now it was just steel girders sticking out of a hole in the ground. I hadn't paid it much attention other than to sign off on the basic layout. As far as I was concerned, by the time it bore fruit—assuming we lived that long—my tenure at the new Agency would probably be just about over and Century would be toast. Every heavy step I took was lightened by the though of that prospect. It was all that was keeping me going right now.

That was a long day, Zack said as I let him out of the box in my mind.

"Tell me about it," I said.

I'm glad Scott was there to save you.

"Me, too," I said, letting the heaviness of my feet trudging across the soft, grassy lawn keep my brain from tumbling into unconsciousness.

You didn't just let me out to ask about your day.

"No," I agreed. "I wanted some company while I walked. Needed to think."

You're not in much shape for thinking.

"This is true."

But you're still mulling over Sovereign? Dreading him?

"Always."

Maybe you should take a break for a little bit. Come back fresh.

I almost smiled, but it was bittersweet. "Head for an island, sandy beaches?"

It would be nice.

"It would be ..." I thought about it, "... irresponsible."

You're nineteen. You're allowed some irresponsibility.

My smile faded. "Not now. Not with the stakes like this."

What was that line from that movie? "If we can't save the earth, you can be damned well sure we'll avenge it?"

"Yeah," I said. "But I don't think Sovereign's going to respond to that threat any better than Loki did." I sighed as I reached the heavy doors of the dormitory, which had emergency shutters secured in a large, rectangular casing over every window in the place. It increased the weight of the door as I opened it, and in my exhausted state, I actually felt it. "If I could even find him to threaten him." I placed my hands over my face as I walked into the lobby area at the front of the dorms. Two security guards stared at me impassively, and I slid my key card through the little reader at the stall that buzzed and opened a gate for me to enter. It wouldn't keep out a meta, but much like the shutters, it wasn't designed to. It was only meant to stall for time.

You think he'd give up this plan if it meant he was going to die along with it if he failed?

I laughed, and the security guards looked at me funny. "Sorry," I said. "I just had a thought." They looked at me as though I was crazy. "A funny thought. A joke, more like. Yeah." *I doubt he thinks he's going to fail,* I thought to Zack, *so I didn't appear like I was talking to myself, since he's currently winning.*

So he's overconfident.

I almost laughed again as I pushed the button for the elevator. *I don't think he's overconfident since, again, he's winning, and winning big. He's wiped out something like five-sixths of our population, so ... he probably thinks he's got this in the bag.* The elevator dinged and I stepped in, forcing a weak smile at the security guards, who were still watching me. I placed my hand on the biometric reader for the elevator and it scanned my hand. More security measures. The idea that Sovereign would come here and try and wipe out our metas was not exactly laughable. I certainly wasn't laughing about it. It gave me nightmares.

Everyone has a weakness.

"The man is a ghost," I said as the elevator doors closed. "I have one person who's seen him in the last twenty years, otherwise he's all hearsay and superstition." I rubbed my eyes as the elevator dinged, heralding our arrival at the top floor. "He'd be a better candidate for the meta bogeyman than I am, given how little he shows up and how scared shitless some really powerful people have been of him."

So he's earned his legend.

"That's the rumor," I said. "But what's he really left behind for us?" I walked to my door, just down the hall, and let my thumbprint get scanned even as I used my badge to unlock it. It was a tandem lock; the hope was that it would at least warn me if something was seriously awry—like someone forcing their way into my quarters to ambush me. Both functioned as they were supposed to, and I heard a beep and a click as the door unlocked and I opened it. "A trail of frightened people."

A lot of dead metas.

"Well, yes, maybe," I said, peeling off my jacket and letting it fall to the floor. "But most of that was Weissman, acting on Sovereign's behalf. He told me that Sovereign wasn't involved in the day-to-day." I let my bare fingers caress my skin, and it felt good. I barely ever got touched skin to skin, and the times that I had usually resulted in something that I could only describe as orgasmic—when my powers worked to their full extent and I ripped someone's soul screaming from their body. Even without that, though, I liked the tactile sensation. It felt good. "What's he really doing? What's he up to?"

You'd probably have to know more about him as a man to

know that. What his goals are, his objectives, what he wants—

"He doesn't want anything, supposedly." I sat down on the edge of the bed and peeled off my shirt. It stuck to me in several places. I tried to decide whether I should shower again before going to bed since I'd sweated on the drive, but I knew that wasn't going to happen. Too tired. "But that's anecdotal, too." I shimmied out of my jeans, sliding them off and feeling the cool sheets against the back of my thighs. "What do we actually know about him? Definitely know, firsthand."

That he destroyed the Agency. That's about it.

"Right," I said. "Mom's the only person we have on hand who's ever met him, ever faced him, ever looked him in the eye and seen who he is and what he's all about." I had a pad of paper next to my bed to make notes on, and I scrawled in big letters: Debrief Mom—RE: Sovereign. Part of me wanted to add AGAIN to it, because I'd sat down with her when we'd started and gone over it, but she had little to say about it. She couldn't remember their exact conversation, she claimed, just that she'd had a sense of being overmatched and afraid he might come after her for some unknown reason. Maybe she had forgotten something. Either way, we were at a dead end and needed to go over what we knew for certain and work outward from there into speculative territory. Something, anything to start working on a plan.

I tossed my bra, sick of it biting into my skin for the day. I lay down, pulling the sheets up. The sheets felt good, so good, like a lover's touch. Which was something I doubted I'd be feeling again anytime soon, given the special intervention it had taken the last time that had happened. I sighed. "I miss you."

I know.

That said, I lay back and stared at the blank, knockdown-textured ceiling above me. Sovereign rolled about in my head, the thought of him, the idea of him, the mystery, the legend. I ran through it all again, and then again, trying to think of everything we knew about him, everything that had come from every living source ...

I drifted off sometime shortly thereafter but scrawled something on the pad in an utter stupor before I went out. It seemed important at the time, and even more so when I woke up ten hours later and read it again, my scrawled handwriting a nearly impossible mess in the morning that light streamed in from the giant window behind me.

Not all of the metas who have encountered Sovereign are still alive. But not all of them are dead and gone, either.

Chapter 24

"Wolfe, Bjorn and Gavrikov have all had encounters with Sovereign," I said, looking at the people arrayed around the conference room in front of me. Everybody of import was there—Breandan, Reed, Scott (still looking a little rough, but present), Karthik, my mother, Ariadne, Li, Kat. Everybody but Foreman. "Wolfe in the 1400s in England, Bjorn in the 1600s in Norway, and Gavrikov here in America sometime in the 1940s or early fifties."

"They don't know the specifics, like a date?" Li asked, leaning on his arm and surveying me coolly.

"They aren't really the 'Dear Diary' types," I said, standing at the front of the room, pacing a little here and there to work off my nervous energy. "So, no, they didn't make a record of the moments they ran into him, but their memories are clear, and with a little persuasion—" I'd had to let them all out of their cages for a while, which was starting to drive me mad again, because I had gotten quite used to not having unexpected voices in my head as I went about my daily business, "they were pretty forthcoming, even going so far as to show me the memories in question."

"You can't just go in there and pick them out, like you do with people you're draining in real time?" Breandan asked, peering at me with heavy curiosity, his tongue pushing out the skin just below his lower lip on the right hand side.

"I could scan through their entire lives," I said, "but without specifics that would take a while, as Gavrikov is over a hundred years old and is the youngest of the three. Otherwise, no, I can't just hop to a specific memory when they're in my head."

"You actually can," my mother said, a little clipped. "But it takes practice. I'll give you some pointers when we have time."

"So that'd be in another few years, after we're dead, then?" Breandan asked with a small, unamused smile.

"No need to be so down, Irish," Reed said with a smirk. "We're doing pretty well so far at swinging down the fastballs Century's been tossing our way."

"And I, for one, certainly hope that lasts," Breandan said. "Because I rather like my petty, thieving life, even though I'm no longer a petty thief."

"Now that we know about these encounters," my mother said, leaning forward against the black glass conference table top, "what do they tell us?"

"A couple of things," I said, frowning. In truth, there really wasn't a ton I could use from the memories. Wolfe had gotten his ass handed to him by Sovereign, and in near-record time. I could feel myself cringe because every strike, every broken bone was mine to relive as I went through the memory, and all of them hurt. "Sovereign dished an epic ass-whooping on Wolfe. That tells us he's mega-tough. He did the same thing to Bjorn, except even quicker. Physical combat with this guy is not something I'm looking forward to." I looked across the table, and saw a sea of unnerved people, so I tried to bring it back to better topics. "He's also got at least some of the powers of Gavrikov—flame skin, flight—"

Ariadne interrupted me. "According to our research, Gavrikov was already something of a hybrid. His father was rumored to be capable of flight, but not—"

"His dad couldn't cast fire, if that's what you're getting at," I said. I'd seen that memory a long while back, and the roots of it were a deeply disturbing journey into how Aleksandr had discovered his power. It was at least a nine on my heebie-jeebie scale, and that was maybe being charitable. His childhood made mine look like a trip to Disney by comparison. I cast a look at Kat, who sat, placid, totally unaware of her part in it. That made her the lucky one, I supposed.

"Right, well," Ariadne said, a little nonplussed, "is this going to be a meta genetics discussion? Because I'm not sure any of us are really qualified for that."

Li's phone chirped, drawing every eye in the room toward him and bringing the momentum of the discussion to a halt. He plucked it out of the front pocket of his suit and took a look. "Excuse me," he said, and stepped out of the conference room without further explanation.

As the door closed, Scott leaned his elbows onto the table. "What's the next move?"

"Continue waiting for actionable intelligence to roll in," I said after a moment's pause.

"Sit back and wait for them to come for us?" Breandan asked, more than a little skeptical. "I don't care for this plan."

"Neither do I," I said with a sigh. "We've hit them hard, made them stagger, in all probability, but we have no idea where to go next. We've got no leads, no line on the specifics of their goals, and thus we're sitting here on our ass until we have some idea of what to do. It's hard to be in a fight when you have no target."

"We have a target," Scott said. "Sovereign."

"Yes. I suppose we do." I almost rolled my eyes but didn't. "But he's not in view. Good luck hitting something you can't see."

"He's like game, and we can't seem to flush him out," Reed said.

"He's like something we can't flush away," Breandan muttered.

"And the Irishman goes for the trusty poop joke," Scott said with a grin. "Figures."

"Go with what you know, I always say." Breandan shot Scott a returned grin of his own.

"That's interesting, because from where I'm sitting it looks like we don't know shit," Reed said, bringing the discussion back down. I waited, and started to clear my throat to voice something when the door swung open and Li reentered, his cheeks flushed. "What?" I asked.

He got as far as the table before slamming the phone against the hard surface, shattering it and causing Breandan, Kat and Ariadne to start in surprise. "That was Foreman. We have a new directive." I kept my mouth firmly shut, waiting for the rest. "Katheryn Hildegarde and her team just killed four FBI agents in Portland." Li put his knuckles down against the smooth surface of the black table, and I heard them crack as he did it. "You're to get your ass on a plane, track her down, and bring her in, however you have to do it."

Chapter 25

"I object to this mission," I said into the stark, slightly crackling silence of the phone.

"Noted," Senator Foreman said on the other end. Because of my enhanced hearing, I could detect all the imperfections that came from the digitalization of the voice that was carried to me now from Washington, D.C. "But you have your marching orders."

"This is taking our eye off the ball," I said as I walked down the cement stairs to the first floor of HQ. "It's a distraction, something that's not in accord with our greater focus—"

"It's something that's vital to the continued existence of your main mission," Foreman said, and I could hear the tension in his voice.

I listened to the echo of my shoes as I took each step. "I disagree. Whatever Hildegarde is doing is bad, I'll grant you that, but—"

"If you don't handle Hildegarde, there won't be anything left of your organization in a month," Foreman said abruptly, surprising me. He wasn't the type to interrupt, preferring to wait until someone had spent their argument so he could counterattack and win. "I have used every ounce of political capital I had to set this up. Every ounce. When the committee looked over the reports, their temptation was to let it all ride, to wait and see. To go with rote instinct and prepare the military to counter any threats from Sovereign and Century. I told them no, that we needed a response force. They countered that not only would it be expensive but that it would take too much time to vet and set up. I told them I'd take care of it, keep it off the books, make sure the revenue didn't come out of the budget and contain any negative publicity.

"Then they pulled out Sovereign's threat, about what he'd do if we got into the meta policing business again." He paused. "I told them it was going to happen anyway, and if they wanted to look like they were caught flatfooted worrying about other things when it did, they could deal with the inevitable outrage from John Q. Public when people find out that they knew and did nothing. But now we have a problem. Hildegarde is killing our agents, and she's killing civilians."

"Li told me," I said. "Four agents is a genuine tragedy, it really is—"

"And two civilians," Foreman said, cutting me off again. "One of them a teenager. It's not playing well on the evening news in Oregon."

I paused, waiting. "I'm not indifferent to their plight, having seen a few innocent bystanders die that shouldn't have—"

"Yes, you are," Foreman said. "You are absolutely indifferent to their plight because it doesn't fit your single-minded obsession." His voice was crackling at the other end of the phone now. "You're waiting for an attack from what you suppose is the greater threat, and I agree, Sovereign is. I wouldn't have put this together if I didn't, and I wouldn't have put you in charge if I didn't believe you were truly obsessed with stopping this extinction. But I'm telling you now, my distinguished colleague from Oregon," he said every word of that with disgust, "who is a prominent member of our committee, is currently back in his home state mourning the loss of two of his constituents, and he wants this solved so he can tell his voters that it's handled." Foreman's voice rose in pitch. "So if you value your mission, get this done and get back to work!"

There wasn't a click like in the old books I read when someone hung up on someone else, but the faint beep-beep that told me he'd cut the connection was dramatic enough. I put my cell phone in my pocket and opened the door to exit the staircase. My mother was waiting in the lobby, arms folded, looking like she was lost in thought. "Ideas?" I asked her as I passed, and she fell in beside me as I headed toward the dorm.

My mother seemed to deflate a little. "Foreman put you on it, huh? No wiggle room to get out?"

"No," I said, shaking my head. "Politics got involved in this one; he seems to think it'll be the end of our little group if we can't convince one of the Oregon senators we're doing everything we can to actually be a meta policing unit."

"I have some experience tracking metas," she suggested.

"So do I," I said. "But I don't really want to waste time on this." I stopped, cursing under my breath. She gave me an amused look. "We're facing the extinction of our entire species, and I've got to go play this small-ball bullshit to keep the government off our backs."

Her eyes flashed and she almost shrugged. "Once you're in deep with these people, you're always in deep with them. They won't let you get away voluntarily."

I laughed. "You make them sound like the mob."

She cocked her head. "The mob would just kill you when they're done. More merciful, I think."

I felt a grimness settle over me. "As opposed to what? The jail time that I've been threatened with?"

She watched me carefully. "You don't think you're getting out of that, do you?"

I turned my gaze to the horizon, and thought about Clyde Clary, about how much blood had bubbled to the surface of the water when he'd died. "I don't know that I deserve to." I turned back to her. "But that's irrelevant. I have a job to do." I smiled, also grimly. "Whatever my final destination ends up being, I've got penance to pay first."

She nodded humorlessly. "Let me go to Portland, then."

"No," I said, shaking my head. "Let's give it a day while we plan a response."

"She could kill more in the meantime," my mother said. "You sure you want that on your head?"

I leaned my head back, letting it loll as I stared up into a cloudless sky. "I don't want any of this on my head, but that has nothing to do with what I'll actually get. This whole thing with Hildegarde is off focus. I thought maybe she could be a help to us. Hell, maybe she still could be, but the appearances are she's in a fighting mood and is looking for—" I paused in the middle of a sentence. "Wait, why was it four FBI agents?"

My mother looked at me, deep in thought, and after a moment, she nodded. "I didn't catch that either, the first time. It's not like FBI agents respond to local crimes, so even if Hildegarde was robbing a bank, she would have ended up killing some locals in with those agents."

"Right," I said. "So the question becomes, what the hell was the FBI doing to run into her?" I reversed course, my feet crunching on the grass as I turned around and started heading back to the HQ building. Something was not right.

"Could have been the FBI's Hostage Rescue Team," my mother said. "They deploy them for crises, and a meta group on the loose might qualify. Or it could be that Hildegarde and her group hit the FBI field office, though I can't see why they'd provoke Century one week and the U.S. government the next. Seems like you'd want to maybe stick to one fight at a time."

"Or none, if I had it my way," I said, opening the front door of HQ and allowing my mother to precede me, "but Hildegarde is clearly in the midst of something entirely different."

We kept quiet all the way to Agent Li's office, up on the fourth floor across the main room from mine. I opened his door without knocking, and he looked up at me, phone in his hand, the receiver up to his ear, completely unsurprised. He waved for us to take a seat across from his desk and I looked over his Spartan office. There were no pictures on the wall, which was pretty standard for our setup. The office furniture was nice enough; we'd had to do a little mixing and matching to get the place filled, taking on remaindered stuff that a local school district hadn't wanted anymore, combined with the finest offerings from some local stores. We could have gone a little more elaborate considering the funding we had to spread around, but I'd kiboshed that idea because I didn't want anyone to be thinking about decor. Their minds were needed elsewhere.

There was a lone spot of color in the room, a potted plant sitting on the corner of Li's desk. He was nodding along with whatever was being said on the phone, and finally he spoke. "Got it. Understood. I'll make sure I pass that along once you send me the file." With that, he hung up, and leaned back in his chair. "What took you so long?"

"What took me so long what?" I asked, frowning at him.

"What took you so long to get here? I expected you minutes ago." He picked up a fresh sheaf of papers from his desk and slid them across to me. "Here."

"What is this?" I asked, picking it up. My eyes scanned the page quickly and I realized it was an FBI report. "This is from Portland? From where Hildegarde—"

"I figured you'd want the details," he said, "since you didn't ask for them in the meeting."

"Long story short it for me," I said, putting the paper aside. "Why was the FBI in contact with Hildegarde?"

"Local investigation," Li said, keeping a straight face. "Portland Field Office was poking into OC—that's our shorthand for organized crime—and they'd flagged Hildegarde, thinking she was some kind of kind of mob enforcer. They were going to bring her in for questioning relating to a string of racketeering charges."

"Organized crime is Omega's MO," I said, and looked at the

paper. "I take it she tore through the agents?"

He shrugged, as if he was trying to be indifferent, but I caught a hint of tension. "Seems like the situation might have escalated when she tried to run and found out she was boxed in. Apparently she has at least one accomplice who can project energy of some sort."

"What type?" My mother asked.

"Don't know," Li responded. "It didn't leave a mark, so it could be anything. Two of the agents had been flung through the air unexpectedly."

"That could have been a straight up hit," I said. "Metas hit pretty hard."

"I suppose," he said. "I don't know much about metas or their capabilities, just the basics. You'll find the crime scene details in there. They didn't get off a shot first, which to me suggested that the assailant did not close on them but hit them at a distance."

I racked my brain, but there was just too much going on for me to process it. "I'll take a look." I shot a sidelong look at my mom. "Is the FBI going to go balls-out crazy for Hildegarde and her gang now that they've killed some of your own?"

Li's reaction was measured, and I still had a hard time getting a sense of what he was really thinking. "Maybe. Maybe not. The head of the local field office has been apprised of what they're up against, and he doesn't seem too eager to cowboy up, so maybe you'll get lucky. When are you leaving for Portland?"

I looked at my mother. "She's going tomorrow. Do they have any leads out there or am I just sending her to chase her tail around and sit in the office doing nothing?"

Li's skin flushed. "They have some leads, yes, but aren't pursuing them because if they were to get in another fight with Hildegarde, the outcome would be just about the same. The Special Agent in Charge—they call them SACs—is waiting for you. The investigation cannot proceed without our assistance."

"And we'll be giving it," I said coolly,

Li stood in a rapid hurry, his face red. "You're gonna wait on this? After all the FBI has done for you?"

"I'm trying to balance the fact that someone is going to kill *all* the metas with the fact that someone might, maybe, kill a few humans," I said. "Not to sound like a dick, but if I'm weighing on the scales, I find one side a little lacking."

"How many bodies does it take before your scales start tipping?" Li said, hot anger bubbling out. "A hundred? Two hundred?"

I kept my cool. "You really think Hildegarde is going to cut loose and start wiping out humans by the hundreds?"

"Probably not," he conceded. "But—"

"But nothing," I said. "Keep this in mind; whenever Sovereign is done killing us, whatever he's got planned for the human race gets rolled out, and I have a feeling it's going to involve some deaths of its own. So I guess you could say I'm trying really hard to take the global view on this one."

"Hard to see the little people from orbit, I suppose," Li said, spitting venom at me.

"I can see the problem clearly enough," I said, still letting the ice in my veins keep me from decking him. "I have eight metas I can send on field operations. Versus one hundred of our enemy. I simply do not have the people to chase down everything that's on our radar right now, because if I did, I wouldn't have had to let a wildfire meta run its course in Nevada two weeks ago." That was true. Some ass had come into his own powers and robbed a jewelry store, killing one of the patrons in the process. He was waiting in the wings to strike again, but I had nothing to root him out with right now unless I wanted to take the focus off of Sovereign.

"Every resource you've been given is at the behest of Senator Foreman," Li said, his voice rising, "including the immunity from prosecution that's enabled you to walk away from five different murders here in the U.S. that we know about—"

I felt my face heat up. "I had nothing to do with murdering Zack."

"What about Wolfe?" Li said. "Your first victim."

"And he was a real prize, too," I said snottily. "I'm sure the FBI would be totally fine with him continuing to walk the streets, since he killed two hundred and fifty-four people in Minneapolis in a string of murders that is still to this day marked 'Unsolved' in your case files—"

"You're still a murderer when it comes to him," Li fired back.

"Prove it," I said with a smirk. "Where's the body?"

"Maybe we could just take a step back from the precipice here—" my mother started to speak, but was cut off.

"I don't need to prove that you killed Wolfe—" Li started.

"Even though it was self-defense," I said, "his hands were wrapped around my throat—"

"—I can prove that you killed Glen Parks and Clyde Clary," Li said, "that you shot up Eve Kappler, left a bloody mess in her apartment. You didn't even bother to try and cover your tracks, you were so arrogant—"

"Maybe I was worried about other things," I said, and I could feel myself shake from some combination of rage, fear and guilt, in proportions I couldn't even put numbers to. "Is that what this is really about?" I looked Li down over the desk.

"Yeah, that's what this is about," Li said hotly. "It's about the fact that Foreman—the senator—took the keys to our last line of defense against the single greatest threat of our time and he put them in the hands of murderer who has zero remorse for what she's done."

His words sent my mind reeling. "You ... have no idea whether I have remorse or not."

"You were almost gleeful about killing Wolfe," Li said,

almost spitting his disdain at me.

"If it had been one of your buddies in the FBI that had brought down a multiple murderer, you're telling me he wouldn't have been at least a little proud about it?" I tossed that one back at him. "He wouldn't have gotten a few beers bought for his achievement?"

"You're not one of us," Li said tightly.

"I AM!" I roared back at him. "I have been all along! I've been training to police metas for the last year, pouring my life into it. I did what I was supposed to do, the responsible thing, by learning how to make sure that no meta ever got out of control again like Wolfe did. I trained to stop maniacs like him, like Gavrikov, like Omega, and I'll be the first to own up to my mistakes, but you can't possibly think I was in the wrong before that." My voice almost crossed to imploring. "I saved the city from Gavrikov. He wanted to give people peace by blowing everything up and I drained him to stop it from happening. I did everything I could to do things right, to avoid killing." My voice grew hoarse. "And it cost me everything."

Li stared at me, and I saw a burning anger behind his eyes. "You killed Zack."

"I did not," I said, feeling the stinging feeling of pain inside me. "I was used. He meant more to me than anything, and I would never have hurt him voluntarily."

I saw a glassy sheet come over Li's eyes. "You're still a murderer. Nothing changes that. You've got blood on your hands. Whatever you thought you were, it changed the day you crossed that line, just as surely as it has with any number of people who set out to do good and let power ruin them." He folded his arms. "You've got nothing to keep your power in check. You think you can just do whatever you want. It's why you didn't worry about cleaning up your crime scenes, it's why you didn't care. You're not as bad as Sovereign, but you're getting there."

I bit my lip and didn't tell him that the reason I didn't care was because I'd been planning to kill myself after killing Winter. That was nobody's business but my own. "Well," I said, "let me quote an old movie for you that was one of Zack's favorites— 'Send a maniac to catch a maniac.'"

Li's face went hard. "Get out."

I started to say something else, something wise-ass, something totally me, the girl who didn't know when to shut up nor how to do it, but I watched his red face, watched his chest heave up and down with emotion and fury, and I just canned it. I turned and walked out, holding the door for my mother, who followed wordlessly. I shut it quietly behind me, taking care not to even rattle it on its hinges.

Chapter 26

"I'm sending you to Portland tonight," I told my mother as we walked across the top floor bullpen of the agency.

"Why?" my mother replied as we walked into my office. I looked at the bare walls and suddenly I hated them; they were even more sparse than the walls of Old Man Winter's old office, but at least I had a wooden desk instead of rocks on top of other rocks.

"Because it's the right thing to do," I said, throwing myself back onto my leather chair. I leaned my head against the plush leather. I hadn't picked it out; Ariadne or someone else in admin had, but I had to admit it was a damned good choice. Between it and the couch against the far wall that I slept on at least one night in four, I felt pretty fortunate in the office furniture department, like I'd won some sort of internal Agency lottery. "Li's right, the FBI has been feeding us intel all along, Foreman's gone out on a limb for us. We owe them."

"It's politics," my mother said. "You were right when you said it takes us off mission for dubious benefit."

"No, I was wrong," I said. "It's a certain benefit; it keeps the other government agencies we're relying on for intelligence happy with us, shows we're willing to do the bidding of our congressional overseers, and builds some good will." *Hopefully,* I didn't bother to add.

She frowned at me, her long, dark hair hanging over her shoulders as she leaned over the chair in front of my desk. It reminded me of me when I looked into the mirror in the mornings. "You can't tell me you changed your mind because of anything besides the way Li just made you feel."

I felt the pressure of the leather against the back of my head, and the scent of it, still new, filled my nose. "Is that such a bad thing?"

"Playing politics?" She snorted. "It's a fast way to forget your mission, to lose yourself in useless trivia and bureaucracy."

"People died," I said quietly. "We need all the leads we can get. Hildegarde seems to at least have some sense of how to hit Century, and we need that or we're just continuing to operate blind, striking out into the darkness until they come for us."

"You let him get to you," she said. "About what you've done."

"I didn't let him do anything," I said, tired. "I didn't let him do anything I haven't already done to myself."

"You shouldn't feel guilty about Wolfe," she said. "That was a righteous kill. Same with Gavrikov. They were both murderers."

"It's not Wolfe and Gavrikov that I feel guilty about," I said. "Nor Bjorn, though I had about as much to do with him getting killed as I did Zack." I let my voice fall. "I murdered Glen Parks. He taught me so much about fighting, about shooting, tracking. He filled in a lot of the cracks that you couldn't. He was a mentor, and what he did to me that night with Zack tore him up inside. He was drinking his life away, and I murdered him. I killed Clyde Clary, too. Big, dumb Clyde. He was an asshole, every inch of him, but he didn't want to do what Winter told him to do. I knew that, and I killed him anyway. Eve wasn't even around when Zack was killed; she dragged Ariadne off to get her out of the way because she was fighting Old Man Winter on it, screaming at him. And Bastian ... he said his piece, followed his orders, and he died for it, ultimately." I looked at her, and she wouldn't meet my gaze, hands white-knuckling the back of the chair, staring down at the black pleather. "I killed them all. Plus Rick, the Primus of Omega, and one of the ministers, Eris. I killed them all, killed all those people." I felt the energy drain from my voice, what was left of it.

"I don't need Li's judgmental eyes to feel guilty. I am guilty."

She looked up, slightly stricken. "You—"

"I want you to remember before you say anything," I said, looking at her with just the slightest amusement, "that you're the same person who used to lock me in a metal box when I broke one of your rules. Whatever reasons you had for it, telling me now that I'm not guilty when you spent all that time punishing me for infractions much less than murder is going to sound ... really screwed up."

I saw her bite back her instinct to snap at me, and she looked to her left. "This is the world I wanted to protect you from. I didn't want you to ..." Her voice trailed off.

"Leave the house?" I asked with bitter amusement but not any rancor. "Get caught up in crazy events? Get in fights? Sleep with boys?"

"Add in drugs and following your guitarist boyfriend around on tour for a summer and I think you'll have hit all the 'parenting fears' high points." She paused, and I watched the emotions roll across her face. "I didn't want you to be like me," she said, and it echoed in the office. "I didn't want you to have to kill. I prepared you for it in hopes you'd never have to do it." Her hands left the back of the leather chair and she cradled them, one upon another. "I never wanted you to have to do what I did. I don't like to kill. Never have. I'm not like Charlie. I'm not like others of our kind. I hated the feeling when I took my first soul." She ran her thin fingers through her hair. "I never wanted you to know what it was like to kill, let alone what it was like to use your power, to lose yourself in the moment of the drain. And I'm glad you're not an addict."

"I'm definitely not that," I said, staring at her. "How many do you have?"

She blinked. "How many souls? Five. But I've got more shadows than I can count."

"That's the partials, right?" I asked. "The ones you only take a little of?"

"Yeah," she said. "It's not the most pleasant thing you can do to a person, but leaving them missing a memory is better than taking their life." She sighed. "I've killed a lot more than that, though. Most were in the line of duty." She looked away. "But some weren't, early on. Some were ..." She brought her eyes back, slow, and I could see depths in them when she turned back to me. "Some were personal. Things I did before I got a tight handle on myself."

"I lived a pretty disciplined life while I was growing up," I said, staring back at her, but not really looking at her.

"I know," she said tonelessly. "Ever since we moved into the house."

"I think I went off the rails this last year," I said.

"It could have gone worse," she said. "Teenage rebellion is always hard."

I looked at her almost pityingly. "What? Like this is my rumspringa, and soon I'll go back to following the ordnung? I killed people."

"So did I," she said quietly. "So did I. But there's nothing you can do about it now except—"

"Penance," I said. "That was what I figured in England. That what I'd done ... seeking revenge was testing the ends of my powers—"

"Pushing societal limits and finding that there aren't that many for a meta, right?" She cocked her head at me. "Not with the old structures of power falling away under Century's scythe."

"I decided I was going to make up for it as best I could," I said. "Try and atone, protect as best I could."

She nodded. "Redemption's a word that gets thrown around a lot nowadays. When I was hiding in Gillette, I watched a lot of TV and inevitably ended up seeing some of that awful reality television. Hollow, vain people clawing for fame and whatever droppings it brings with it. They toss around the word redemption after a failure like it's something you do after you make a simple slip up, like bumping into someone in the street." She looked at me, and I could feel the power in her eyes, the truth, that she knew what she was saying. "You and I both know it's deeper than that. Redemption isn't as simple or cheap as they'd suggest; not as easy as winning some vapid and pointless competition. Redemption for us means saving our souls from the abyss that most of our kind dwell in." Her blue-green eyes glimmered in the half-light of the office. "I saw my sister go down that road, and there's nothing in this world that can redeem her now."

"I know how that feels," I said, and I did, all the way to the bone, my body feeling like it might suddenly sink through the chair, it was so heavy.

"You're not her," my mother said. "The ones I killed ... they still weigh on me, every day, even the ones I killed in the line of duty. You don't have to sink like Charlie. There is redemption out there, if you want it badly enough. This might just be your chance."

"I don't know that I can ever make up for what I've done," I said, shaking my head.

"Not make up for it. Not even offset it. Just ... do your best to try and tilt the balance back in the other direction." She sighed. "Live a life where you're doing your best to fight back from what you were, what you did. Become a person who's the opposite of what you were when you dove deep into the waters of revenge. Someone who stands up for what's right."

"I may have to kill again before this is all over," I said. "I may have to kill Weissman and Sovereign. There aren't any easy solutions for these men, there are no prisons that can hold them, no places to send them where they won't harm others."

"Then we'll have to kill them," she said. "And that's part of your redemption, too. You'll have to make the hard decisions others can't because your soul has taken damage that others shouldn't have to experience." She caught my gaze, and hers was haunted. "It's a terrible burden. A terrible price. But because of what you've done—if you really want to redeem yourself in your own eyes—you have to carry it without complaint."

I nodded. "I had a feeling it would come down to me."

"You got yourself into it," she said sadly, "and you're the only one who can carry you through. Trust me on that. I've been carrying it myself for more years than I can count."

"Yeah," I said. "Take Reed and Karthik and go to Portland." I thought about it for a piece. "Bring Kurt with you."

She frowned. "That pudgy agent?"

"Yeah," I said. "He's good in a scrape." Kurt Hannegan had been one of the first people I'd had Ariadne hire back when I got put in charge, though I'd kept him at a distance because we didn't necessarily work all that well together.

She nodded. "We'll get out there, see what we can find, and get back in a day or two, at most."

"Take your time," I said. "Do it right. And while you're out there, have Karthik, Reed and J.J. try and locate local Omega safehouses—"

"I'm not a rookie," she said with a hint of impatience. "I was planning on working all the angles to find Hildegarde. I've tracked a person or two, after all."

"Sorry," I said, more tired than contrite. "Just covering all my bases. When you get back, I need to debrief you again about your encounter with Sovereign."

She stiffened. "All right. I'll start thinking, see if I can remember anything else about it."

I nodded. "Do that. We need every bit of information we can get about him. Talk to Ariadne on your way out, have her charter a plane for you."

"Will do," she said coolly and headed for my office door. She stopped, her plain, unpainted fingernails resting on the frame. "Foreman made the right call putting you in charge."

I blinked. "What?"

"You're all grown up," she said, a little wistful. "You're making the right moves. It makes me wonder what happened to my little girl."

I didn't even think to go with a bitter response, because all my bitterness toward her was nearly gone at this point. It had dissipated sometime over the last six months. Still, I didn't know what to say, and after a few seconds she drummed on the edge of the doorframe with her hand and left. She disappeared into the bullpen, leaving me sitting in my office chair, marveling at the fact that we had made it through an entire conversation without any hostility at all.

Chapter 27

I stayed in my office until well after midnight, as was my habit of late. I was combing intelligence reports that had nothing to do with any of our suspects, hoping that somehow one of them would hold a little nugget, a key to what Century's next move was. Murder rates were within fairly normal parameters in the border cities, and the list of metas known to the U.S. government wasn't getting shorter because of unexpected deaths—yet. I knew it was coming, but based on what I was looking at, it seemed that Century wasn't in position yet.

These thoughts were swirling in my head as I slept, and the smell of my office laser printer was still hanging in my nose as I curled up on my couch, which sat against the wall next to the office door. The soft leather had its own distinct smell, and it filled my nose as I lay there, cheek pressed against it, mind still sprinting even in my exhaustion.

Little Doll worries too much.

"Thanks, Wolfe," I said. "Your concern is touching."

Little Doll should worry about herself, not others. Sovereign is coming, the telepath told you. Said he was coming for you.

"Not much I can do about that," I said. "Except be ready." I had a Glock 22 in my shoulder holster and a Walther PPK in my ankle holster. I knew I was tough enough to take a meta in a fair fight, but I was under no illusions after being captured in the airport that I was in any way faster than a speeding bullet. The best I could do was dodge maybe one guy with a gun if I was lucky. A firing line would be the end of me just the same as it would anyone else.

There is no preparing for ... him. This from Bjorn, who

always sounded a little scared when he talked about Sovereign, like the guy was going to jump out of the nearest closet and rip Bjorn's soul clean out of me.

"I'm as ready as I'm ever going to be," I said.

Little Doll should run. Run far, far away. Even she can't stop Sovereign. Best not to try.

"Because I hear you telling me what to do, I immediately know to do just the opposite," I said, settling in on the couch.

He is too strong, too wily, too powerful. He has crushed metas who would make Little Doll look like ... a little doll by comparison.

"You know, if you really tried, Wolfe, I think you could be even more sneeringly condescending." I paused for comic effect. "No, wait, no you couldn't. I'm making my stand here. If anyone doesn't like it, you know where to find the door to your little cages."

Don't be foolish, Little Doll. We can help you, help you hide from him.

"I don't want to hide from him!" I said, my fury boiling over. "I want to go straight at him, to feel my fingers around his neck as I sap the life from him! If I knew where he was right now, I would go to him, find him, and do my level best to kill him just so we could get this over with, one way or another." My anger spent, I felt the seething on my lips die down. "I'm tired. I want to be done with this."

Little Doll should not be so cavalier with her life—

"What life?" I said with a laugh. "What life do I have? I'm in the service of my government now, in the service of my people, and that's all I've got going. Forgive me for trying to figure out the shortest way possible to end this crisis. I just want it to be over so that maybe I can take a breath, maybe feel like I've paid some of my debt to society. I'd even be glad to be hunting troublesome metas again if it meant I didn't have the extinction of my entire species hanging over my head. So again, Wolfe, what life? The one where I wake up in the morning, think about this all day long, and go to bed wondering if this will be the night that it starts here in the U.S.? Where I wonder when the axe will begin to fall, and if I'll even be able to stop it when it does? So I can wake up to another day and wonder if this is my last one alive, if they'll be coming for me now or at the end of it all, after I've seen the body counts rack up? Another day to wonder if I'll get to watch every one of my friends die because Sovereign wants me alive and all of them dead?" I sighed. "And I don't even know why he wants me alive."

The Little Doll is special. Wolfe knew this from Omega, from the others, but they didn't tell Wolfe how special you were, that you were one of the offspring of the master. Of Death.

"They kept you in the dark? Big surprise." I laughed ruefully. "That's all anybody does, isn't it? Layers of secrets on top of secrets, burying one after another." I felt a little stab. "It's what Omega did to Adelaide, too. What Old Man Winter did to me. Sovereign and Weissman are doing it to at least some of their people, maybe all of them, who knows." I sighed in the dark and felt the pressure of my body resting against the couch. "Too many secrets. I've lost count of all the ones I'm supposed to be finding answers to."

Beware the secrets of scary people, Gavrikov said. *They will consume you, wrap you up within them, and carry you away.*

"I think I've already been carried away, Aleksandr." I felt a little mournful as I said it. I longed for the simplicity of my house. No, that wasn't true. What I really longed for was the nine months or so that I'd been part of the Directorate, when things were simple and I had a boyfriend who loved me, friends who watched my back. I thought about Scott and Kat, and how I hadn't really spoken to them outside of a meeting, or about anything other than work in the six months since we'd started this endeavor. Hell, even Breandan and Karthik were nothing more than work colleagues at this point, at a distance. The conversation I'd had earlier with my mother was one of the deepest ones we'd ever had, and one of the first outside of a meeting or a discussion of straight business of the agency. "I've been carried along by this river of secrets since day one, with only a little bitty break somewhere in the middle." I blinked. "I wonder if I'll look back on this in five years and still think of my time at the Directorate as the best days of my life." I didn't say it, but I wondered if I'd even be around to look back on it in five years. The odds were not great.

There was a beep from the phone on my desk announcing the intercom. I rolled off the couch and walked over to hit the accept button, and I heard loud, crackling noises through the phone. "What?" I said, feeling a sense of unease.

A loud klaxon sounded throughout the building, a howling sound, and I saw a red emergency light begin to flash outside my office, casting the cubicles of the bullpen in a deep red light. "Ms. Nealon, this is dormitory security, we are under fire—" The voice was cut off by the staccato sound of gunshots in the background. "—overwhelming numbers—" The phone hissed and squealed from the feedback noise and the howl of what was coming through it. The sound of gunshots was steady now, and I could tell that a pitched firefight was going on. "They are in the building—"

"Activate the shutters!" I shouted, but the sound cut out. I waited there for an awful moment, then turned and looked out my office window. Light from muzzle flare flashed across the way at the dormitory. Black shapes were entering the building now, swarming in, too many to count, flooding out of vans parked right up on the curb. It was an army of men, and their purpose was clear.

We were being invaded.

Chapter 28

I took the elevator even though I shouldn't have, stopping at the first floor and shouting at the security detail to lock down the building. I saw the shutters begin to clink into place even as the doors closed again and I descended to the basement. We had built directly on top of the old Headquarters and the previous dormitory because for all their faults, the space was already excavated. A little too excavated, after the explosions, but that was easier to fix than digging a new hole in the ground in winter, so we just let the construction guys clear the mess and start building. There was an additional advantage to this, though, one that I didn't readily advertise.

I hit the armory first, throwing on a Kevlar assault vest, the kind used by our security teams when they needed to clear a difficult target. I hadn't had to deploy the security teams yet, which was just as well. They might have to come into play in a few minutes, but I didn't care for that idea much. I grabbed a walkie talkie off the rack and set it to the emergency channel. "Get the FBI's Hostage Rescue Team on the line, get them out here."

"Understood," I heard a clipped, familiar voice on the other end of the radio. "I've already contacted them."

"Li?" I asked. "I sent my mother along with Karthik and Reed to Portland to get on that manhunt for Hildegarde. I need you to see if you can locate any of our other metas. I need Scott and Breandan." I cursed. "But they're probably in the dorms."

"I'll see what I can find," Li said.

"Sienna," Ariadne's voice broke in. "What are you going to do?"

"Ever seen the movie *Die Hard*?" I asked, snugging a

submachine gun strap tight across my shoulders.

"Oh, dear God," Ariadne said.

"It's all right," I said. "As soon as the FBI HRT gets here, let them know the situation and have them start setting up. I didn't see the shutters deployed a minute ago, but if the Century force has gained access to security, it's more than probable that they'll be locking the building down to repel our efforts to retake it." I burst out the door of the armory and kept talking as I ran down the hallway of HQ toward the far side of the building.

"At which point you'll be locked inside with them," Ariadne said.

"I run this place," I said, "good luck locking me in anywhere. I can override any door I want opened. No, if they trigger the shutters—and they should, to keep us from dusting them with snipers—then they'll be the ones locked in. Security will be the only place they'll be able to raise and lower the shutters."

"But that keeps our people trapped," Ariadne said, "and we have an awful lot of young metas over there."

"No argument here," I said as I hit the edge of the building and reached a locked room. I ran a card key over the door and it beeped, sliding open to admit me. "Hopefully they're not dug in, because I need to deal with the Century force on my own."

There was a pause before Ariadne spoke again. "You're not a one-woman army, Sienna."

"Oh, yes, I am." I took a breath as I entered the tunnel that led from HQ to the dormitory's basement. The overhead fluorescent lights clicked on in a long sequential pattern that left me staring at a dank, acrid-smelling hallway. The tunnel was left over from the original Directorate, designed to be used when periods of snowfall made transiting from building to building uncomfortable. I hadn't used them since shortly after I came to the Directorate because they tended to lock them down in the summertime, but they had survived the destruction of the Directorate with only a nasty, smoky smell to show for it. I ran down the hall, feet pounding against the concrete as I headed straight for my target. "Coordinate a response, Ariadne. Keep them contained, because if they're with Century—and I can't imagine they're not—then their objective is to wipe us all out, so we're effectively already dead. Make sure they don't survive the attempt."

Ariadne's reply came back eight octaves higher than usual, coated in frustration. "That's insane—"

"Do it," I said. "That's the position of the head of Ops, okay? Do not negotiate, do not bargain, kill them all as soon as you can, because I guarantee you that they'll be trying to do that to our people."

"Why not just blow up the building then, and save ourselves the trouble?" Ariadne asked with measured sarcasm.

"Why, that's a lovely idea," I said. "I might just have to do that."

There was a pause. "Tell me you're joking."

"I'm joking." I took a breath as I came to the end of the hallway. "Probably."

"You cannot be serious—"

"I'm entering the dormitory and switching to silent," I said, placing a small headset on my ear and clicking the volume lower. "Do what I've asked. I'll contact you if I need anything, otherwise maintain radio silence."

"But—"

"Radio silence begins now," I said, cutting her off as I ran my key card over the scanner next to the door. It beeped and I placed my hand over the biometric scanner. It read my palm quickly, probably noting that my lifeline was getting shorter by the moment, and the door hissed open into the dormitory basement. The good news was that it wouldn't open for anyone but me, and only while I was alive. The bad news was that whoever Century had sent, I doubt they knew or cared about that little detail.

I crept into the basement, my senses hyper alert and listening for any sound. There was plenty of it; scuffling of feet, gunfire from above, shouting. Either the extermination of my people was well underway or there was still a fight going on. The shouting led me to believe it was the latter, which meant I had a chance to tip the balance. Most of the metas who were here in the dorms weren't much in the way of fighters and were low on the power scale. That meant that while they were stronger and faster than a human, they didn't stand half the chance I did of being able to outmaneuver someone pointing a gun at me or being able to completely overwhelm a group of armed mercenaries with my superior speed and reflexes.

I pondered the fact that the force assaulting us was carrying guns. I'd run across some of that kind before, armed mercenaries whom Century had employed to take out smaller groups of metas a few at a time. I suspected that meant that we weren't facing much in the way of metas this round, just men with guns. I kept my hand firmly on my submachine gun. Men with guns I could handle, so long as I was armed. Hell, I could handle metas, too, but this might actually be easier if I did it right.

I got to the nearest staircase and ascended. I knew where I was, and it was in a back hallway of the dormitory building. I opened the door to the corridor and didn't hear any noise nearby. I dodged out with my weapon covering the corners, sweeping for enemies. I didn't look in any direction that I wasn't already pointing the gun, and I started to move forward, toward the main lobby. This had been the way to my room, and a line of windows to my left was shuttered closed, steel grey metal blocking any light from coming in from outside. The lamps flickered above, on emergency lighting, and red emergency lights flashed from boxes mounted every twenty or thirty feet at the sides of the hallway. In the distance I could see the entrance to the lobby and could hear gunfire coming in bursts.

I slipped along the wall, trying to make myself invisible, melting into the shadows where possible. I could see men advancing across the mouth of the hallway ahead, firing their weapons as they headed not toward the cafeteria but toward the long hallway opposite mine, the one where most of the metas we had on campus were staying. We'd kept almost everyone on one side of the building because it was easier to keep things regulated. I had worried at the time that it might make them more vulnerable, but I thought cloistering them together might also be more defensible. It appeared I had been right on both counts.

And of course the beauteous thing about it was that my enemies had left their backs totally exposed to a flanking attack by yours truly.

I stuck to the shadows, moving slowly, quietly, though the gunfire was deafening, echoing down the hall. The smell of discharged gunpowder hung thick and heavy in the air as I eased along through the red light, the faint clouds of smoke from so much weapons discharge casting a thin haze into the air. I kept on, trying to remain as quiet as possible even though I could probably have driven a truck down the hallway, honked the horn, and run right into their midst without them noticing until the treads were upon them.

I came to the mouth of the hallway, where it met the opening, and saw what I was up against. There were twenty or thirty of them, all spread throughout the lobby. They were totally focused on the hall, and gunfire was coming steadily from that direction, which made me wonder who on my team had guns and was resisting their advance. Whoever it was, they were doing a pretty good job of stymieing the mercs, holding them back from charging. They were all wearing Kevlar vests and tactical helmets, which had the potential to stop a bullet, though it was hardly a foregone conclusion. Shooting them would still hurt them, and although they were cushioned, I knew I could break bones through their padding and armor. For maximum effect, though, I really needed to get those helmets off.

The good news was that I had a plan to do just that.

I slipped on a gas mask as I stood in the shadows, unobserved by everyone. It was a newer model with a wider lens for me to see out of, one that dipped back further so it didn't obstruct my field of vision like a lot of the old bug-eyed models did. I thumbed a canister of tear gas off the belt I had grabbed from the armory and then another, pulling the pins loose with my index finger before I heaved them toward the middle of the lobby.

That drew attention immediately, causing three mercs to look back at me. I met their gaze with quick bursts from my submachine gun, which roared in the hall and lit the walls with muzzle flash. I ran forward and slid feet-first like a baseball player behind a makeshift barricade that the mercs had set up from a table they'd dragged out of the security room. I fired blind over it twice, letting the rounds rip with the best aim I could from my hidden position. I heard bullets come back at me, tearing into the surface of the table and ripping through, showering me with splinters. I tried not to pay attention to how close they were getting, but it's tough to ignore it when bullets are tearing through your cover.

I heard the sound of the tear gas canisters burst, and I smiled. I counted to five then rolled right, coming out and surprising a guy who had been creeping toward me trying to flank me. I pegged him in the head, landing a few rounds in his neck before I kept rolling right, coming up in a squatting position after my next roll. I shot to my feet and fired left, hitting another guy who was emerging from the growing fog as he looked up, shocked to see someone coming at him.

I could see flashes in the tear gas, could hear the sound of gunfire and coughing in the midst of it, my finely tuned meta senses combining with adrenaline to keep me on point. I dodged left as I felt bullets whipping to my right and I grabbed at another dark figure emerging from the mist as he came within arm's length of me. I threw him without letting him get close, just whirled and tossed him by the front of his vest before he could whip his gun around or react to me in any way. I heard him land after a twenty-foot flight, and it didn't sound like one he'd walk away from. I was already moving on, though.

I came upon two more figures, huddled behind the security desk. They were emerging as they coughed, and I mercilessly hit the first in the neck with a knifehand strike that sent him to his knees, choking even worse than he already was. The next caught a perfectly aimed kick to the knee that caused him to scream in pain as he fell toward me, head thumping against the Kevlar on my chest. I saw him fumbling for his gun and knew I couldn't chance it. I grabbed him around the neck just like you see in the movies, and I wrenched it so hard it broke his vertebrae. It was instinctual, it was thoughtless, and he fell from my grip like the dead weight he now was. I shoved aside the thought of what I'd done, pushing it off to the back of my mind for later.

I was in my groove now, and the tear gas was starting to clear, dispersing in the massive atrium of the dormitory building. As it thinned, I caught glimpse of another cluster of three, just catching their collective breath, hands still on their guns. They were carrying European assault rifles, bullpup design, which I didn't recognize right off because of the fog of tear gas in the room. My face was starting to sweat inside my mask, making it more difficult to see.

I charged the three of them and swatted away the barrel the first pointed at me as he fired. I heard glass breaking as the rounds shattered the windows out front and then a sound of clanging metal as the round met the shutters outside. I jerked the barrel down even as I felt the hot metal in my hand and pulled my weapon around, firing a three-shot burst under his visor, which looked like an oversized motorcycle helmet. Crimson splattered the clear mask, and blood pumped down his neck as he fell limp to the floor.

I didn't spare any mercy for the next either, booting him in the groin with a kick that would have scored a fifty-yard field goal if it had been aimed at a football. The man on the receiving team screamed and dropped to his knees, all thoughts of keeping a grip on his rifle forgotten. I raised a knee to knock his helmet off and then finished him with a backhand to the face that shattered any semblance of a nose that he might have started out with.

The last of the triad caught a shot in the gut, and when he doubled over I knocked his helmet off and planted a palm on his forehead, then shoved as hard as I could. From a normal human, it probably would have staggered him. Because it was me, the back of his neck cracked, his feet flew out from underneath him, and his skull hit the floor hard enough that it made a wet spot on my shoes that probably wouldn't ever come off.

I grabbed his gun as he fell and braced the stock against my shoulder. Seeing action heroes fire two guns in movies always made me cringe because normal humans can't really do it effectively. The aim goes all to hell because the recoil throws it off with every shot and their reflexes aren't good enough to bring it back to center in a time-efficient manner. Rapid fire is an even worse idea because accuracy progressively deteriorates every time the gun fires and the barrel rocks back.

I had meta strength, however, and the recoil didn't affect me at all. I kept the submachine gun and the rifle fairly steady as I fired them both at two clusters of targets, men in black who were emerging from the fog. Six of them came out firing or ready to, and I pegged the first with enough bullets to send him to the ground with a pain in the chest. The next two on each side took rounds to the chest and neck respectively, ending at least one of their breathing careers. I adjusted my aim upward for the third on my left, and he took three bullets to the helmet, shattering the visor and splattering it with gore. The other guy got hit in the chest and staggered back, landing hard. I surged forward and kicked one of the survivors in the guts, taking all the wind out of him, sending him flipping in a roll straight into a wall. Another was starting to get up, gun in hand, so I raised the rifle and fired into him only a few feet away. I could see the bullets penetrate his Kevlar and red begin to run down the black vest he wore. I shot the next two who were also moving, scoring a hit to the side of the helmet that penetrated through and one to the other guy's legs that hit his femoral artery. His leg started to gush blood, and I knew he had only a minute or two of life left in him before he bled to death.

"Looks like you guys are the Expendables," I said, "but without the benefit of having Sly Stallone as the brains of your operation."

The tear gas was almost clear, and I knocked my mask off my head with an offhand flick of my wrist. The once-stale air now caused a sharp tingle when I breathed it, like I'd bitten into a jalapeno. I could see five more guys ahead, toward the hallway opposite where I'd entered, and I fired at the first with the rifle because they were far enough away I didn't want to chance it with the submachine gun. I veered right and ducked behind the corner of the wall before peering out and firing again, using my precision to blast one of the guys in the head. I didn't see him for more than a second before I had to duck behind the corner of the wall as it started to absorb a hail of bullets, but I knew he wasn't getting back up.

I took a few steps back from the corner as the drywall continued to break down from the gunfire of my adversaries. The entire corner was just about chipped off now, with a half-foot indentation from where they'd tried to shoot through the wall to get to me. It wasn't a bad idea, actually, but I'd backed about six feet away from the corner, anticipating that exact strategy. The further away I got, the less likely they were going to hit me on a blind shot.

My shoe squeaked on the tile and I was thankful yet again that I always stuck with flats instead of heels. I was also wearing pants instead of a skirt because I knew what kind of job I was really in. Paperwork and desk bullshit aside, this was my office, in the thick of the fight. My purpose was to save metakind, and wearing heels and a skirt while sitting behind a desk was never in the job description.

I dropped the submachine gun and took off at a run for the corner. Just as I reached it I slid like a baseball player, letting the seat of my pants slide on the tile. My momentum carried me forward across the unresistant surface and I went sliding across the mouth of the hallway, rifle at the ready. As I went past, I heard the remaining three open fire, but they were too slow and I was too fast. I opened up with the rifle and caught the first one under the chin. He sagged, all the starch taken out of him. The next I caught lower, just under his vest, bullets tearing into his belly, and he groaned in pain and started to drop.

I couldn't get a bead on the last of them before I disappeared behind the corner of the other side of the hallway. I pulled the rifle sling off my shoulders because I knew I was just about out of ammo. I reached to my hip and pulled my Glock and sprang to my feet. I ran at the corner again, but this time instead of sliding I jumped into the air, starting to execute a flip.

In the movies, they show this sort of thing in slow motion, two guns firing simultaneously. It was utterly ludicrous for a normal person to even think about trying, but again, I was not normal. Even with my dexterity and reflexes, though, it was a hard shot with just the one gun I was holding. I managed to land two out of the five shots I fired, one hitting the last mercenary in the torso, the other knocking his helmet off without breaking through it. I could see him trying to shake off the shock of what had just happened, even as he staggered under the pain and bruising from the gunshot to the chest. He bounced off the wall, trying to catch his balance, and took aim at me just as I landed, flat on my back.

I absorbed the shock well, spreading it out over my back, my buttocks, my legs where possible, and one arm. The other I tried to keep focused on him, my gun hand still extended, but the impact sent my aim wide, and I'd pulled my finger off the trigger just before I landed in order to keep from accidentally firing. It took me a moment to readjust myself, to bring my gun up after the landing, and I knew as I brought it into alignment that I was too slow, that my gamble with the last blitz hadn't paid off. I kept on, trying to get my gun up in time, but when the shots rang out, I was aiming at his leg at best, and I knew I was done.

It came as a surprise when he was the one who slumped, a cloud of red mist around his head as if someone had blown a puff of blood into the air. He hit his knees, then pitched forward on his face, dead. I still had my gun up, aiming at him now, in case somehow I had missed something.

"Sienna, is that you?" I heard Scott's voice from somewhere ahead, beyond the barricades of furniture and tables that were blocking the hallway.

I took a breath then another, as the adrenaline started to fade. "Yeah. It's me. Who else would it be?"

There was no response for a moment. "Did you get them all?" Scott asked finally.

I looked back into the foyer of the dormitories, into the mass of dead, dying and wounded. "I think so. Just a minute." I got to my feet, which were a little unsteady, and worked my way back into the foyer. There were a few men moaning, still bleeding, and I kicked their guns away as I made my way through, disarming them and punching a few in the jaw to put their lights out as needed. When I reached the security desk, I swiped my card and hit the button that started to retract the shutters. There was an incredible clatter as the building began to exit lockdown, and I saw men in tactical vests—familiar faces from our security detail—come pouring in through the main doors. I waved them in, and said, "Secure the area, sweep the building floor by floor to make sure it's clear."

I heard someone acknowledge me but I paid little attention. I was already on my way back down the corridor where I'd heard Scott's voice only a minute earlier. I pushed aside the first barricade, a desk turned on its side, and started picking my way around the obstacles in the way. "You okay in there?" I asked as I vaulted over an upturned table, its four legs jutting into the air. Bodies of mercenaries were littered through the debris, as if they'd gotten turned back on at least one advance down the hall. I took a breath. That defeat had made my job easier.

Then I came to the first body that wasn't a mercenary. Men from our security detail had died back in the foyer, I'd seen their corpses, but here, lying against an overturned chair, was one of the clerks from Omega whom I'd brought over from England. I remembered his face but not his name, recalled that he'd stood with me in the last fight against Weissman and Raymond over in London. His eyes stared straight ahead now, whatever had been behind them long gone. I knelt down and closed them for him, and saw another familiar body just past him.

This one was another from the battle in London. She was older, in her late fifties by human years, and I thought her name was Rochelle. I remembered it because it was so distinctive. Her neck was covered in blood and her body was still, head pitched to the side at an awkward angle. I reached out to touch her; she was still lukewarm but far colder than a living human being would have been.

"Scott?" I called out again as I stood, my legs feeling like they were going to buckle under me.

"Yeah," came the weary voice from ahead. Why wasn't he coming to me? Why wasn't he leading them out, whoever was left? I started toward him, climbing over a couch that had been ripped apart by bullets, and on the other side I found three more bodies of our own—a security man who'd died with a gun in his hand, a meta from England whose name I couldn't recall, and another, a girl, whose name was Athena.

I sagged next to Athena and let my fingers touch my face as I dropped my weapon. The smell of gunpowder and spent rounds was heavy in the hallway, and as my face sunk into my hands I smelled it on me, like the scent of death, strong in my nose. I reached over and touched Athena's face, the black powder smudges on my fingers rubbing off on her skin. I'd recruited her to join Omega, and now her lifeless brown eyes stared back at me from the floor. She'd been shot in the back while trying to run away, here in this place where I couldn't protect her. Even though I'd told her and all the others to come here, told them to leave London and come here to die, so far from home—

I felt a little noise of horror escape me and clamped a hand over my mouth as I settled back on my haunches, sitting down in a pool of wet blood. I didn't even know whose it was. I didn't care. I stared at Athena's lifeless body and tried to process it all, tried to fight back the horror.

"Sienna?" Scott's voice came from down the hall in the direction I had been heading only a moment earlier. "Sienna, are you all right?"

I pulled myself together in an instant, pushing aside the shock, the horror, pretending there was a hole somewhere deep in my soul and I could dump everything down into it. This was no time for tears; there were others waiting for me on the other side of the barricade, the last barricade from the sound of Scott's voice. "I'm coming," I said. "I'll be right there."

I stood on unsteady legs, shuffling with as careful a balance as I could, dodging around the last overturned desk. I could see the recreation room behind it, full of metas, the survivors of our little band. There were far more of them than there were of the dead, I knew that much, and I felt a rush of gratitude. I let out a weary sigh, mixed with more than a little relief to see so many still standing, peering out into the hallway, looking at the spot behind the desk—

I came around the desk to find Scott just sitting there, his back against it, his face red and shot through with emotion. I started to say something but stopped myself just in time. There were little sobs coming from the recreation room, the sounds of mourning and fear, and as much as I wanted to reassure them, I couldn't when I saw what they were weeping about.

There was another body next to Scott, a man whose face was at peace in spite of the angry red wound in the middle of his forehead. He wore a slightly upturned smile—just a hint—under his waxed mustache. His once-lively eyes were now staring off into the distance, and his distinctive cologne had been overcome by the heavy odor of gunpowder that still lingered in the air. The sobs of the survivors drowned out any other noises, and my knees gave out and I fell to his side. He did not respond even as I shook him, Breandan's head lolling around with the motion of his body as I tried desperately, desperately, to shake back to life a man whose luck had finally run out.

Chapter 29

Jon Traeger
Lake Superior
November 10, 1975

They nicknamed the ship the *Mighty Fitz*. He'd barely made it on board; just in time, really. The wind was howling and the squall was pitching the sides of the massive freighter he'd found passage on at the last moment. They didn't normally take passengers, even though they had two cabins for it, but a lot of money had changed hands and the deal was done just moments before the *Fitzgerald* left port. It was worth it for Jon to get her out of here, to get her away from the Midwest.

"We're safe now," Jon said to the woman who sat a little distance away from him. He'd been reassuring her since they'd gotten on board, but it didn't seem to be having much effect. Not that he could blame her.

Her name was Elizabeth, and she was huddled against the chill that was seeping into the passenger cabin. The steady wash of the water against the sides of the ship was getting more dramatic as the hours passed, and the freighter was listing to the side. They'd been awakened in the early hours of the morning and been unable to get back to sleep. The storm seemed to have worsened. A couple of hours earlier when Jon had tried to talk to the captain, the man had ordered them to stay off the deck.

She shook her head, her dark hair and smeared makeup distinctive. "I don't know that we'll ever be safe. Not from him."

Traeger felt the swell of uncertainty as he stared at the walls of the freighter's cabin. There was a drape covering the porthole, and every few minutes he'd find himself pacing the deep-pile carpeting to pull it back and look out into the darkness, where the rain and waves lashed at the ship. "He's not invincible. He's not infallible. We lost him in Duluth, before we crossed the Wisconsin line, simple as that. You're free now." He sank down to the bed as the ship rocked to the side again, almost throwing him against the wall. "He can't hurt you now."

She swallowed so heavily he could hear the *gulp!* over the sound of the storm outside. "I don't think he wanted to hurt me, exactly."

Traeger could smell the oily residue of the ship's reprocessed air. "No? Why do you think he wanted you?"

She started to answer when a grinding thud and the squeal of metal cut her off. A shudder louder than any the storm had produced ran through the ship. Elizabeth's eyes went wide, and she jumped for the bundle on the bed next to her, laid out asleep. Jon moved for them both, protectively, as another grunt of stressed metal echoed through the whole ship and the world pitched on them, turning sideways, the hardest list of the ship yet.

"He's found us." Her voice was low, filled with quiet desperation as she clutched the bundle in her arms. It was long enough that it ran across her body, legs sticking out the side, oblivious to the commotion taking place around her. Jon threw his arms around them, grasping Elizabeth and the child in a tight embrace.

"Impossible," Jon said, almost under his breath. The sound had stopped, just for a moment. "We left port over a day ago. No one could track us like this. No meta could find us over open water like—"

The hatch to the cabin opened with a slow, grinding squeak, the mechanism squealing as it turned, in desperate need of oil. Jon stared at it in a kind of fixed horror, trying to figure out his next move. *Can I fly them out? The girl, maybe, but not both,* he realized grimly. *Not in this storm.*

Jon looked down at the bundle in the woman's arms. It squirmed, a little girl, eight years old, looking up at him with wide eyes, still blinking from her sudden awakening.

"Shhhh," he whispered, and the door creaked again, squealing the lock open the last little bit, popping as it swung wide. The ship was still listing, the waves rocking it in the waters of Lake Superior.

The door swung open, framing a figure silhouetted in the light coming from the corridor outside. There was a shadow at first and that was all, a great silhouette dripping rain onto the carpeting, and then the man took a step over the lip of the hatch threshold, and shut it behind him, turning the heavy wheel to crank it shut. Once it was closed he stepped away, and Jon could see him wearing a coat that was soaked through, black, and boots that oozed water when he took a step. *Did he fly all the way out to us from Duluth? That's a long flight, even for a—*

"Hello, there," the man said, breaking his silence. "I've been looking for you, Elizabeth."

Jon felt iron descend down his back bone, and he stood, ramrod straight. "She doesn't want to go with you." He protectively an arm out.

"She doesn't know what she wants yet," the man said, staring at Jon with slight mirth in his eyes. "She's been running from me because of legends that have no basis in reality. I don't want to hurt her. I'm not here to cause trouble—"

"Then what did you do to the ship?" Jon asked, staring him down. "Because it sounds like you may have caused some trouble."

"I didn't do anything to the ship. Yet," the man said. There was a little hint of darkness in his eyes now, menace and malice. "I have no interest in fighting with either of you. I just want an opportunity to talk with her."

"You've picked an awkward way to go about it," Jon said. "Chasing her down. You can't just let her go?"

The man hesitated at that. "I wouldn't have preferred it this way. I'm a man who doesn't want ... well, anything, most of the time, honestly. But ... I need to talk to her. I've been looking for her for a long time—"

"Hence the reason she's running," Jon said. "Not usually a good sign when a man of your reputation is hunting someone down. Tends to be a little ominous."

The man laughed humorlessly. "What do you know about me?"

"You're Sovereign," Jon said without hesitation. "Not just a local legend, but it seems like you've spent more than your fair share of time in the Midwest for the last few hundred years."

The man smirked. "What can I say? I like the Nordic people, and I'm a sucker for a good hotdish."

"You've killed a lot of metas," Jon went on, "and more than a few humans."

"Dangerous ones," Sovereign said darkly. "Ones that were extorting their fellow man, taking advantage. What about you, Jon Traeger?" Jon bristled at the mention of his own name. "You've got a little bit of a reputation, too. Working for Alpha, crisscrossing the world, looking to solve other peoples' problems, even when they haven't asked—"

"Usually those problems involve Omega," Jon said, "and let's face it, when it comes to dealing with them, most folks don't know there's any other option."

Sovereign smiled. He didn't look terribly sinister, Jon had to admit. "So you're watching out for your fellow human beings, guarding them against the dangerous and criminal brotherhood of Omega."

"It's a sisterhood, too," Jon said. "Just ... you know, in the name of equality."

"Right," Sovereign said. "So here you are, protecting a girl from a dangerous threat."

"Potentially the most dangerous," Jon said, staring back at Sovereign. "According to what I've heard, at least."

"'What you've heard'?" Sovereign's bleak amusement filled the cabin. "Do you find there's typically a lot of truth in rumors?"

"A grain," Jon replied. "Enough to concern me."

"Let me put you at ease," Sovereign said. "I'm not taking the girl without her permission. I've been seeking her out—"

"That much is plain," Jon said.

Sovereign smiled. "I need to talk to her."

Jon stared back at him. "So talk." He looked back at Elizabeth. "She's listening."

Sovereign stood quietly for a moment as the little girl quivered wordlessly in her mother's arms, and a look of discomfort came across his face. "Look, I don't know what you've heard about me, but I've not been after you to hurt you in any way." He laughed nervously, surprising Jon. *A man this powerful gets nervous?* "I mean, we haven't even had a chance to meet face to face until now. I don't know why you were so afraid of me—"

"Because I have a child, sir," she said, staring at him, the little girl clutched across her chest, a blanket separating them, wrapping the little girl up wholly so that she looked like a waif. "And when a powerful man starts inquiring about you, trying to find you, track you down, if you're in my position you don't wait to find out his intention." She looked away. "I know the intentions of most men—"

"I promise you, mine are different," Sovereign said.

"Yeah, well, it hasn't worked out so well with any of them," she said bitterly.

"It would be different with me," Sovereign said, "because I'm different." He took a step forward and Jon held out a hand to stay him. "Put your hand down before you hurt someone," Sovereign said.

Jon shook his head. "Just keep your distance until she asks you to get closer."

Sovereign's face reddened. "I'm not here to hurt her."

"Fair enough," Jon said calmly, "then you won't mind keeping your distance, will you?"

Sovereign's nostrils flared. "You're a creature of the wind, are you not?"

Jon stared at him levelly. *Looks like this is about to turn hostile.* "I'm an Aeolus, yes."

"Let's call you what you are," Sovereign said. "A Windkeeper. A creature of the wind." His face darkened. "And all that's left of you when I'm finished with you will be able to float away on the wind, so don't tell me what to do. I don't take kindly to being interfered with."

Jon stared at him, felt the fury and fear rise in equal measure in his gullet. *This isn't going to get any prettier by waiting. He'll kill me in an instant.* He closed his eyes, took a breath, and hurled a burst of wind so hard that the man called Sovereign was flung bodily into the wall.

"Let's go!" Jon shouted, grabbing for Elizabeth's arm. He caught her by the wrist and she ran with him, unbattening the hatch and slamming it behind them, leaving Sovereign behind, shaking his head from where it had struck the bulkhead. A little bit of blood was visible on the man's face in the flickering light of the *Edmund Fitzgerald*'s passenger cabin as Jon slammed the door and cranked the wheel to batten it shut.

Jon's feet pounded as Elizabeth followed, the child in her arms. The little girl was crying, but the sound was barely audible as they crossed metal stairs toward the deck. *Out into the storm. I can carry us in the storm, maybe lose him in the clouds ... with wind drifts like these, even the woman and child might not be too much for me to carry ... Just have to harness it, tame it.*

They burst onto the deck as a wave crashed over the bow and the ship tilted. Jon felt his balance tested, but he caught himself on the side of the conning tower, holding Elizabeth steady along with him. The night was dark, the driving rain highlighted in the deck lamps, coming in nearly sideways and frigid cold as they steadied themselves between waves. "Hold tight to me!" he shouted as the world started to list again.

There was a grinding of metal once more, and something burst in the middle of the ship. The deck peeled back and Jon saw it split, the forecastle of the ship breaking off from the strength of the impact. He adjusted to grab for Elizabeth but failed, snagging the little girl's blanket instead.

Elizabeth let out a cry as the deck pitched, a wave crashing over the side with such force that the whole thing shuddered, and Jon watched as the *Edmund Fitzgerald* was snapped in half, the damage done beneath the deck compounded and revealed by the strength of the waves. He grabbed hold of a recess in the conning tower, feeling every tendon in his shoulder yanked tight by the sudden drop of his entire body, the shift in gravity as the ship dipped, sinking into the waves.

It happened so fast he barely knew it. He found himself hanging on vertically, the girl's blanket bunched tightly in his fist, and he watched as Elizabeth dropped away into the water beneath him, screaming as she fell into the frothy, roiling surface of the lake. He cried out, shouting into the storm, and felt the conning tower of the *Fitzgerald* pitch forward, tilting over with the strength of the waves. He jerked the blanket upward, snugging the child into his arms and letting the sodden, wet mess of it fall away as he clutched her tight to him. As another wave came at them, he realized that if he didn't leave now, he would surely be carried down with the wreckage of the *Fitzgerald*, and Elizabeth, down to the bottom of the lake.

He started the wind with his free hand, a tornado that carried them up, him and the little girl, whose cries were lost in the screaming of the gale. They broke the clouds after a few minutes of turbulent upthrust, and he held her, cold, wet and sobbing against his chest as he flew them into the night, toward a shore that was somewhere in the distance.

They reached land less than an hour later, but by then Jon's arm had grown numb and weary from carrying the girl crooked in it, his skin cold from the frigid storm. As his feet set down gently upon the shores of Lake Superior, Jon Traeger looked down at the girl, now sleeping in his arms, and let out a sigh.

"I'll take you to England," he whispered, the clouds above brewing, ready to bring forth the harbinger of the storm he'd just outrun. "To Alpha. Maybe Hera can find your living relatives." He let a weary sigh, and cradled her with his other arm. "If not, I'll take care of you myself." He felt her warm against him, even through the layers of wet clothing. "I won't let any harm come to you ... Adelaide."

Chapter 30

Sienna Nealon
Now

"So the question is, did they wait to strike until we were more vulnerable or did they happen to catch us at a convenient moment?" My mother's voice echoed over the speaker of the phone. I held it in my hand, pushed against my ear, my head back against the chair.

"I read the minds of a few of the surviving mercenaries," I said, replying slowly, as if I were prying the words out of my own mouth. "They didn't seem to know we'd be at half capacity. Their task wasn't even to kill the metas they did, they were supposed to secure them and barter for the telepaths."

There was a pause on the other end of the line as my mother took a deep breath. Morning was shining in from outside the windows, the sun gazing down on what should have been a perfect day. Under normal circumstances, I wouldn't even have noticed. Now I not only noticed but was painfully aware of the disparity between the weather as it was and what it should have been—dark clouds, gloom, rain, torrential downpours. Between the security detail and the metas I'd said I would protect, we'd lost enough people last night that it could only be classified as a catastrophe.

"So they were there solely to take back—"

"The telepaths we captured in Florida, yes," I said dully, staring out onto the green, sunlit campus grounds. When I looked over at the dormitory building in the distance, it showed little outward sign of the assault that had done so much damage only hours earlier. I felt a burning in my chest, like bile waiting to be thrown up, as though I could expunge all the feelings I was denying in that way. "Apparently, Century thinks we're still holding them alive."

I could hear her thinking at the other end of the phone, and I was virtually certain I knew what she was going to say. "I know you don't want to hear this—"

"You're right," I said, "I don't."

"—but this is a silver lining."

"It's a lot of dead people that I brought over here from London saying I'd protect." The words tasted disgusting in my mouth, like meatloaf.

"But this tells us that Century is not omniscient."

"I already knew that." I didn't need the bodies that were stacked up in the morgue downstairs to drive that point home.

"But," my mother went on, heedless of my clear desire not to have this conversation, "this means that they'll think we still have the telepaths."

"I said I understood it." My voice was just tired. I hadn't slept at all that night, just sat in a chair in the corner of the medical unit and stared at Perugini's back while she sighed and did the post-mortem work she had to do. Surprisingly, she didn't pick at me once. She probably knew it wouldn't do a damned bit of good.

"Then they'll—"

"Be coming back at us again, yes," I said. "I told you I got it. You graded my papers for years, you know I'm not stupid."

She sounded tired, too. "I just want to make sure you don't miss the important implications here. This is potentially vital to our efforts."

"It is," I agreed. "And I promise I'll be all over it ... when I'm capable of thinking again. When I'm capable of drawing a breath without remembering that once again I've failed people that I've made promises to, that I've gotten people killed again—"

"This was not your fault," she said. "This is war—"

"This is my fault," I said. "They would have been safe if they'd stayed in London."

My mother let out a bitter laugh that crackled through the phone. "Sweetheart, this is war. Real war. Waged by the baddest, meanest meta on the planet with a hundred of the strongest, most capable people following in his wake. Thinking that anywhere is safe is folly." Her voice hardened, and I felt compelled to listen on rather than interrupt her. "You've seen what men do when they mean to wage war—because war is will against collective will, and the will of Sovereign and Century is to wipe us all out. You can't go beating yourself up because you stood your soldiers all in a line against theirs and said you wouldn't let them do it unchecked because it was inevitable that they were going to challenge you on it at some point. It was inevitable that he'd eventually send someone to knock you down, to pitch you back on your heels, and hit you hard enough to put you out of the fight. That's how they do it, men like that. Like Winter." Her voice hardened. "You did what you could for them. Mourn. Get it out of your system. Because what you can do for the dead is exactly nothing. But what you can do for those still standing with you is lead. And you need to get back to that as soon as possible."

I swallowed heavily, listening to her words. I knew she was right, even though I didn't want to hear it. "Okay. What about you?"

"We're fine," she said. "I'll tell Reed and Karthik once I'm off the phone with you. I'm sure they won't take it too well, so I'll try to break it gently." I didn't feel any actual amusement at the thought of my mother trying to break anything gently to anyone, ever, but there was definitely a ghost of it in there somewhere. "We have a line on an Omega safehouse, so we'll be checking it out in a couple hours once everyone's all woken up." She sniffed. "Pacific time is a little bit of an adjustment for the team, apparently."

"Just be safe," I said.

"Can do," she replied. "And Sienna ..." She hesitated. "Don't beat yourself up. You did everything you could for those people, and you still have a mission to get on with."

I bit my lip as I heard the click of the line going dead and lay my head back into the softness of the seat, staring out the window of my office into the bright sunshine of a day that should have been storms and darkness.

Chapter 31

I sniffed as Ariadne and Scott stared at me from across the desk. I'd cried some, no lie, but that was past now. I'd addressed the troops as best I could, but they were morose and scared. I tried to motivate them, tell them how we weren't finished yet, how Sovereign had taken his shot at us and failed to do anything more than bruise our spirit, but I didn't think they bought it entirely. I didn't blame them, not with our dead friends as visible evidence to the contrary. I didn't buy it, either.

"We need options," I said, staring at Ariadne and Scott, both sitting quietly across the desk from me. "We have a dispatch point for the mercenaries, at least—"

"I had Li call surveillance on it," Ariadne said, looking up, her red hair catching the sunlight filtering through my window.

"You did what?" I leaned forward, incredulous.

"There's no one there," she said. "I had them watch from a distance, and after eight hours of observation, they were ordered in. Nothing there, it's just an empty warehouse on Chicago's south side. They used it for staging, but cleared it out either before or after the mercenaries left for here."

"Any idea where they came from?" Scott asked. "Other than Chicago."

"All over," Ariadne said. "I'll forward you the dossier, but we've got IDs on most of the dead and the handful of survivors. They're mostly foreign nationals, the types that go where the money takes them. They were filtered into the U.S. in a few waves, met up in Chicago, and got sent out on this mission." She pursed her lips. "It was supposed to be the first of many."

"Looks like Century plans to keep up their tradition of using human mercs to supplement their ethnic cleansing efforts," I said, looking down at my bare desk. The light grain of the wood running across the near-white surface caught my attention.

"Why stop running a play that's working?" Scott asked. "These guys managed to handle the small-scale dirty work, freeing up their metas to hit the cloisters."

"Which is even more important now that they've lost their big gun." I thought again of Raymond, the man who had been my great uncle, and of how I'd watched him die in London. It was uncharitable to think of it this way, but his death had bought us months of time. Time which I felt like I was wasting, one grain through the hourglass at a time. I sighed, pissed off and more than a little desperate.

"So what now?" Scott asked. "We've got no more leads than we did before they attacked. We're back to square one and minus a few really good people."

I thought about that. We had lost good people, decent people, and had gotten a handful of pawns in return. The only thing I'd learned from the mercenaries was the address of that warehouse in Chicago, and that Weissman—that turd—had given the orders, right before he'd caught a flight back to an undisclosed location. Presumably wherever he was setting up the next phase of the extermination. I'd also caught one other thing—each and every one of the mercs had been shown a photo of me and was told not to kill me, on pain of his own death. Of course, they couldn't have known it was me fighting through a cloud of tear gas and jumping through the air to distract them, but that was almost irrelevant.

Something bothered me, though, something about my conversation with mother. "Actually, we do know a little more." I chewed my lower lip. "They either don't have us under enough surveillance or penetrated enough to know that the telepaths are dead. Hell, it's why they sent these guys."

Scott looked at me in askance. "You can't think that this was a serious attempt to get back the telepaths."

"It was a decent operational concept," I said. "Hardly foolproof, or a sign they were tossing everything they had at us, but it was a workable plan. It could have been carried off, forcing us to negotiate with them for the release of the telepaths." I felt slightly warm, and I knew it was more than the beam of light that was shining in across my seat. "They think we have something that they want. That they need."

Scott looked at Ariadne. "And this is good news ... how? Unless you want to bring the wrath of Century down on us even quicker than it would otherwise come landing on our heads?" His face went serious. "Because if that's your plan, uhm ... let me know so I can vacate the premises immediately, please."

"That's my plan," I said, nodding as I thought it through.

"Okay," Scott said. "I was sort of kidding about the running thing, but I have to admit I'm a little uneasy now that your confessed desire is to bring them down on us—"

"Think about it," I said. "Those telepaths make their job so much easier. Without them, it's going to take twice as long to do what they mean to do. They're going to divert other forces here so long as they think the telepaths are alive. It's a game of resources, and they started with the most expendable thing they had, the same way you don't expose the queen to danger in a chess game if you can accomplish something with a pawn. We beat that, and now it's going to take more of their attention to get the job done, so they'll send more because the alternative is adding months or years to their schedule of extermination." I folded my arms and leaned back in my chair. "They'll be coming again, no doubt about it."

Ariadne looked from me to Scott then back. "I still fail to see the good news. They've proven that they'll come at you in treacherous ways—taking hostages—in order to get the telepaths back. Wouldn't we be better off delaying our confrontation with them until we've worn them down a little better? Make the odds less overwhelming?"

"No," I said, shaking my head. "Because right now we're the lightning rod, drawing the strikes away from other things they could be concentrating on. This is good, because every day we can delay them is another day we buy time to counter them."

Scott cocked his head sideways. "The problem you're obviously missing is that if you're a lightning rod, you're pretty much asking to be struck by lightning."

I looked across at the two of them and smiled, just smiled, because in spite of all the other crap that had happened, I knew what to do now. I knew exactly what the next move was, how to play it, and how to slap Century hard enough to bloody its nose. "Yep. That's exactly what we're going to do."

Chapter 32

It took a few days to make the preparations, days of quiet around the campus where we were still mourning. The funerals took place at a ceremony in an Eden Prairie cemetery a couple days after the attack. I stood there in my black dress on a warm day and thought of all the people we'd lost since I'd had the audacity to walk out my own front door one frozen day in January only a year and a half ago.

Two hundred and fifty-four people died in the first few days, starting with two guys in a parking lot who had dared to stand up on my behalf and interfere with Wolfe's attempts to kidnap me for Omega. There were agents in that number, random families from Minneapolis and Saint Paul, police officers. Wolfe wasn't in the number, but he was in my thoughts, even though I'd locked him away again for now.

Aleksandr Gavrikov was dead because of me. I didn't blame myself for it, but a few thousand people in Glencoe, Minnesota, had been vaporized because of him, because of the message he'd been trying to get to us.

Andromeda. I'd watched her die before my eyes, powerless to help her. She'd fallen to her knees in front of me, a bullet wound spreading red across her shirt like paint spilled onto a blank canvas. She'd been abandoned, forgotten, held captive by Omega for reasons that none of us knew, and to this day I was the only one who seemed to care that she had died. Unfortunately, I had yet to get a chance to pay back those responsible for her death.

Dr. Ronald Sessions. Dr. Quinton Zollers on the run. Kat had lost her memories of Scott, her lover, because of me, because of a mission I led. Zack dead. Joshua Harding. He'd died trying to save the lives of the metas that I'd sent away and abandoned to make their way on their own while I hid in the box for days, trying to keep out of sight of my sins.

And M-Squad. Some of them had been my friends, and I'd killed them, every one.

Hera. The Ministers of Omega. Rick. I had his blood on my hands.

I glanced over at Ariadne during the ceremony and she met my eyes with a dull look. Part of me wanted to ask her if she was thinking about Eve right now, but that was the part that wished she would just lash out at me, once and for all, get it over with. I could see the flashes of repressed anger in her eyes, but she was too much of a pro to come at me with it. She had a job to do, she had to work with me, and she did it.

I still wished she'd give me the hell I so richly deserved for it, though.

We hadn't waited for the team to come back from Portland to do this, and part of me wished we had. I'd never had a funeral for Zack, didn't see what became of his body, though I'd checked after I got back from London and got ensconced in my current job. I'd found out it had been returned to his family, who'd had a cremation and a funeral a few days after I'd left for England.

Some girlfriend I was. I left his family behind to do the cleanup while I took his soul and jetted off to Europe.

The pastor intoned some words about flesh being transitory, and the list of my failures ran through my head again, without allowing me to settle in on any of them. I should have been in utter misery, but I wasn't, not really. I was detached about the whole thing, pondering it, trying to figure out where I fit in. I'd lived through so much, had so many people die for me, that there had to be a reason for it. Only a moment separated me and Andromeda—the time it took for a rifle bolt to slide the next round into the chamber—from being dead right there with her in the forest in

Western Wisconsin. Only luck had kept me from dying in an explosion like Dr. Sessions, luck or the watchful eye of Janus making sure his prize wasn't killed in the destruction he'd wrought.

I thought of Janus, lying near dead in the medical unit as I tossed the first shovel full of dirt onto the casket in Breandan's grave. Breandan's family was all presumed dead in Ireland, his love had gone before him by the better part of a year, killed by Century, and I was the only family of any sort he had left. I thrust the shovel back into the mound of upturned earth, my symbolic part of the funeral over with. I looked across the thinned herd of English metas, knowing that no one had left in the wake of the attack. That was a little bit of a surprise, but not too much. Where else would they go? Back to London?

The sun was hot on the back of my head as I played it through my mind again. The funeral was starting to disperse, people wandering back to cars. I stood over the grave of the Irishman who'd let me believe I could trust people again and I agonized over the fact that I'd failed him. I wanted to say I was sorry, whisper my heartache away over his loss, but the words would be worth no more than the warm breath I issued them upon. I had failed him. That was done and over with.

The hard part was yet to come.

"You're thinking about all of them too, aren't you?" I heard the soft sound of Scott's voice at my shoulder. I could feel his presence behind me, staring at the grave in solemn stillness. "The ones we've watched slip away before us."

"It's been a deadly year," I said. "I was thinking about the body count since I left my house." I didn't turn. "You remember. Your aunt and uncle were in there."

"I don't blame you for that, you know," he said quickly. A little too quickly.

"Sure you don't," I said, voice flat. "What about Kat?"

"Like I said before, that was all Clary, and you settled his hash, so ..."

I glanced back at him. "You don't really think Clary deserved to die over that, do you?"

He shrugged. "I don't know. There's a lot of people who haven't deserved to die since we started this thing, but they're dead just the same. Guys like Sovereign don't seem to care about 'deserve,' so why should I waste a lot of time thinking about it?"

I inclined my head as I looked back on the open grave. A backhoe in the distance started up, and I knew that he'd be heading this way, coming over here to start filling the graves that were lying open in front of me, the gaping holes in the earth that should still have been full, grass growing atop them. "Sovereign," I said quietly. "I've never even met the man and I hate him."

"Kinda gives you all the more reason to stick a thumb in his eye when you get a chance, huh?" Scott wasn't exactly smiling when I turned to him, but there was a grim satisfaction in the way he said it.

"Let's hope we get the chance," I said, tugging on the skirt I was wearing. It was black and fell below the knee, totally uncharacteristic of me and not something I'd wear anywhere but to a funeral. "I don't want to think that anyone's died in vain."

"There's definitely a *Wrath of Khan* line to be quoted here," he said as I fell in next to him, walking back toward where his car waited. "These guys ... they may actually have bought us a chance. Maybe."

"I love how equivocal you are about that."

"We've got the might of the meta world against us," Scott said with a shrug. "I think a strong 'maybe' is a hell of a lot more chance than we had last week. I'll take it."

I nodded as we walked along. Birds chirped in the trees as a soft breeze rustled the boughs. I hated them for their cheery disposition. "It's all we're gonna get, I know that much. One shot.

After that, it's all bound to come raining down on us."

Scott gave me a bitter smile. "Straight to the end, huh? At least it'll be over with."

"I was kind of hoping to drag it on a little longer," I said. "Got a few things I'd like to do before I check out of this life." I stopped at the door to his car and looked back over the sunny graveyard. "I'm not ready to end up in a place like this. Not yet."

Scott smiled. "Too young to die, huh?"

I felt any trace of emotion frost over, like the ground in winter. "Too many people left to send before me."

Chapter 33

My mother's helicopter touched down on the helipad that I'd stood on what felt like a thousand times. She slid the door to the Black Hawk open and was the first to get out, Reed, Karthik and Kurt a few steps behind her. Kurt walked with a little bit of a limp, as if he'd had his knees taken out from beneath him. I couldn't recall him walking like that when he left, so I nodded to him as my mother approached me. The day was a little more overcast. It would have been better funeral weather.

"Oh, him?" My mother dipped her head in Kurt's direction. "He slipped getting out of the van when we were going in to the Omega safehouse. He's fine."

I nodded to her as the rotors began to spin down on the helicopter. It was loud out on the helipad, loud enough that I was content to wait until things had quieted slightly before I spoke again. I didn't get a chance to say anything else before Reed stepped up, enfolding me in his arms in a tight hug that I reciprocated.

When he pulled away, he said with a ragged breath filled with emotion, "I hope you kept yourself far out of the way of that craziness, but I know you didn't."

I gave him a tight smile, but there was no joy in it. "I didn't have anyone else to delegate to taking back the dorms. It was me or nobody."

"I guess it wouldn't be possible for you to let it be nobody, huh?"

"It's not really who I am," I said. "Standing by and doing nothing isn't my thing anymore. Did too much of that once before; I won't do it again."

"We didn't find much at the Omega safehouse," my mother said, interrupting whatever else Reed might have said to that. "But this is worth a look." She held out her hand. A cell phone sat in her palm, a slightly older model of disposable phone, the kind you could buy at Wal-Mart for fairly cheap.

I took it from her outstretched hand and flipped it open. "I assume it's been checked for—"

"It's clear on explosives, tracking worms, all that fun stuff," she said. "J.J. talked us through shutting down the GPS on it before we got on the plane. Not that it matters, since pretty much everyone knows where we are, but I figured we'd best take no chances."

"Good call," I said, looking at the screen. It was a simple, small-screen flip phone with very few options available. I thumbed the button for Contacts, and only five were listed. Home, Murphy, Richards, corner store and Hildegarde.

I looked up at my mother and she nodded. "I didn't call it yet, but we did do a trace on all those numbers. The home one went to the safehouse's line, corner store rings a convenience place just down the road that delivers pizza—we checked it out, nothing seemed particularly funny about it, and they had records of dozens of orders going to the safehouse address—and the last three look like Omega operatives, one of which corresponds to the ID of one of the dead from Hildegarde's team." She smiled. "If you wanted a way to get in contact with Katheryn Hildegarde, I believe you may have it now, assuming she hasn't cut off her phone."

I stared at the little piece of plastic perched in my hand. "Is it likely she's kept the same phone? She is on the run, after all."

"J.J. says the phone in question is still in use but masked from easy tracking." My mother shifted her weight from one leg to the other, altering her posture the way she did when she was impatient. "It's set up to roam on non-native networks, the ones that don't belong to the phone company that sold it to her, and it comes up under a different signature every time it hits a network. Long story short, you can call her, but the minute you do, she'll be able to jump to using a different ID on the phone and it'll keep us from being able to track her without jumping through some significant hoops."

"But we could track her?" I looked at my mother carefully. "She's a dangerous person, a wanted fugitive."

"We might be able to," she replied. "Key word there is might. Our little tech geek didn't seem heartened by the idea."

I sighed. "We might as well call her, then." I turned to Reed. "Go talk to J.J. and tell him what we're about to do. Get him ready to do what he can to find her." Reed nodded, hesitating for a moment. "I'm fine," I told him. "Really." I don't know how convincing I sounded, because I was pretty sure I sounded like I was dead inside by this point. A sensation I was rapidly approaching in actual fact.

"We need to talk later," Reed said, and I could tell by his eyes he meant business.

"We do indeed," I said, resigned. He took the hint and headed toward HQ at a jog. I looked back at Kurt. "How are you holding up, Kurt?"

"Feel like I've been kicked in the knee by a horse," he grunted.

"Go see Dr. Perugini," I replied. I had a great line about how it looked like he'd been kicked in the face by a horse, but I kept it to myself. It wasn't worth it. I waved him off and he headed toward the building as well.

"Have anything for me to do?" Karthik asked, and I thought I caught a note of faint hope. He seemed a little down—more than a little, actually. I knew how he felt, and I suspected he was blaming himself for not being here when the battle had gone down.

"I have lots for you to do, Karthik," I replied. "But first, we need to try and make contact with Hildegarde. Why don't you come along? You can take a listen if we get her on the phone, tell us what you think."

He nodded and fell in behind me as we walked into HQ and across the lobby toward the elevators. Security checked our badges scrupulously even though they'd seen me exit the building only moments before. The head guard watched us all carefully, his hand on a submachine gun, finger lingering just above the trigger. I'd been told by Scott that they were taking the incident at the dorm personally, those who remained. A few had quit in the wake of the incident, but the ones who were staying were almost all ex-military and were more than a little pissed that so many of their brethren had died in a sucker punch attack. Personally, I wouldn't have wanted to be in their crosshairs at the moment.

We passed through the security checkpoint and hit the elevator, riding in silence to the fourth floor. When it dinged and we exited, I led them in silence to my office. I saw Ariadne through the window, her head down, working on a stack of file folders that was sitting on her desk. I was glad I didn't have her job, I reflected as I passed.

When we got into my office, I sat in my chair and gestured for my mother and Karthik to take the seats across from me. They didn't, though; my mother joined me on my side of the desk, hovering near the window, and Karthik remained standing next to the door, in a perfect position to ambush some poor bastard who stopped in to drop off a report. I didn't say that, though, because he looked tense enough to actually do it.

There came a knock a minute later and when the door opened, Reed was there, J.J. in tow behind him. The nerd still wore his hipster glasses, though he'd grown something of a beard in the last few months. I say something of one because it was not the sort of thing a normal man would have looked at with pride. It was stringy and patchy, the kind you'd expect to see on a prepubescent teen. "Hey," he said as he entered, flopping down into one of the chairs opposite me before I even had a chance to offer him a seat. "So, we're going to try and track down Katheryn Hildegarde, killer of FBI agents?" He templed his fingers and stretched them, and I grimaced as he cracked his knuckles. I was fine with the sound of my own joints doing that but when other people did, it I got a little creeped out. "This should be fun. She's got someone devilishly tricky working her network security; this little thing they've pulled to mask her is absolutely masterful stuff. It's kind of new for me, too, I'll admit. I'm a little envious—"

"J.J.," I said, cutting him off. "Can you do it?"

"Maybe," he said. "I mean, I've never tried it before."

I held my breath and my annoyance. "What do you need?"

He shrugged. "Nothing. I'm hooked into our phone system," he gestured at the little laptop sitting on my desk in front of him, "I'm watching the networks. I'm good to go. You may dial when ready." I shook my head at him, then picked up my office phone and dialed the number out of the contacts list on the phone I still held.

It rang as I stared over the team sitting around my office. Karthik waited nervously behind the door, still looking like he was going to take a swipe at whoever was next to walk in. Reed fidgeted on my couch, his ponytail making a slight swishing noise against the leather surface. The ringing in my ear was louder than I remembered, and had an atonal, electronic buzzing noise to it.

There was a popping on the line, and I heard the sound of someone answering. "Hello?" came a female voice, strong yet tentative.

"Katheryn, this is Sienna Nealon. Do you know who I am?" I paused, hoping that the next sound I heard wasn't a click and a dial tone.

"It'd be hard not to know who you are," she said, and I could hear the caution in her voice. "How'd you get this number?"

"We picked up one of your colleagues' phones at a safe house in Portland," I said. "Do you know what my current job is?"

I heard a sigh at the other end of the line. "I've heard rumors about a few jobs you have. Primus of Omega? Operations Director for the U.S. government's new meta Agency? Oh, and the last person on earth that Sovereign wants to see dead. So," she went on, "in which official capacity are you calling me today?"

"In my official capacity as someone whose sole focus is beating the holy hell out of every member of Century. Preferably with their own limbs after I've ripped them from their bodies." I let a little heat sizzle through the line. It wasn't feigned.

She didn't say anything for a long moment. "You've got my attention."

"I'm calling you because I was under the impression you might be a person who's of a similar mindset," I said. "Someone who'd like to put Sovereign's back against the wall and nail him tight to it."

I heard her breathe on the other end of the line, and I could almost hear her contemplating my words. "I don't know what you've heard, but if you think you're going to beat Sovereign, I'm going to go ahead and say you're either crazy, naïve, or you don't know what you're up against."

I waited to see if she would say anything else. She didn't, so I spoke. "But you're not hanging up." I paused for a second. "And you've gone and stuck a splinter in Century's paw yourself."

She was thinking it over, I was sure of it. "What have you got in mind? Since I assume you're not calling me to let me know what you're going to do just so I can write it up in a declaration of intent and frame it for you."

"I don't know what your penmanship looks like, but I would definitely be looking to outsource that work," I said. I looked at my mom, who stared back at me with a look of annoyance that was all too familiar. I shrugged. Cracking wise was not something I was going to give up at this late stage in my life. "No, I'm calling you because I figured that as two people who have a common goal, i.e. kicking Century in the dangly parts, I figured we might be able to accomplish more together than individually."

There was a long pause after that, and only her light breathing every few seconds convinced me that she hadn't hung up out of hand. I wanted to give her time to think, but at the same time, I was wondering what was going on in her thought process. It felt like forever, but was probably only a few seconds before she came back with, "What did you have in mind? Specifically?"

"I'm planning to put a severe hurting on Century," I said. "Soon. I could use a few more metas in my camp. Any chance you'd like to visit us here in Minnesota?"

She didn't hesitate much this time around. "I was planning on heading south, but it's just too damned hot in California. Going east sounds like a real good idea." There was a hoarse amusement in the way she said it. "Strength in numbers, right?"

"Seems less intimidating when it's not a hundred versus one, doesn't it?" I asked.

There was a stark, humorless laugh. "Only marginally. Is this a number I can reach you on?"

"Yeah," I said, and clutched the phone a little tighter. "It's my direct line; it'll find me, day or night, unless I'm in the middle of punching someone in the face at the time."

"Then, from what I've heard about you, it'll barely ever catch you at all?" Her voice was laced with irony.

"I've slowed down a lot lately," I said. "Saving all my face punching for Sovereign and his crew, and they've yet to do much to present their chins for a solid hit."

I heard her click her tongue. "True enough. We'll be there in a few days, and maybe together we can find a way to change that up a little bit." There was a clicking noise, and the line cut off. I set the phone gently back down in the cradle, running through everything I'd just heard. I looked around at my team, and found them staring back at me. Reed in particularly looked jaded about the whole exchange. "She came around pretty fast."

"Not to sound cliché," Reed said, "but anyone else think it was a little too fast? Especially considering she knows she's killed government agents and that you're working for said government."

I chewed my lower lip. "Could be she's just anxious because she feels the heat of Century's breath coming down her neck. The enemy you know ..."

"Versus the one you don't?" My mother spoke from behind me. "She might prefer the possibility of jail to the certainty of Century eventually killing her. It allows her to abdicate responsibility for keeping her group on the run."

"Let's not plan on her good graces," I said, tapping my fingers on the desk. "J.J., any luck tracking her?"

"That's a negatory," J.J. said, shaking his head, still staring at his laptop screen. "I'll dig a little deeper, but based on what I'm seeing here, I'm not even hopeful about giving you a location based on what tower she was using on the network. Which would be cheerfully vague, in any case, and several hours out of date by the time I ran it down." He picked up his laptop and stood, heading toward the door. He paused next to Karthik, just as he was about to reach for the handle. "By the way, about that other thing I sent you ..." His voice trailed off. "I ... um ... sorry I couldn't be more specific."

I frowned. "What other thing?" I tried to remember if I'd gotten some email of consequence from him, but nothing was standing out.

"The tracking notice," he said, looking at me blankly. "I sent it to Ariadne. I figured she would have forwarded it to you by now." He pursed his lips, and looked very uncomfortable. "She probably hasn't gotten to it yet. I just sent it an hour or so ago. Never mind." He started to turn, but a look from me to Karthik caused a hand to be placed in front of the door, shutting it tight.

"J.J ..." I said, trying not to be too menacing but probably failing. "Why don't you save Ariadne the trouble and just tell me what you found?"

"Um, right," he said, adjusting his black-rimmed glasses as he turned back to me. He kept his head down, staring at the carpet. "I, uh, was combing airline reservation computers along with some NSA PRISM intercepts, and I caught a little bit of a pattern."

I wanted to thump him on the head or throw a stapler at him, but I refrained. "And?"

"And, well, I found some receipts for a credit card," he said. "And a couple plane tickets under different aliases." He still wasn't looking up.

"Lots of people travel every day," I said. "You're going to need to be more specific."

"Right," he said, and looked up at me furtively, just for a second. "The names were Richard Snow and Edgar Stark."

"So, other than both being from Winterfell, what do these names have in common?" I asked with blunted irritation. I looked over at Reed, but he already looked stricken, a sick look engulfing his face.

"They're aliases generated by our travel department at the Directorate," J.J. said. "Well, not really the travel department. They were generated by me, when I was doing work for the travel department—"

"J.J.," I said, catching his attention, "if you don't cut right to the point with your next sentence, I am going to stick you in a heavy bag and beat the living snot out of you to work out my frustration. I may or may not take your glasses off first." I slapped my hand against the table hard enough to make him jump at the sound. "So. Speak now."

He adjusted his glasses with shaking hands. "These are vintage."

"J.J.!"

"Um, sorry. Uh." His hand left his glasses and fell to his side, leaving him supporting the laptop with one hand. "I generated the IDs myself, for a specific person, and the names were, um ... well, they were kind of an in-joke," he laughed a little then swallowed heavily. "I tracked them from Los Angeles to Denver, and the next leg brought him here, to Minneapolis, yesterday." He licked his lips. "So he's here, in town. And, uh ... it's, uh ... well, you know, it's ..."

I didn't answer him. I didn't need to. I just stared coldly into the distance, feeling the wild, heart-pounding sense of rage, the desire for revenge that hadn't left me in the last six months. It hadn't left at all; it had just faded slightly into the background.

Winter was here.

Chapter 34

Are you going to kill him? Zack's soft voice asked later that night when I was alone in my room. I hadn't really paid much attention to anything said after J.J.'s little revelation, because nothing else needed to be said. We were in a holding pattern and would remain there until something broke loose and gave us a sign of the direction we needed to head in. It was not my chosen method of conducting business, being reactive instead of proactive, but waiting for someone to screw up was all I was left with. I just hoped when the time came it wouldn't be me.

"I don't know," I answered Zack quietly. I was sitting on the edge of my bed, a lit candle filling the room with the faint aroma of vanilla. I wasn't really a candle type of person, but Kat had bought it for me as a peace offering or a friendship gift or something along those lines, and I had accepted it without gnashing my teeth too much. Now it was burning silently in the corner, filling the room with something that was supposed to help soothe me. It was an open question whether it was actually working. I could almost taste the vanilla, heavy, waxy, filling the air.

I closed my eyes and waited for the inevitable backlash from Zack, the angry reply shouted in my head, the snappish remark about how I didn't care enough about him to bother killing his murderer even when the man was in town. It didn't come, and after a moment I opened my eyes again to see the darkness outside my expansive window. *He's not a threat at this point,* Zack said.

"I wouldn't go that far," I whispered. "We underestimate Erich Winter at our peril. He's a dangerous man in any environment. Just because the government has impounded most of his assets and he's had his organization cut out from under him doesn't mean he's a toothless, clawless tabby." I sighed. "I just don't know what to do. I don't want to drop back into vengeance mode and forget ... everything that's really important." I hesitated. "Not that you're not important—"

I got it, he said gently. *Going after Winter to kill him puts you in a sticky position, causes you to lose focus on what's most important. Makes you divert attention from this impending confrontation with Century. I don't need you to kill him for me.* He strained, and I could almost see him in the back of my mind. *I don't* want *you to kill him for me.*

"I'll make sure he faces justice," I said. "That's within my power. If he shows himself, he'll get taken down by us."

You have bigger fish to fry.

I let myself fall back on my bed, curling up with a pillow in my arms. "Always. I always have something else I need to be doing nowadays. Always another thought for what we're going to do next, how we're going to gain advantage."

You should spare a thought for yourself in there somewhere.

"I'll think about that tomorrow," I said then frowned. "Or the next day." The fatigue was setting in, and I was weary. It was well after midnight, and I needed to be up by six. There was so much planning to do, things to consider and move into place, given what was coming our way. The soft bed against my face was a relief.

Like Zollers used to say, Zack went on, *you can only do what you can do. After that, maybe it's time to take a step back and let the rest handle itself?*

It wasn't terrible advice, but I was so tired. "Zollers ..." I murmured. Where was the good doctor, anyway?

I fell into a world of darkness and emerged in the waiting room of his office, the fishtank bubbling in the corner. The chair was hard underneath me, and I wondered for the thousandth time if he'd had any part in selecting them. Then I realized I wasn't in his actual waiting room, I was in a dream, and everything had a fuzzy, surreal quality. It took me only a second after that to realize it wasn't actually a dream.

"Ugh," I said. "Dreamwalking."

"Sienna Nealon," came an echoing voice from beyond the door to his office, "Come on in."

I appeared in the office, not bothering to walk through the door, and found myself on the sofa. Zollers was sitting in his usual chair, a pad of paper across his lap. He looked at me over his glasses, his hair grey around the temples.

"Well, well," I said, "here we are, not really here."

He shrugged expansively, and answered in his low, smooth voice, "So it would appear. You summoned me?"

"Not intentionally," I said. I could feel tension, even in the dream. "I was talking about you before I fell asleep."

He nodded, as though taking it all in. "So that's how it works. Simple enough."

"Yeah," I agreed. "I'm usually better about avoiding it, so ... sorry for the mix-up."

"So you weren't actually looking for me?"

I started to roll my eyes again but stopped. "I suppose I should be," I said, a little reluctantly. "I mean, you do know more about the workings of Century than anyone else."

"I do," he agreed, wearing a little halfhearted smile. "And you've been in the business of putting a fight in place for them for the last six months. I'll admit I'm a little ... disappointed you haven't come to me for help."

I gave him a cockeyed look. "You really want to come out of hiding for a hopeless fight?"

He shrugged. "Just being asked would mean something."

I let a breath out through my teeth, making a low, hissing noise that wasn't frustration so much as a reluctance to admit the truth. "I don't like to dreamwalk. I hate it, actually."

"Oh?" He looked at me over his glasses then pulled them off and held them up. "Do I really need these in a dream?"

"No," I replied. "Or didn't you catch my teleportation gimmick earlier? You only need them if I think you need them." I waved a hand at him. "Now you don't, anymore, so ... enjoy the benefits of clear vision."

"Much appreciated, at least for as long as it lasts." He put aside the glasses and stared at the pad on his lap. "Remarkable."

"Yeah, I'm a real cornucopia of useless talents," I said, folding my arms.

"I wouldn't call them useless," he said, looking back up at me with clear, unimpeded eyes. "But why don't you like to dreamwalk?"

"God, this is surreal, even for a dream," I said, looking at him with marked impatience. "Are you really counseling me in your office while I'm sleeping?"

"We fall back into familiar roles," he said with a smile. "But as always, you don't have to talk about it if you don't want to."

"No, it's fine," I said, a little deflated. "Of course I don't really want to talk about it, but I probably should. I don't like to dreamwalk because it always reminds me of the person who I most often did it with." I paused, and felt a cauldron full of regret burn inside me. Dream me or real me? Maybe they were the same person. Or maybe I just had heartburn. "It reminds me of what Zack and I used to do in dreams." The burn was more pronounced when I gave it voice, but it felt better after a moment. "So now I only use it when I have to."

"Ahh," he said, like it was a true revelation. "And since that's the only way you have to contact me ..."

"Yeah." I folded my arms tighter. "That's why I haven't contacted you."

"But you've used it to contact others?" He peered at me. I wanted to look away, but didn't.

"Once," I hissed regretfully.

"Who was that with?" he asked, watching me with the most peculiar expression. I couldn't tell quite what he was thinking.

"Scott," I admitted after a moment's pause. "When I needed a ride home from the airport."

He gave me something bordering on a smirk. "I'm the most knowledgeable person about Century that you know, and you wouldn't contact me via the only method you have because of the feelings it generates, but you would use it to save yourself cab fare." It was definitely a smirk now.

I felt a sizzle of impatience and embarrassment. "When you say it like that, I feel stupid."

"I wouldn't feel stupid," he said casually. "I would perhaps suggest that there may be more complexity to your feelings about this particular power, though." He let one eyebrow creep higher, and I could see nothing but amusement. "Perhaps something to do with the predominant purpose of use coloring how you view using it now—"

"Thanks for the psychoanalysis, Doc," I said, and I used my control over the dreamwalk to dispel the feverish blushing sensation I felt under my collar and up my cheekbones. I stared at him, trying to overcome the emotion. "Fine, well, we're talking now. What can you tell me about him?"

"Hmmm," he said, pondering. "Sovereign? He's very strong. He knows this. His reputation is well earned, something he's spent time building, cultivating."

"So he's prideful about it," I said. "Got a little bit of an ego."

"Perhaps," Zollers said, a little too coyly for my taste. "But it really doesn't matter because you won't be able to beat him."

I narrowed my eyes as I looked at him, my first sliver of suspicion poking at me. "I heard he can change his face."

"Could be," Zollers said, a little more brusquely now. "I only met him for a few minutes, and that wasn't an ability he demonstrated to me." He seemed to get a little thoughtful. "Still, I suppose it's possible. Never heard of a meta who could do that, but it's not as though we know every type of meta in the world, do we?" He smiled thinly. "After all, Sovereign is still a mystery."

It felt just the littlest bit like he was fishing, and I leaned forward. "You said Century had scared the hell out of you when last we met. You told me they wanted me dead, that this storm that was coming would consume me."

He nodded slowly. "I told you they wanted to kill you back then because it was true. A man named Weissman was my contact with Century, and he quietly made his position plain—he wanted you dead."

"Why?" I asked, still leaning forward.

"I wasn't in a position to ask," he said.

"They changed their minds since," I said, settling back in the chair. "Weissman said the order came down from Sovereign himself."

"Did it?" Zollers gave me a slow nod then a smile. "I suppose that's a good thing for you, then."

"Or a bad thing for him," I said, watching him through the haze of the dreamwalk. He wasn't being evasive, but his eyes were clouded.

"I think you may be harboring some ill-considered notions here," Zollers said, leaning forward himself. "If you think you can take Sovereign ... you're wrong. He will destroy you if you try. His power is unlike anything—"

"I thought you said that Weissman was your sole contact with Century?" I asked in a muted tone.

"He was," Zollers said, and I could see a hint of hesitation in him. "Before—"

"Before you ran from them because they were going to kill you?" I asked, feeling myself smile a little, like a dog who's caught the scent of fresh meat. "Which, by the way, they seem to be doing a pretty mediocre job of." I watched him react only a little to my goad. "You ran into him after that?"

"I did," Zollers said, and I could see him start to hesitate, could sense the emotional friction from him. "He's ... fearsome—"

"And he let you live," I said with a twisted smile. "Just let you walk away after you betrayed his organization and left their target—me—alive in spite of their strict orders?" I felt my lips curl up at the corners. "You know what I think? Once a liar, twice a liar—"

"I get the rough sense of what you're thinking here—"

"That telepathy is real handy," I snarled, and I was on him in an instant, had him by his faux shirt. "Let me show you the other side of what I can do in a dreamwalk." I touched a finger to his forehead before he could speak, and I heard a scream rip from his throat in agony, pure anguish and pain that was the absolute opposite of what I'd done with Zack. "Too bad you couldn't read my mind to know THAT was coming."

He writhed on the floor and looked up at me with a pained expression. "You have no idea what trouble you're in."

"I know that you killed my friends," I said, looking down at him in silent fury. "Read my mind, Sovereign. Know what I'm thinking—that I'm going to find you and kill you, whatever it takes. You and your one hundred closest pals are going to die by my hand, one at a time or all in bunches. Because that reputation you've got of being the biggest badass on the planet?" I started to reach for him and he disappeared, gone from the dreamwalk in a cold second, nothing left behind but a faint wisp of his essence, a surreal haze marking the place where he'd left. "I'm going to take it for my own by killing you."

Chapter 35

"That was mighty bravadocious of you," Scott said to me from across the conference table. It was morning, the sun glimmering in from behind him, and I was looking at him across fingers templed in front of my mouth. Ariadne's coffee was the dominant smell in the room. It carried a hint of hazelnut. It was honestly making me reconsider my personal ban on coffee, it smelled so good.

"I had the upper hand," I said. "It was my dreamwalk."

Scott's eyes got a little dodgy. "Um ... when you touched me the time you dreamwalked to me, it didn't cause me any pain at all. It was, uh ..." his face got red, "... quite the opposite."

"It's something I figured out a while back," I said, covering my own embarrassment by looking away and catching my mother's half smile. I'm sure that made me flush harder. "With Zack, unfortunately for him. It's controlled by mood, and if you dreamwalk while angry ..." I let my voice trail off.

"I made a man go into a coma one time by doing that to him," my mother added.

"Which was it?" Reed asked, a little sarcastic. "Pain or pleasure?"

She smiled thinly at him. "Wouldn't you like to know?"

"Please stop the world of ugh," I said, ready to throw a flag down between the two of them. "And don't ever talk like that to each other in my presence again. Ever. There are way too many naughty stepmother ebooks out there for me to feel at all comfortable with that exchange." She just rolled her eyes.

"If I might interject," Karthik said a little hesitantly, "you just told the man who has been called the most powerful meta in the world to step off, essentially. Was that the wisest move?"

"I made him angry," I said. "I aimed to provoke him."

"Which brings us back to Karthik's question," Reed said sourly.

"It worked," I said, trying to reassure them. "I needed him focused on one thing and one thing only—being pissed off at me, afraid of me, even. I needed to get him seeing red." I looked down the quiet table, saw Scott looking at the black glass surface. Li hadn't spoken throughout the entire meeting, and he was sitting next to Ariadne looking somewhat dead of disposition.

"I suppose if that's what you were aiming for, then well played," Reed said acidly. "Can I just say that I'm not thrilled by your plan?"

"That's all right," I said. "You don't have to be thrilled by it."

"I also have grave reservations," Karthik said.

"If this was a democracy, I'd be all ears," I said. "We could set up a voting booth and everything, hand out little stickers once we were done. But as it is, if you don't want to follow through with it, leave. Please." I tried not to be brutally blunt but probably fell shy by miles. "This is going to require total buy-in from all of you. It's a risk, I know—"

"And you're sure that Quinton Zollers is Sovereign?" Ariadne asked, her hands folded uneasily in front of her. There was a faint twitch at her eye that I wondered about.

"It certainly fits the timeline," I said. "Century was dead set on killing me the day that they murdered Andromeda, but then after that they decided not to? I think it was Zollers. He decided to spare me. It was his judgment call, nobody else's, that kept me alive. He told Weissman to let me live, for whatever reason."

"What is that reason?" Reed asked, humoring me more than anything. He was just as sarcastic as I was, dammit.

"I think he liked me," I said. "That he felt sorry for me."

"Well, I'd say you've done a fine job of wiping that slate clean," Reed said. "His mercy is probably good and over by now.

That means next time he'll kill you. You're walking into a fight with the most powerful meta in the world after you've provoked the hell out of him; his restraint is bound to have left town."

"It was always going to come down to this sooner or later," I said. "The kid gloves had to come off; we were eventually going to get serious and mix it up with him. Better now than later."

"Yeah, that way you can get that pesky dying thing crossed off your To Do list ASAP and leave the rest of us to clean up the mess," Reed said, and stood, buttoning his suit coat. "This is ridiculous. You want to fight him, fine. I signed on to draw a line against him and Century, and death was always understood to be a risk, maybe even a big one. But what you're doing now is just pure, patterned suicide." He took out his agency ID and tossed it on the table. "I didn't sign on to watch you kill yourself." Without another word, he left, walking out the door.

I took a close look around the table, watching for any other signs of anyone following him. "Anybody?" I asked, finally. "Anybody?" I waited another second. "Bueller?" No one laughed. "Never mind. We've got work to do. I did just work over the face of the supposedly most powerful meta on the planet, after all." I stood without any other preamble. "You know what to do." I turned and walked out of the room myself, afraid to stay and hear what they might be saying about me after I was gone.

Chapter 36

I walked into the medical unit without any sort of fanfare. It was quiet in there, the steady beep of Janus's monitoring equipment set to the lowest audio level. It was still loud and obvious for a meta, and I waited for a minute to see if Perugini would come lunging out at me, shrieking about some perceived evil I'd done or had had committed on my behalf. She didn't appear, so I made my way slowly over to Janus, who lay on his back, a breathing tube sticking out of his mouth.

I took a slow breath, a long inhale through the nose and a long exhale out my mouth, the cool air carrying its own air-conditioned smell, a filtered, sterile aroma. I looked at him. He was so frail. He didn't look like the man who had confronted me in the basement of this very building, standing so confidently even as I had a gun pointed at him. I could have easily killed him that day, but he'd faced me down because he knew in his heart that I wouldn't shoot him. I wondered how much of that was because he could feel and control my emotions and how much of it was motivated by the simple conviction that I wasn't the sort of person who would do that. A part of me wanted to cry because only minutes afterward I had become that sort of person, and things hadn't been the same since.

"What would you do?" I asked the empty room, the figure in the bed. All the larger than life personality, all the exuberance had fled, and now he was just a shell. Something that Century made him. "What would you do if you were in my position? Maybe we wouldn't be here if you were in my position." I stared down at him. "You knew the secret, after all, the key to whatever the hell Century is trying to keep us from knowing." I brushed the stringy silver hairs off his forehead where they were out of place. The Janus I knew was impeccably kempt at all times. This man with his hair askew, his glasses missing ... he wasn't Janus. "You would have led us right through the middle of it. And I would have followed you. All the way to the end." I sighed again. "You or Hera. Because you both—even though I didn't know her for that long—actually projected the image that you cared. About me. About metas." I bowed my head. "But then again, I got taken in by someone else who said the same things once before."

I drifted toward a brown, plastileather-covered chair that was by the bedside. It had a slight impression in it, a circular pucker where Kat's bony butt probably sat in it day in and day out. I lowered myself into it, making a much larger imprint and frowning as I did so. "Were you different?" I leaned back and found the chair distinctly uncomfortable. It didn't make me move, though. "I thought you were. I still think you are." I felt myself begin to chew my lip. "What is it about me that causes me to seek out these father figures to replace a man I never even knew? Winter, Zollers, you ..." I looked at him, hoping to see some sign, some movement, but all I saw was the motion of his chest moving up and down with the steady pulsing of the ventilator pumping air into his lungs.

"I mean, what did he really leave me?" I asked. "I didn't even know his name until I was eighteen. Jon. Jonathan. Traeger." I smiled almost morbidly. "I guess I could be Sienna Traeger if I wanted. Would she be a different person?" I felt the smile disappear. It wasn't real, anyway. "No, he didn't leave me anything. At least Winter gave me something." I clenched my hand on the arm of the chair. "He gave me pain. Motivation to go past the moral line I'd drawn against killing. That could end up being important." I looked at the stainless steel surface of the wall by the door and remembered one exactly like it in the old medical unit of the Directorate. "I've been past that line more times than I can count now. I live past that line, killing whenever I feel like there's a need." I sniffed and sat up straighter in my seat. "I killed half a dozen men in the last week alone. Watched even more than that die." I stared straight into the distance, at the metal wall, and wondered if I'd see Wolfe's face in it this time.

I didn't. Just my own looking back at me.

I leaned toward Janus. "Do you remember that time in the elevator at Omega? When I asked you if I was monster?" I felt myself fill with emotion. "You told me a monster wouldn't care." I held my hand over my mouth, like I was trying to hold in what was attempting to force its way out. "I'm not sure I care anymore, not when it comes to Century. I want to stop them, mostly, but it's more than that now. I want to hurt them. Hurt Weissman for what he did to you, to the others. For how he made me feel—powerless, like I was a nothing. I want to break him," I said, and felt the burn in my words. "I want to crush him, him and his boss." I felt myself sniff a little. "It makes me wonder if you would think me a monster for wanting to do that, or if you'd reassure me the way you did in that elevator." I felt a little warmth in my eyes. "Because I can't remember anyone doing that for me before, not like that." I sniffled, and felt the wetness on my cheeks. "Like my dad maybe would have done, if he'd been alive to do it."

I heard the door swish open and I hurriedly wiped my cheeks clear. I kept my head turned away from the door even as I heard light footsteps make their way over to me. I kept my eyes on Janus, turned away from the figure approaching me, even though I knew who it was.

"It's so sweet of you to come visit," Kat said as she stopped next to the chair. "I know it means a lot to him."

"Yeah?" I rubbed my wrist under my nose and tried to avoid sniffling. "I've heard they can hear us, even in a coma."

"I've heard that too." She put a hand lightly on my shoulder.

"I need to get him out of here," I said, and stood abruptly.

"We need to move him quietly to somewhere safe, off campus, like a hospital elsewhere in the country. No one's going to know who he is if he's at Abbott Northwestern in Minneapolis. Here, with us, he's a sitting duck. It's an invitation for Century to murder him while he's sleeping."

"No," Kat said quietly. I had yet to look her in the face. "He trusted you, Sienna. He believed in you. He would want to be here."

"The storm's here, Kat," I said, toneless, watching the monitor above his bed. "The one we've heard about, it's arriving, and it's going to hit us right here on campus—again. I practically called it down on us. I need the few metas who can still fight, and I need them up front with me, not protecting others." I looked sidelong at her, just a glance, and saw her trying to catch my eye. I quickly looked away. "He's not safe here."

"He's not safe anywhere," she replied. "He wouldn't want to leave. I don't want to leave."

"Did Karthik come talk to you?"

"He did," she said. "Sienna, you don't need to worry about us. We'll stay out of your way. I'll protect him as best I can, and if I can't ..." She shrugged, and I saw it out of the corner of my eye. "Then it's the way things will be. I'm not going to run from them. Not now." She took his hand, holding it carefully in her own. "I'm tired of running from them, and he wouldn't want to hide in anonymity, waiting for the world to end around him."

"Here he's just another lightning rod," I said, staring at the frail figure on the bed. "Just another target that Century wants dead."

"Maybe we'll buy you some time to hit them back," she said, and I caught the hint of wistfulness in her voice.

"I don't want you to buy me time," I said, and looked up at her. "I don't want anyone to buy me time."

There was a silence for a few minutes after that, a kind of

peaceful calm punctuated only by the beeping of the machine.

"What is it about him?" I asked, and looked at her. "What brought you two together?"

"Oh, I don't know," Kat said, and took his hand in hers, holding his limp fingers in her grip. "When I met him, I was ... completely blank. I didn't know my name, what had happened, I had no idea what I was or anything about myself." She squeezed his hand in hers as the respirator pushed up and down behind us with a gasp. "He was so kind. My only friend, really." She looked at me, but I didn't look back. "Do you know what that's like? To be alone in a sea of people, not really sure about yourself, trying to figure out if there's a friendly face in it somewhere?"

"Yes," I whispered. "I believe I'm familiar with that."

"It's a lonely experience," she said. "He was there for me during that, guiding me along, making me feel like someone cared." Her hand let his go. "He made it easier, learning again, finding out who I was. He helped me define myself, figure out who I was just by being him."

"But you forgot him," I said, staring at Janus's closed eyes, his slack face.

"Yes," she said. "I did." It was barely a whisper.

"How did it happen?" I asked, cocking my head to look at her.

"I ... I don't remember," she said. "I honestly have no idea. Sometimes I think I get ... little flashes? But nothing that sticks. It's like there's a wall, and the things I can see of him are on the other side of it, but there are things I'm missing now, too, like ..." she looked over her shoulder, "... like Scott. It's still so uncomfortable to walk past him in the hallways, did you know that?"

"I can imagine," I said. "I don't think it'd be easy to deal with the fact that your first love has completely forgotten you."

"Yeah," she said. "Anyway, I can't imagine leaving this place again before the storm. If nothing else, maybe we draw some of Century in and keep them busy for you." She turned and looked at me. "He was in this fight. He believed in beating them, believed you could do it, that you'd save us all somehow. I can't take him away now, even if it means his death. He'd be so upset with me."

"All right," I said, and tasted the bitter reluctance. "You can stay. Just ... be careful. And ..." I looked her over. "Are you armed?" She nodded. "Good. You're a fair shot with a pistol, and you may be dealing with mercenaries again. Either way, aim for the head and the heart, because if you're fighting metas, that's the only thing that'll kill a strong one."

"I've got my powers, too," she said with a little twinkle in her eyes. "I can do things you haven't seen yet."

"I'll take your word for it," I said and brushed past her on the way to the exit. "Take care, Kat."

"Sienna," she called to me, and I turned, looking back as the doors opened for me. "I believe in you, too. That you can save us. I believe it with everything I have."

I tried to take a breath, tried to feel the calm of her words, but there was no solace in them. Not for me, the person everyone was counting on. "I wish everyone felt the same as you did." I turned and walked out, thinking to myself that what I really wished was that I was one of them.

Chapter 37

Night fell, darkness swooping down on us like an unwelcome guest. Preparations had been made, quietly, and some were off attending to them even now. Karthik and my mother were absent, as was Reed, still. I hadn't seen him since he'd thrown his badge down at the meeting. I stared at Scott, who sat on the arm of my couch, rubbing his fingers against his leather jacket. Ariadne sat in the chair across from me, as did Li, who was studying the smartphone in his hands as though it carried the secrets of life itself. Kurt was in the corner, looking surly but representing the human agents, what few of them we had.

"Where are we at?" I announced, breaking the grim silence.

"Dormitory is locked down," Kurt said. "Only way in or out is through HQ, the basement tunnel."

"Good," I said, nodding, my stomach churning.

"All non-security personnel are furloughed," Ariadne said, looking up at me. "All the essential ones are working out of the FBI building for the foreseeable future. Hopefully Century will restrict their activities to our metahumans, for now."

I nodded. That was a careful calculation; honestly Sovereign could jump the rails at any time, could go hold someone like J.J. hostage in his apartment, but I simply did not have the resources to try and protect every employee in the Agency. "Just like old times, huh?" I asked Ariadne with a weak smile.

"You mean like just before the last time our campus was utterly destroyed?" She was completely devoid of humor. "As I recall, the aftermath of that one left us with quite the prodigious body count as well."

"You should get out while you can," I said gently, staring at her. "Just ... go, run."

"To Bora Bora?" She looked like a world of sad had descended on her. "Now more than ever, I don't have anywhere else to go."

"Any clue where Reed went?" I asked the room, pretty sure I wasn't going to get an answer.

"Your mom talked to him," Scott said. "He's with her."

I blinked. "Really? Like ... dead in her trunk?"

Scott let out a low guffaw. "I don't think so. Pretty sure he's guarding the metas with her and Karthik." He gave me a sideways wink. "He's still pissed at you for picking suicide detail, but he knows he's got a role to fill, and he'll fill it."

I turned my chair sideways so I could look out the window to the dark campus behind me. In the distance I could see the dormitory building, a dark shadow on a dark night. I knew that just beyond it, the science building was still out there, and I could see the faint hints of the girders rising above the woods that circled the campus. "Good for him," I said. I turned back around and looked at Li, his smartphone in hand. "Mr. Li, I believe it'd be better for your health if you joined our associates at the FBI building for the next week or two."

He looked at me with something that looked like burning fury, just for a moment, and then I caught a hint of relief. "I'll think about it."

"They could use some watchful eyes on them," I said gently. "And if we fall out here, someone's going to need to be in place to pick up where we leave off."

I saw him grit his teeth. "I'm no coward."

"Not saying you are. This isn't your fight, though." He started to argue, and I held up a hand. "Not yet, anyway. If you wanted to delay, you're certainly welcome to an off-campus assignment."

"I think I'll stay here, thanks," he said tightly. "But if there's nothing else, I've got a few more reports I should be checking on in my office."

"Sure," I said with a nod, and he stood, leaving in a smoking big hurry.

Kurt watched him go then looked over at me. "I'm gonna go line up the agents one more time, tell them that as crazy as they are, at least their families will get a nice payout if they buy it." I started to say something, but he stopped me. "That's not really what I'm gonna say. I'll come up with something appropriate." He licked his lips. "Maybe something from *Patton*. These kids are young enough they've probably never even seen it." With that, he exited, letting the door shut behind him quietly.

"I suppose I'll go comb some reports, too," Ariadne said and stood slowly, like an old woman, weary and aged. She probably wasn't but a year or two over forty, but she walked like someone who had had all the life taken out of her. I wondered how much of it was my fault and decided to take the balance of the blame on myself.

"Ariadne," I said, and she stopped at the door. "For what it's worth—and probably zero, I'm sure—I'm sorry."

She stiffened, not even turning back, and then walked out, shutting the door behind her.

"That was tense," Scott said. "It's like these people think they're going to die or something."

"I'm surprised you can find room for a joke in a moment like this."

"Reminds me of that time when Century was about to shoot us dead," Scott said with a slight smile. "And you called me an asshole."

"I did not." I frowned at him.

"Well, that was the subtext," he said and shot me a grin.

"You didn't have to be here for this," I said and looked at him sadly.

"Last time, I checked out before the big dance with Omega,"

he said, "and ... Zack died. I should have been here. Maybe I could have done something, changed things somehow." His expression turned serious. "I'll always think I could have done something, even if the truth is that I might have died right along with him."

I nodded slowly. "I doubt Winter would have killed you. Probably just had Clary knock you out or something." Scott sauntered on over to my desk and made his way around the edge. "You know, because he was looking to turn me into a killer, not just murder people for the sake of it." I paused, frowning. "Well, except for Bjorn."

Scott gingerly lowered himself down onto the desk in front of me, sitting at an angle, legs hanging over the edge. It was a more natural way to talk, I supposed, than doing so from across the office. "Do you remember that road trip we took?"

"Kinda hard to forget it, since it ended in the aforementioned episode of us running through the woods and almost getting killed by Century mercenaries." I frowned in concentration as a thought occurred to me. "Where do they find this endless supply of gun thugs?"

"I was a pretty bad influence on you that trip." He ignored my wry observation and gave me a twisted smile. "How much did you end up drinking?"

"A lot," I admitted. "Enough to nearly land me in bed with that—actual, real—asshole Fries."

"I could kind of understand that," he said. "You and Zack had broken up," I felt a twinge at the mention of Zack's name, "you were ... tired of not being able to ..." he shrugged, "... do what ... couples do."

"You know what really pushed it over the edge?" I asked, leaning back in my chair. "It was watching you and Kat all the time. It was like I got my first look at what a happy couple should be, outside of the television, and I wanted my life to look like that. I wanted to be able to sleep with my boyfriend without killing him." I laughed, kind of rueful. "Stupid, huh?"

"I don't think it's stupid at all," he said and shifted on the desk. "I think it's pretty natural."

"Yeah, well, it didn't end so well."

"What, like that was your fault?"

I sighed. "My skin killed him. My touch killed him. So, yeah, if you want to look at it at a literal level, yes, it was my fault. If you want to zoom out to the metaphorical level, if he hadn't been my boyfriend, Winter wouldn't have used him as leverage against me, so he'd still be alive." I waved my hand at him. "I've made my peace with it long ago, but yes, I still think it's my fault."

"Hum." He looked down, cupping his hands together. "Zack was one of my best friends, you know."

"He thought of you the same way," I said gently.

"I didn't hear about you two breaking up right away," he said. "Not on that trip."

"Well, no," I said, "because you were wasted."

"Right," he said and I caught the chagrin. "But when I did hear, it was the weirdest thing. Because Kat told me, and the first thing that came to mind—and I feel like such an ass for saying this—was that I was glad."

"What?" Part of me wanted to ask him to clarify. Another part very much didn't.

"I know, it's terrible." His jaw clenched between words, and I could see it stand out on his tanned face. "But I was, I was glad. And, uh ... it kind of took me a while to narrow down why, so I just sort of ignored it." He glanced at me. "But, uh, after you came back here, and we started working together, I figured it out."

Oh, God.

He must have seen it on my face, the look like the train was barreling toward me, and there I was standing on the tracks like I was paralyzed or something. "It kind of does make me an asshole, doesn't it?" He looked away. "Like, really for real, subtext of your comments aside. But, uh ... seeing you work. How you work. How serious you are about it, how committed you are. I mean, you're the real deal. You've thrown yourself into certain death over and over—"

"I don't ... I mean, I wouldn't say I've ever thrown myself into *certain* death—" I stammered, trying to interrupt him.

"You're just so brave," he said. "You're the most gutsy, fearless person I've ever met. You take the hits and keep bouncing back. You're like this epic badass everyone keeps underestimating until she completely wrecks them, and it's so awesome to watch." He was focused on me now. "I respect the hell out of you, I watch in constant amazement, and, uh ... even a meathead like me can finally get the message sooner or later." He leaned in closer, and I was trapped. My chair could have tilted back a little farther, but I didn't lean it back.

"I, um ... don't remember sending any messages?" I said weakly. "Maybe you misread an email?"

"I know you don't feel the same," he said, and his face was just ... THIS close to me. Like inches. "And I'm totally okay with that. I will follow you into the jaws of death, whatever comes, because I believe in you, that you're the one who can stop this. But I wanted you to know that ..." He started to incline his head, tilting it to the side. My eyes were so wide, I felt like my eyelids were going to break at any second. His were closed, shut tight, and I was pretty sure my jaw was open just as wide as my eyes.

Still he kissed me, because apparently my lips actually WERE closed, and my eyes followed, and for about a second and a half, which was as long as it lasted, it was really, really good. After that he broke off, and I just sat there, eyes still closed, my head back against the soft, leather padding of my chair.

"I just figured I ought to tell you before this all broke loose," he said, and I opened my eyes to see him taking slow, small steps toward the door. I watched him go without uttering a word, just staring at him shell shocked, as he opened the door and smiled faintly at me. "When it's all over, we can talk about this, if you want. Or just ... let it be. Up to you." With that he closed the door, a soft click that sounded like a vault shutting in my mind, a cascade of emotions running over me, too many, too numerous to count.

I sat in that silence for a full minute after he left, just staring at the door, remembering the kiss, before I finally spoke. "He really does taste a little like the ocean," I mused, and my fingers found my lips and the warmth and memory of the kiss that lingered there long after Scott left.

Chapter 38

Sierra Nealon
Minneapolis, Minnesota
March 18, 1993

She hadn't felt the baby move yet, which the doctor had told her was unsurprising. She was only eight weeks along, after all, and they didn't move until long after that. It was a little disconcerting, though, something she felt like she should be feeling, would hope to be feeling, especially now. It would be just a little bit reassuring.

Fires were blazing all around her, and she was catching lungfuls of the smoke, the dark, choking, chemical kind that came from the walls of the Agency's office building being fully engulfed in flames. Sierra crawled on her hands and knees, trying to keep underneath the flames that swirled on the ceiling above her, trying to keep from breathing any more of it than she had to. *This can't be good for the baby.* Her worried eyes shifted toward the stairwell door just ahead. She was on the fifth floor and needed to get down. She had yet to run across another person, not surprising given the time of night.

The fire had come in one massive burst, an explosion that rocked the Agency's headquarters, flinging her out of her desk chair and causing her to black out for a moment. When she had come to, everything was burning and she knew she had to get out quickly. She could hear the fire alarms going off faintly in the distance but couldn't decide if that meant that they'd gone out in this section of the building, or if she was just having trouble hearing. *It was a loud explosion,* she thought. *So loud. I don't hear ringing, though. Is that a good sign or a bad one?*

She reached the door to the stairs and splintered it when it resisted her, breaking through it at the bottom, like she was carving a dog door out for herself. She paused when she punched through, expecting a backdraft to come shooting out at her. She braced to roll aside, but when it didn't, she finished ripping it from its hinges and crawled inside the stairwell, the gritty concrete texture pushing into her palms as she crawled. Grit and debris dotted the ground, and she steered around the more obvious pieces, ignoring the little flecks of broken glass as they cut her hands.

The smoke billowed up the stairwell, smoking skyward and obscuring the floors above from her view. She got to her knees, then to a crouch, the tight neck of her blouse pulled over her nose. *I have to find Jon. I have to protect our baby.*

Her life was a succession of surprises of late: *marrying Jon, the pregnancy, and now this. I've had enough surprises for one lifetime.* She held the shirt tightly over her face, trying to let the cloth material filter out some of the acrid smoke as she descended. *He's got to be on the first floor, if he's still ...* She felt a dryness in her mouth that had nothing to do with the heat or the smoke. *He has to be. Has to be on the first floor.*

She reached the next-to-last landing and hurried down to find the fire door open, the first floor ablaze. The pillars that held up the ceiling were already engulfed in flame, the desks and chairs that filled the bullpen-like space of the Agency's lower floor a charred mess. It was black ground in the middle, cratered, like a bomb had gone off, and the ceiling was open ahead. Debris tumbled down from an upper floor, and she noticed that the crater opened to the basement.

How do I get out of here? Her mind raced, looking over the sea of flames. The heat was overwhelming, but the smoke was almost worse, overcoming her. *One way out, one way only, and it's right through the middle of it.* She ducked and ran, felt the flames licking at her as she sped across the floor, dodging around the crater, only opening her eyes the barest amount here and there as needed. *Almost there ...*

She got close to the front windows which had shattered; all that remained was the lip of the wall and she jumped over it like a champion hurdler, bursting free into the cool air outside, the suffocating smoke clearing as she kept going, further from the fire. She stopped after a hundred or so feet, standing out from the corner of the square, oblong building. It was technically in Golden Valley Minnesota, but right on the edge of Minneapolis, which was what the postal codes all said. *Was,* she thought. *Now it's nothing but wreckage. So long, Agency. I guess they'll have to build a new—*

She heard a noise from behind her and turned to see Jon lying there, eyes open, staring up at the sky above. She took in the scene with a steady onrush of horror, and it occurred to her after a moment that there was someone else there as well, a man, impeccably dressed. It didn't immediately occur to her to think of him as anyone other than someone who had been passing by when the explosion happened. She ran, still coughing and hacking from the smoke she'd breathed in, a thousand thoughts clouding her mind. Her shoes slapped loudly against the asphalt of the parking lot, and she cleared an island of grass with a tree planted in the middle of it with a leap, landing next to Jon.

His eyes were open, staring up at her lifelessly, his face placid and slack. She fell to her knees and shook him. *Sometimes he sleeps with his eyes open. Creepiest damned thing I've ever seen.* She grasped his burnt, pinstriped dress shirt and lifted his chest, jerking his upper body into motion. His neck lolled back, following its path of least resistance and his eyes didn't react at all to the motion.

"He's already dead," the man said in a quiet voice, solemn.

His hands were clasped in front of him, and Sierra had a sudden vision of him as a funeral home director, giving only the coldest comfort to the bereaved he was forced to deal with. "I'm sorry."

"What ..." She let him settle back and ran her hands over him, but there was no sign of blood, no sign of trauma, of burns past some minor blackening of his dress shirt. She looked up into the face of the stranger, oddly stricken. "How?" The man didn't say anything at first, and she read his hesitation. "How?" she asked, again, the harsh edge to her tone.

"He made a mistake," the man said at last, not looking at her. "A long time ago."

"Did you do this?" She held the back of Jon's neck in her hand, felt the odd weight of it, the heaviness as his head lolled. There was no burning in her fingers, no swelling of her power from the touch as there should have been. The man did not answer her. "Did you?" She clutched Jon tighter. "Did you do this?"

The man did not speak, but his feet left the ground and he hovered, lightly, a few feet away from her. "This isn't how I wanted us to meet. It isn't how I would have planned to run into you, Sierra, not for the first time."

"You wouldn't have planned this?" She laughed through the first tears, the words were so absurd. "How would you have planned it? Something to make a better first impression, I take it? Something other than killing my husband? The father of my unborn child?" She stood, letting the body slump to the side. Her fists balled and she readied herself. She could feel the weight of the pistol at her side, the duty weapon she carried, and she drew it fast, firing five rounds perfectly, snapping off each shot with precision, her eye focused on putting the front sight of the gun just above his heart.

The man didn't even move, didn't shrug, just stood there and took the bullets, absorbing them into his body like they were nothing. He watched her with mournful eyes, dark eyes. "You can't kill me."

"Oh, really?" Sierra adjusted the aim higher and fired again, this time aiming for the hovering man's skull. Every shot was flawless, but he just stood there, staring back at her, dully, with each subsequent shot.

Her gun clicked empty, the last round spent, and Sierra stared at him, the action slid open and smoked slightly in the cool night. Still, the man stood, hovering on air, arms folded, apparently undisturbed by the fifteen shots that had just been fired straight into him. Sierra screamed at him in fury and flung the gun at his head, charging at him and leaping. He disappeared before she could make contact, and she fell to the hard pavement of the parking lot, grunting at the pain of her landing, asphalt scraping across her elbow.

"You can't hurt me, either," the man said, and she turned to find him still hovering, watching her. "I'm sorry."

"You don't know what sorry means, yet," she said, her voice a snarl. She leapt back to her feet and flung herself at him. It was rage, pure and simple, and the detached part of her mind knew it, but she did it anyway because that cold, rational part of her was long gone, buried under the howling grief for Jon. *He was the one. The only one who ever—*

Suddenly there was a hand around her neck, gripping her throat, squeezing hard, firm and choking the life's breath out of her. Her feet were suspended off the ground, and she fought for a grip on the arms attached to the hands around her neck, hoping to get something—anything—out of them. Willing her power to work, mostly.

"I didn't know you were married," the man said quietly, and his hand stayed tight around her neck. "But your husband was mine. He defied me, he knew he had crossed me, and he had to know that on this day, the day I met him again, the penalty was going to be utter horror." The man looked past her at the flaming wreckage of the Agency. "Combine that with your little shakedown operation here, and I had the perfect reason to destroy this whole place." He adjusted his grip and Sierra took one breath and one only before he tightened his grip around her neck. "I understand you're angry, but now you're just being foolish. I could crush you with minimal effort. I could break you with less trouble than a normal person would have cracking a walnut shell. Just ask Erich Winter—he took one look at me and ran, and I haven't seen him for over a hundred years." He loosened his grip. "Cross me, and you're just asking to die. Push me, and I'll push you over the edge. Come at me for revenge, and you'll die for no good reason. You can't fight me, you can't hurt me, and you damned sure can't stop me from doing anything."

Sierra felt his grip reverse, turning her head around. She hung in his arms, his hands holding her by the scruff of her neck, ten feet off the ground. "I'm sorry about your husband." He shook her head, forcing her to look down at Jon's body, empty-eyed and lifeless, staring up at her. "But you need to think clearly. You have a child to worry about, after all." He spun her around, and she felt gravity shift, felt her feet touch the ground. "His child. Your child." The man smoothed out her collar, and let her go. Sierra fell to the ground, felt the pavement hit her backside when she landed. "Maybe it'll be a little girl like you." He smiled faintly. "Maybe she and I will meet one day."

He seemed to grow smaller in her sight. It took her a moment to realize he actually was drawing away, hovering out of her reach. "I'm going to leave now. I'm sorry for your loss." His face grew hard. "But don't make me take more from you. I'll be watching." With that, he flew straight up, disappearing into the low-hanging clouds that covered the night sky. Sierra could see them burning with light from the fire.

I'll be watching.

She felt a bitter taste of disgust in her mouth and leaned over again toward Jon's body, felt it cold under her hands. The burning was gone, the fire he let her feel sometimes when they'd touch skin to skin for too long. She pulled her hands back, touching her own neck. She could feel the bruising from where the man had grabbed her. *No one's ever done that to me before. No one. Never. Not even Dad ...*

"Sierra?" The voice was cold, the accent Germanic, and she looked up to see him coming toward her—Winter. Erich Winter. "I saw you talking to him. Was it you? Did you tell him where to find us?"

I'll be watching.

She thought again about the hands on her neck, the tightness in her throat. She thought she felt a quiver in her belly. *Maybe it'll be a little girl like you.* Sierra felt the cold chill run through her even as she looked past Erich at the fire raging in the remains of the Agency building.

Maybe she and I will meet one day.

With a loud, groaning crack the upper floors gave way and came crashing down, sending the building into a flaming destruction, a burning mess throwing clouds of smoke and debris across the parking lot. Winter disappeared in the dust and smoke, as did Jon as she staggered back. She thought about fighting her way back to him for one last touch, one last kiss, anything.

I'll be watching.

Touch hadn't been the thing that they'd built their relationship on. The smoke covered her, the dust concealed her, and she made her way, as quietly as possible, to the edge of the parking lot while everything was obscured. One thought pounded in her head with the blood, even as the pain from where he'd gripped her faded with every step. She crept off into the night, mind outracing her body by a factor of ten.

Have to lose him. Have to hide. I will not let that ... man ... ever meet my child. Not ever.

Chapter 39

Sienna Nealon
Now

I read three FBI criminal activity reports after I got my wits back about me. That took me until well after midnight, at which point I sat back in my chair, leaning at a forty-five degree angle, pondering just giving up and going to sleep right there. I heard the creak of the chair again, wondered if it was saying something about my weight and my sedentary lifestyle, and shrugged it off. I let my head loll to the right and looked out the window.

I blinked as I stared out, something catching my attention. There was movement in the construction site of the new science building. I turned the chair around and leaned closer to the glass. A light was bobbing around in the unfinished windows of the first floor, where they were still doing the basic framing. I stood and moved closer to the window, peering out, trying to catch a glimpse of whatever it was, but it was far, far too dark of a night and the view was partially obscured by the dormitory building. I frowned as my mind raced, wondering at the possibilities, from the mundane (a construction worker doing some unscheduled overtime, a thief using our building site to improve his home at a rock bottom discount) to the fearsome (the entirety of Century hiding in the site, preparing to stage an assault on us.

I crossed my office and flung open the door. "Who's still here?" I called out, and waited a beat for an answer.

"Me," Ariadne's voice came from the office next door.

"I am." I saw Scott appear toward the end of a cube row, peeking his head out into the main aisle.

"We've got something going on," I said.

"Hooboy," Scott said and pounded his way down the aisle at a fast jog. I moved aside and led him over to the window. Ariadne followed behind a moment later.

"See that light?" I pointed out the window. "In the construction site?"

"No," Ariadne said, and I watched her squint into the darkness.

"Yes," Scott answered immediately.

"I'm thinking ..." I looked again. "I'm thinking it's probably not a construction worker or someone doing some thieving."

"The odds are definitely a little too coincidental for that," Scott agreed.

I flashed a look at Ariadne. "Can you take care of Li? I don't want things to get fouled here."

"Yep," she said and disappeared back into her office.

"I'm gonna go scout," I said, opening the cabinet behind my desk and pulling out a submachine gun, pulling the strap over my shoulders.

"Are you freaking kidding me?" Scott asked, looking at me in disbelief. "That is not in the plan."

"The plan is for an attack," I said. "This could just be a prowler, in which case I need to scare the bejeezus out of him."

"Umm, or it could be a Century ambush, designed to lure one of our best people out by themselves so they can sucker punch them," he said. "Walking into a dark construction site in the middle of the night? Not your smartest move ever."

I hesitated. "You have a point."

"Thank you," he said graciously. "I may not present a compelling argument very often, but when I do, boy, is it a doozy."

I started to answer back when my phone started ringing, making both of us jump a little. I started to reach for it, and Scott slapped my hand away. I looked at him with irritation, a *What was that for?* kind of look. "I've seen this movie," he said. "Do not answer that phone."

"This isn't a horror movie," I said, "and I'm not played by Neve Campbell." I picked up the receiver. "Hello?"

"Sienna Nealon?" The woman's voice was a little out of breath but recognizable.

"Katheryn Hildegarde?" I asked, though I was sure it was her.

"One and the same," she replied, still trying to catch her breath. "We're, uh ... out on the construction site on your campus. Me and my crew. We, uh ... ran across something. If the rumors are true, you can even call it a gift for you."

"Oh, really?" I asked, and shared a look with Scott, who was giving me the *Don't be an idiot* look. I knew it because I'd sent it his way enough times while working with him.

"Yeah," she replied, sounding pretty matter of fact. "Caught someone snooping while we were making our way to your front door. I think you know him." I heard the sound of flesh hitting flesh, a dull thud, and then Hildegarde spoke again. "Say hello, asshole."

The voice that followed was deep, pronounced, a familiar one that would be burned into my memory until my dying day.

"Hello, Sienna," Erich Winter said. "I believe you are sitting in my chair."

Chapter 40

I crossed the campus, the combination of minimal light sources and my meta eyes keeping my feet on the straight and narrow, avoiding the subtle dips in the lawn where I might twist an ankle. It was a warm night but not hot, still being early summer, and I drew a deep breath as I went along toward the building site.

Scott had argued, had tried to dig in his heels, had fussed, but ultimately conceded that he'd stay back. Which was fortunate, because I wasn't looking to spook Katheryn Hildegarde. I needed to keep things on a cool level. I needed to assess the situation. I tried not to think about the other thing—the other person—who was with her.

Him.

I made it past the dormitory at a steady walk, not running. I didn't want to raise my heart rate any more than I had to. I needed to keep calm heading into this situation. I ducked under a low hanging wooden beam that hadn't been properly placed yet and looked into the dark. "Katheryn?" I asked cautiously, looking down what appeared to be a long hallway to my right. The science building was different than the one that had been here before, something new because the old one's design was a remnant of the time before the Directorate when the campus had been a failed junior college.

"Over here," came a voice from the corner of the building. I saw stacks of rebar and concrete blocks crowding one of the walls of the hall where were they were building it in, making it as strong as possible, and I picked my way around and cut through the open center of the building. Looking up, I saw the latticed rebar where they were starting to construct the floor, like a net of metal that hung over a large, open, square space. I came out in the middle of the building and found them there. Katheryn Hildegarde, one of her cronies ... and Erich Winter.

He stood nearly seven feet tall, head slightly bowed, and he was wrapped tightly in a light mesh around his chest and shoulders. It took me a minute to realize that it trailed off to Hildegarde, and she smiled as she gestured to her ponytail, which connected to the mesh via a snaking segment on the ground. "Medusa type," I said, and she nodded. "That hair is really quite something."

"Thank you," she said, a little brusquely. "You didn't bring any of your other people with you?"

"We're running a little low on staff at the moment," I said, smiling tightly. "Figured I'd make it a little easier on you, not coming at you with overwhelming numbers." I shrugged. "I wanted to keep things polite and on the level."

She flattened her lips like she was giving it all due contemplation. "That's ... very considerate of you. Really courteous and thoughtful." She turned her neck to try and look past the incomplete walls. "And did you station snipers at the corners of the building to keep overwatch?"

"Wouldn't matter if I did," I said with a shrug, "since they can't see into the building." I gestured at the unfinished walls. "This would be a sniper's nightmare, trying to find a way to manage a shot through this, don't you think?"

"Yeah," she said, like she was surveying it all over, giving it thought. "So, we're here. What's on your mind? What are you thinking?" She glanced down at her wrist, then put her hand down to her leg and tapped her fingers against her jeans. She really was an elegant woman but severe.

"The end of our world," I said. "It's all I think about. What's on your mind?"

She looked around again, as if looking for something

unexpected. "We're free to talk here? The FBI isn't listening in on us?"

"Nope," I said. "I'm trying to keep my FBI liaison out of the loop at present since you killed a bunch of his fellow agents."

"Nice," she said. "I didn't mean to do that. When they're coming at you with guns, things tend to get out of control pretty quickly. Anyway, yeah. Century. The greatest threat of our time. Probably the greatest since ... I dunno, I wasn't around for it, but I heard the Hades situation was pretty bad. World War One still gets mentioned quite a bit among the older crowd. Anyway, yeah, it's bad."

"What do you know about Century?" I asked.

She shrugged. "Standard line. Sovereign, the most powerful meta in the world, a man capable of things that don't really seem possible given normal meta abilities, has joined up with a hundred of the world's mightiest. Together, they've successfully wiped out around twenty-five hundred people so far, with about another five or six hundred to follow." She smiled thinly. "Including anyone who's not in that Top 100."

"You make it sound a little like a Who's Who list."

"Maybe it is," she said. "Anyone who doesn't make the list is definitely not getting an invite to the world's most exclusive party, where the door prize is survival."

"What are they going to do after that?" I asked, watching her carefully.

She walked to a nearby wall and leaned against the corner, her hair still stringing behind her, binding Old Man Winter, who stood, stoic and silent, watching us talk. "Take over the world? Give each other facials and perms?" She gestured to her long knot of hair. "Which, in my case, would be an expensive proposition. Hell if I know." She looked to Winter. "What about you? Do you know?"

"I know it is nothing good," Winter said in his low, slow

timbre. "One does not start a plan by wiping out all of metakind and end with something benevolent, such as a benefit to raise money for the American Red Cross."

Hildegarde looked at him before giving him a concessionary nod. "The old man's got a point. For those who aren't on the bus for the select few, it's not looking so grand."

I looked over at her. "You keep mentioning the select few. Any idea how they were chosen?"

She tapped her fingers against her leg. "No idea."

I watched her, sussing it out. She set her jaw, and I looked over at her compatriot. He was big, almost swollen. "You must be a Hercules," I said, and he nodded. "My grandfather was one."

"Interesting bit of family history," Hildegarde said. "He still alive?"

"No," I said with a slight smile. "Omega killed him."

"Oh," she said, and things just felt awkward. "Uh, gosh. That's, uh ..."

I shrugged lightly. "It was a long time ago and across an ocean, plus I didn't know him, so ..." I looked at Hildegarde again. "So how do you want to do this?"

She froze, and I got the sense that her head was spinning as she was looking for a response. "Do what?" The pitch of her voice was off, was wrong somehow, but I couldn't quite put my finger on how.

I didn't get a chance to ask my next question, either, because a hand reached out from behind the wall and grabbed her head, slamming it into the concrete block. Hildegarde dropped to the ground as someone stepped out from behind the wall, a shadowy figure that glared coldly down at her before looking up at me and giving me a slight nod.

I recognized him even though it had been months since I'd last seen him; his short brown hair framing his young features. He was missing his glasses, though. When last I'd seen him he was wearing ridiculously oversized glasses, like the biggest nerd on the planet. They were gone now, and he looked young, handsome. He took a deep breath as he watched me through his brown eyes and then sighed. "Hey, Sienna. Did you know that she was betraying you to Century?"

"I was starting to get that feeling, yes," I said, letting my eyes scan between him, Winter, and Hildegarde's goon, who was standing almost stunned, unsure of what to do. "I'd ask what you're doing here, but I think I already know."

"You always were a clever one," he replied. "And, hey, I told you last time we met I'd see you again."

"I vaguely recall that," I said to Joshua Harding, "but I kind of figured that Century killing you would have put the kibosh on that."

"Century didn't kill me," Joshua replied, that enigmatic little smile on his face. "Do you know why?"

"Of course," I said tightly, feeling every muscle in my body tense as I looked at him. "Because you're Sovereign."

Chapter 41

"The kids—your friends—were sure you were dead," I said, looking uneasily at him. Winter was to my right, still tangled in the solid weave of Hildegarde's hair, though he looked like he was very nearly shivering, as though the warm summer air was chilling him. Hildegarde's last remaining flunky was just past him, still looking stunned.

"I let 'em think it," he said. I looked at him very carefully. He was the same kid, but now I was seeing him differently. Suddenly his boundless confidence didn't seem so out of place, and he didn't really look fifteen or twelve or whatever anymore. He didn't look old, but there was wisdom in his eyes that I could discern even in the dark. "Hey, I saved their lives from the squad Century sent out. Does that earn me any points in your book?"

"Very few," I said, letting my weight shift back and forth between my legs, ready to spring. "Since you're also in charge of the organization that's killing all of our kind."

"That wasn't really my idea," he said, and I caught a hint of mortification from him. "But I guess I can't really dodge the responsibility for it, can I?"

"Not really."

"Would it help if I told you it was for a good cause?" He gave me a sly smile. "Because at the end of it all, it really is."

"It might help if you told me what the real cause was," I said. I didn't know if I should spring or not, find out if he was really as badass as everyone seemed to think he was. I looked to Winter and Hildegarde's flunky; part of me was hoping they'd test the theory for me.

"Winter's not going to come at me," Sovereign said with that same smile. "He's a broken man, still scared of me since I burned and crippled him after he tried to shake me down outside Peshtigo a hundred years ago. Neither is that nameless Omega red shirt, either, because I'm mentally paralyzing him right now."

You're a telepath? I asked in my head.

"Yes," he said. "But it'd be rude to have this conversation in our heads. Also, probably a little too forward for me. I don't want to be too presumptuous; I know you've got enough business going on in that head of yours to keep it spinning. I don't want to add to your problems."

"Bub," I said, "you are my problems, every last one of them."

"Now, now," he said, and took a couple steps along the wall, keeping his distance from me, "don't exaggerate. Weissman is at least ... like 95% of your problems. I may be the big gun backing everything up, but I did not put this in motion."

"You know, let's just cut the shit," I said, keeping a wary eye on him. "What do you want?"

His face creased a little as he smiled, tightly. "That's a funny question to ask. Do you know why it's funny?"

"Because you're not a guy known for wanting things."

"Mm, sorry, you didn't phrase your answer in the form of a question," he said with that same smile. "Kidding. It's a Jeopardy joke. You didn't watch that, I guess."

"I only got an hour of TV a day, so no, a quiz show wasn't high on my list of teenage priorities."

"Aww, Jeopardy is more than a quiz show," he said with good humor. I got the feeling he was trying to out-irony me, to let me know he was in on my sarcastic little view of the world, that he wanted to share my wavelength. It was the same thing he tried when I thought he was a fifteen-year old boy who was trying to hit on me, and it wasn't any more effective. "Listen, I have walked the world. For ... a long time," he said, stopping before telling me his actual age, probably concerned it would affect my opinion of him. "I've seen horror and wonder, sometimes within a breath of each other. I've seen humans at their best, and their worst. I've seen a lot, and the one constant is that there are terrible things happening out there." He kept a sense of quiet sadness about him for his soliloquy, and I wondered if he was using his power to influence me. "It could be a better world, if we troubled ourselves to act, to make it one."

"And here comes you," I said, "ready to take that first step. Of course, it involves completely destroying anyone who might oppose your plans first, so naturally it has to be the bestest plan ever. Because we base our designs for a better world on ... what? Body count?" I saw him recoil only slightly. He was keeping his cool. "Hey, the good news is you're not Hitler, Mao or Stalin, yet, though since I don't know how phase two is going to end, you're still in the running."

"You don't understand," he said quietly. "And no, that's not an invitation to ask me more about the plan. You'll see what we do. You'll be around to realize the rewards of what we're going to accomplish. Eventually you'll discover that we were right, that the world could be a better, safer place—"

"For those who survive," I said, winning the award for most irony. "Go ahead, pick your broken egg/omelet rebuttal metaphor of choice, and let me know why people have to die in order to make your better world."

"People are dying anyway," he said, and I caught a hint of sadness in how he said it. "People die every day, and for a lot less purpose than making the world a better place."

"Well, since your definition of 'acceptable breakage' and mine differ, I'm going to go out on a limb and guess my definition of a 'better world' isn't going to jibe real well with yours, either." I cracked my knuckles, and he looked at me with a sense of uncertainty, as if he felt a little sick. "Why don't we just get this fight underway?"

"I'm not here to fight you," he said, shaking his head. "I don't *want* to fight you, Sienna."

"If you want to build your 'better world' on a pile of corpses, you'd better be prepared for mine to be one of them," I said as I assumed a fighting stance. "Because I'm not just going to lie down and let you kill everyone I care about."

His hand came up, covering his face for a moment, and when it came away he looked tired, older. Same guy, just weary. "Are you even willing to listen to reason? What is it with you?"

"Maybe it's something you said, maybe it's something you did." I dipped a shoulder, my version of shrugging when I was in a fighting stance. "Could be the company you keep. Like Weissman. Not a huge fan of your BFF."

"He's not my ..." Sovereign looked chagrined, like I'd caught him doing something embarrassing. "He's an ally of convenience, okay?"

"I've had those before," I said, and indicated Hildegarde's prostrate body with a nod of my head. "See how well it works out?"

"She was going to betray you, you know that, right?" He looked uncertain again.

"So you've said." I was still waiting for the fight to break loose, and I was beginning to wonder if he was using the same power to hold me back that he was employing on Hildegarde's Hercules, who still had not said one damned thing. "I'm a little unclear on the why."

"She was trying to prove her worth, buy her way into Century by clearing a few spots off our roster," he said.

"You mean she thought that if she killed a few members of your club, you'd let her into the club?" I raised an eyebrow at the Hercules, who still stood there, looking like a helpless thing, overinflated and unsure of himself, looking haplessly from Sovereign to me. "Not the greatest plan ever."

He looked down at her unconscious form. "She's *your* ally." He looked up, and was smiling again. "Maybe you should pick them more carefully."

"Maybe you should stop killing all the good ones," I replied with a smugness I didn't really feel. "Or at least the more effective ones."

"Hey, I didn't beat the Primus of Omega to death with his own chair," Sovereign said, stepping around Hildegarde's body to lean against the wall, his black leather coat making a little noise as he did so. "I don't typically go in much for wrath, but I heard you really put it to him."

I sighed. "Are we going to discuss my greatest hits or can we just get to the fighting already?"

"Why are you so eager to fight me?" He let out a sigh. "I don't want to fight you."

"Then why are you here?" I asked. "To get back your telepaths?"

"What?" He frowned. "No, I know they're dead."

"Then why the hell did you send an army of mercs in here to shoot us up a few days ago?"

"That was Weissman," he said quickly. "He didn't know they were dead. Also, he is eventually going to try and kill all your friends."

"It seems like you're trying to make a good impression on me," I said. "Keeping it polite and all. You know what would make a really good impression? Not killing the people I care about. Not killing random strangers. And not letting your boy Weissman do any of that, either."

He grimaced, and I could tell he was genuinely pained. "I would if I could." He pushed off the wall and walked over to Old Man Winter and stood behind him. Winter, for his part, stiffened as the shorter Sovereign hovered over him. "But I can't. You know why?"

"Because you're a neo-fascist and you just can't get this killing of your inferiors out of your system?"

He made a face, something between a smile and a frown. "I'm not a neo-anything."

"So does that make you a paleo-something?"

"You know why Winter did what he did to you?" Sovereign clapped both hands onto Winter's shoulders, causing the giant man to blanch. "Because he believed that pushing you to kill was the right thing to do." He leaned toward Winter and peeked around his arm. "Isn't that right, Erich?"

Winter looked me in the eye. "I did what I did to make you stronger. To make you the kind of person who could—"

"That's enough of that," Sovereign said, and Winter stopped speaking. "She gets the point. He did something horrifying to you because he believed it was the right thing to do. What do you think about that?"

I paused, caught a little flatfooted. "I ..." I blinked, not really sure how to answer.

"Come on," Sovereign said, encouraging. "You know how it makes you feel, don't you? What it felt like when he did what he did? When he ordered you to be held while—"

"Shut up," I said, my cheeks flushing hotly. "I don't need a reminder."

"So how did it make you feel," Sovereign went on, "when your father figure, your newly adopted parent, replacing the old, inferior one who'd abandoned you, turned out to be even worse?" He didn't smile.

"He's not my father," I said a little too abruptly.

"No, of course not," Sovereign said, "because you've never actually met your father, the real one. He died before you were born. Would you like to talk to him?"

"You are such an asshole," I said and meant it.

"I am just pointing out that the people who have helped shape you and influence you may not have been the most morally centered individuals." He stepped out from behind Winter and spread his arms. "All your outrage at what I'm doing is at least partially grounded in the judgment given to you by a mother who locked you in a metal box regularly and a ..." He glanced back at Winter, "... a father figure who forced you to kill your first love."

"So I should take instruction from you instead?" I asked. "Because you're morally superior, having never locked me in a box or caused me to kill someone I care about?"

"I saved your life," he said calmly. "Three times now and counting. No, I don't expect you to take instruction from me. I don't expect your opinion of me is going to change one way or another tonight. I'm just here ... to save you. To help you. I don't care about telepaths who are already dead," he waved a hand at the sky, "and I'm not gonna tell Weissman that you sent your mother, your brother and your British friend away with all your junior metas so you could try and draw out some of his people and kill them in a rather obvious trap." He smiled. "He's probably figured that one out already, anyway, if you want to know the truth."

I felt gut-clenching fear. I had been so sure I was being clever, even though everyone but me had practically cursed me for being a fool. The dormitories were sealed tight but completely empty, wired to explode if I ordered it. And I had planned to order it, too, as soon as Weissman's latest gambit showed up.

"It was a good plan," Sovereign went on. "But I can read minds. The good news for you is that I'm not fussy. I'm not in a hurry. I'm more worried about doing this right and not being harsh with you than I am about running over all your friends and getting them killed. I can be flexible. There's room for mercy in my plan. I promise you that we can build a better world, one where people aren't starving to death or being killed in wars every day that they didn't start or want, where the planet isn't being killed because of selfish desires." He didn't smile, just looked at me grimly. "You could help. You could be the greatest force for good that the world has ever known, saving more lives over the next five thousand years or more that you're going to live than the piddly few that we're going to have to take to start setting things right." He cocked his head to look at me, and his tone turned imploring. "I know it haunts you, what you've done. Who you've killed. What you've become in the process. You worry about the cost to your soul. Make that sacrifice mean something by truly balancing the scales." He took in everything with a sweep of his hand. "I know you think you're fighting the good fight against the grand evil here, but what you're really doing is perpetuating a system that creates outcasts, isolation, alienation, fear, starvation and death. You're fighting for everything bad and ignoble and horrible in life but you think you're on the side of the righteous because ..." He gestured to Old Man Winter. "Because of something he told you? Because of something your mother instilled in you? These people fight to keep the status quo. Why is he even here?" He poked Winter in the chest with an outstretched finger.

"To tell the truth," Winter said finally.

"Which you could have told her at any point previously, if you'd been of a mind to," Sovereign said. "No, now you're here because you're scared. Because a system that you helped prop up, that made you wealthy and gave you power, is about to crumble. That scares you, scares you enough that you'd scar a teenage girl for life in hopes that she'd protect you—your position, your power—from the change that's coming." He shook his head at Winter. "Your legacy is going to be that you did it all for naught."

"Don't be so sure about that," I said. By now I was just cocking off, still hesitating. I didn't want to attack him, and I didn't know why. He was just being so damned ... polite.

"Don't you realize what's going on here?" Sovereign turned on the passion, and I could feel it exude from him. "He's got you fighting for a world where the people who were supposed to show you the most care betrayed you, hurt you, left you. You're lined up to defend a world that has made you lonely, bitter and mournful. I know you don't want to hear it, and this whole ... this extinction, you call it ... this isn't how I would want to get to where we're going. But there aren't any other viable options. The old world has to be torn down to bring about a new one." I could hear the remorse in his voice, and I knew— somehow *knew*—that he actually felt the pain; he wasn't just putting me on. "I don't want to do what we have to do. It took a long time to convince myself that it was right. I don't expect you'll come around until you see the result, I really don't. You've been beaten down, broken, shattered by people you trusted. I don't think you'll look at me and see someone who's trustworthy for a long time, not with what I'm doing, how we're going about this. But I know that when we're done, you'll be able to look out on what we've built, and it'll be a shining world, something new and bright without the rough edges and cruelty you've come to know from this one."

"And who's going to live in this world of yours?" I asked, practically choking up. "The five people who haven't ever done anything bad, haven't ever hurt a soul?" I glared at him.

"Everyone could have a place in that world, that's the point," Sovereign said. "It won't take as much as you think."

"I don't think I have a place there," I said. "I don't think I could live in your world." I put my hands up one last time. "I'm going to fight you now."

"I won't fight you, Sienna," he said, shaking his head. "I won't. I'm not here to harm you. I'm here to save you."

I felt a curious swell of emotion, some great sadness and longing that I didn't want to feel, but it was there anyway. "Well, I'm here to save the world, so I don't think you're going to have a choice."

I launched myself at him, a little slow, halfhearted, and he dodged by hovering right out of my path. I landed and turned, and he hung a couple feet off the ground behind me, watching me with sad eyes. "I told you I don't want to fight you."

"I don't feel the same," I said and pulled my gun. I ran through the magazine, sixteen rounds, and he stood there all the while, never moving. When the smoke from the chamber cleared and the action was open, he still hovered, and I heard a faint clinking. I looked down to see the bullets falling off of him, hitting the concrete floor of the construction site one by one.

"You can't hurt me," he said, shaking his head. "And I won't hurt you." He swept to my right, hovering just behind Winter. "But I'll tell you what ... here's a gift for you. Take Winter. Do what you want to him."

Winter's eyes widened, but he said nothing.

"You think I give a damn about Winter now?" I shook my head at him, incredulous. "You're a pretty lousy mind reader if you think I'm going to waste my effort on him while you're still hovering over there, ready to destroy everything—everything I hold dear."

"Sweetheart ... all the things you hold dear are things you shouldn't," he said, looking down on me with sadness. "The things that have hurt you."

"Sure, tell me how to feel, that'll fix everything." I nodded at Winter. "What I see is this—another guy who just has plans to make the world over in whatever image he wants, not really caring that everyone else might not want to share his vision. Sure, yours is grander than his, but your intentions are exactly the same. Remake your corner of the sky to your exacting specifications, and to hell with the consequences for the people who don't fit into your plan." I almost spat at his feet. "You want to talk about legacy? Yours is a mass grave."

He gave me a haunted smile, a kind of half-hearted expression that didn't even look like he was remotely happy. "The people who change the world? They almost always have a mass grave under their feet. Most of the time that doesn't end up being their legacy, though." He stared me down. "What about you? You're digging a pretty large gravesite at this point. You don't want to at least examine the reason why it's happening?"

"I ..." I started to answer, then found I couldn't. I didn't really have one. Everything that had happened, everything I'd done, I had no words to reason for it, not now. I just stood there, blinking, not sure what to say to the surprisingly warm brown eyes that were staring at me expectantly, as if I should know the reason why I'd killed so many people.

And then Old Man Winter was flung through the air into Sovereign's back, knocking him over, and the need to craft an answer became completely irrelevant.

Chapter 42

Hildegarde rose to her feet, her hair whipping back behind her, retracting from where she'd thrown Winter into Sovereign's exposed back. She took one look at me, then at her crony, and bolted, running full out around the corner of the wall segment that Sovereign had appeared from behind. I stood there, a little confused, not really sure if I should be doing something or if continuing to do nothing was the appropriate play. After only a moment's pause, her Hercules followed suit, running off in the opposite direction, dodging behind a corner and out of view.

"Excuse me for a moment," Sovereign said, and rose into the air as Winter fell off his back. Sovereign shook his head then flashed into flight around the corner where Hildegarde had just vanished. I was left staring at Erich Winter, whose hunched frame was slowly getting up off the ground.

"He will destroy you, you know," Winter said. "Whatever he says is lies."

I blinked, as though I could clear my head of the surreal imagery I had just seen merely by doing that. "I guess you two have that in common, then."

"I never lied to you," he said, easing to his feet, shoulders still stooped. "I may not have always told you everything, but I did it to try to protect you—"

"Spare me the warmed over, empty air that you're flinging in my direction," I said. "Your excuses are doing nothing but adding carbon dioxide to the atmosphere." He quieted, and a long, piercing scream came from somewhere in the distance. It was male, and it cut off after a moment. "I guess we just found out who's stronger than Hercules."

"He will kill everyone," Winter said. "You heard him admit as much yourself."

"I did," I said. "I also watched you order your goons to force me to drain Bjorn, then my boyfriend, in order to piss me off and make me kill people."

"You needed to prepare," he said. "You needed to lose your hesitation." Another scream followed his words, this one from a woman, and only slightly farther away, judging by the sound. "He is coming."

"Yeah," I said. "If he doesn't kill you, by the way, you're under arrest." Winter cocked his head at me, most curiously. "Senator Foreman sends his regards. He's a little miffed that you fled the country rather than making at least some report to him."

"I had important work to attend to," Winter said.

"Yeah, I bet fleeing my impending wrath was crucial to your strategy of saving your own ass to work another day."

"Sorry about that," Sovereign said as he flew back around the corner, sweeping low to avoid the rebar ceiling. "I, uh ..." He met my gaze. "I hope you don't mind, but I had to kill those two. I don't normally go for killing if I can avoid it—witness this guy here," he waved at Winter, "but in this case, I mean, their time was pretty limited anyway, and hitting me in the back of the head with a Norseman? I can only handle so much insult from someone who's already killed my people while trying to impress me." He looked from me to Winter. "Sorry, did I interrupt? I can wait. Really. If you two have business to hash out, you go right ahead."

I let out an impatient exhalation. "I'm pretty sure we're supposed to fight. This is how it always ends—talk, fight, done. It's a cycle. Don't mess with the process."

"Sorry," Sovereign said. "I'm not going to fight you. I'm sure Weissman will, when you stick your nose in his end of the operation again, but not me." He didn't look like a fifteen-year-old, not anymore, and he had sadness aplenty that differentiated him from someone that young. "I've warned him about killing you, though." His jaw tightened. "I thought he knew better before, but ... I had to teach him a lesson after Andromeda. That never should have happened. And for that, as well, you have my apologies." He bowed his head in contrition.

"Oh, for the love of—" I said, groaning. "You're here to apologize me to death?"

"No, I came here to save you," he said. "From Hildegarde. Like I said, she was planning to betray you, to capture you, and turn you over to us. She figured it was her way in."

"I don't think I needed saving from some over-muscled louse or some lady with really bad hair extensions."

"But you're not going to turn it down, right?" He raised his arms at each side, like he was questioning. "In fairness, there were a couple other reasons to come visit. One was to ... introduce myself. Formally. Now that some of the cards are on the table and things are in motion." He turned to Winter. "There is one more, though."

Winter stood off against him, lowering his frame to a defensive stance. "No. You won't—"

Sovereign moved against him in a flash, grasping him by the front of his shirt and lifting him up. "Yeah. I think we established a long time ago who has the power between you and me, Erich." He turned to me. "Anything you want to say to Old Man Winter before I finish him off?"

"Ummm ..." I stuttered a little, not really sure what I could say. It came to me after about a second. "Don't kill him," I said quietly. "He's not worth it. I'll put him in a jail cell and he can sit the rest of this fight out."

I saw him think about it for a second or two, a grimace plastered all over his youthful face. "No. I'm sorry, no. I think the world needs to know something, and he's going to be my messenger, my example." He turned and looked Winter in the eye.

"If you inflict pain on Sienna Nealon, I will visit it one thousand fold back upon you." He reached out with his free hand and touched Winter in the chest, just touched him, delicately, as if he were administering the slightest of pokes.

Winter grunted, then moaned, and fire sprang from the spot on his chest where Sovereign had touched him, fanning out in an explosive burst across his clothing and his body. His screams rose over the sound of the crackling flames as they raced over him, consuming his flesh.

I dodged away, my hands over my face, turning from the light of the burning pyre as it consumed him, burned him, and the screaming didn't cease until I heard the thud of a body hitting the ground, followed by muffled moans from the scorched and blackened form of Erich Winter. The smell was horrific, like someone had char-roasted something under my nose, and it smelled nothing like chicken.

"I'm sorry you had to see that," Sovereign said, sighing. "I could have flown him off, I guess, before I did it, but I figured you two might have some last words to exchange afterward." He hovered closer to me, but not so close I felt like I could take a swipe at him. After what I'd seen, I wasn't sure I even wanted to. "I like that you wanted to spare him. I think it shows that ... whatever he did to you, it didn't really work. It didn't change your heart." He started to reach out, and I stayed right where I was, frozen in place, as he came closer, as he brushed my cheek then let his hand hover there. "Whatever you've done, there's still an abundance of good in you."

I looked up at him, felt the gentle touch of his hand on my cheek, and I stared into those deep, brown eyes. "Are you sure?" I asked.

"I'm sure," he said so soothingly it was like the most heartfelt reassurance I've ever heard. "I've never been so sure of anything in my life. There's so much good in you."

"Really?" I tried to keep my voice level and reached up for his hand, brushing it, holding it against my cheek. "You think there's good in me?" I reached up with my other hand and anchored his open palm to my face as I pulled his face close to mine. My voice turned low and harsh. "Why don't you come inside and find out for yourself?"

I forced his hand against my skin, hard, pressing it to me as he stood there, dumbstruck, and I counted the seconds, waiting for something to happen. I expected him to flee, to fight back, to run, and I waited for my power to work over the sound of the wind blowing sporadically through the construction site, counting the moments and waiting for it to do something, anything.

After a minute passed, he gently tugged his hand away. "I know you didn't intend for that to be meaningful ... but for me it kind of was."

"How did you do that?" I asked, staring at him, my last desperate gambit blown.

"You've met someone else before that your touch didn't effect, didn't you?" He was a little coy, acting mysterious, but I could see just the hint of hurt behind his eyes.

"Andromeda?" I asked, feeling my bare fingers brush against my palm and remembering the touch of the girl who had died almost without a friend. And now, I knew, completely in vain.

He nodded slowly. "She must have made a hell of an impression. I should be going. Thank you for reminding me, though, Sienna."

"Reminding you about what?" I asked, my voice hoarse. It was the middle of the damned night, and I was completely drained. I hadn't fought, but I felt like I'd been through twelve rounds with him.

"Reminding me why I'm doing this," he said. "Every once in a while I waver, I think maybe it's not worth the cost. But you— you're the reason. You're who this is for."

"I don't want it," I said, almost croaking it out. "Just stop it. I don't need your ... pity or whatever it is."

"You know what it is," he said, and there was a glimmer in his eye. "I'll see you again." With that, he stopped hovering and flew straight up, melting through the rebar like it wasn't even there, and arched off into the dark sky.

Chapter 43

"Sienna," Old Man Winter croaked, rasping my name out from his burnt, blackened husk.

I started toward him, then stopped, waiting a few feet away. "What do you want, old man?"

"I ... can help you ..." he said, and every word was a battle for him.

"I don't need your help," I said, keeping my distance. "Why don't you just die in peace?"

"Please," he said, and turned his scorched face toward me. The deep lines were all burned away, and I could see the sinew and bone, the last of the blackened flesh that remained, and it reminded me of a time when I'd lost a hand to fire. "I can ... help you ..."

"Fine," I said. "Help me. Tell me what you know, and be quick about it." I looked him over. "Even as a meta, I'm guessing you've got minutes remaining, if that."

He struggled, and blood pumped out from his open skin, searing and hissing with heat as it poured out onto the dusty concrete floor. "Take me ... take me with you ..."

"There's no medical unit that can save you now," I said, and stooped down next to him, still taking care to keep a foot or so of distance between us. "You're ... uh ... toast. Literally."

"Take me with you," he said again, and his long arm came out. I didn't bother to dodge, and his blackened fingers landed on my arm. "*With* you."

I looked at his scorched flesh touching my pale arm, and I shook it off. It left a trail of carbonized ash and dust marring my bare skin. "No." I felt a rage build up inside me, welling up with disgust. "No. No, I will not."

"I can help you defeat him. Help you ..."

"I don't want your fucking help," I said, and I felt my body and my voice shake. "I don't *need* your help."

"Together, we could save the world," he whispered, his voice starting to fade.

"You could have helped me save the world months ago," I said. "Instead you forced me to kill the only man I've ever loved." I stood and took a step back from him. "You made me a murderer."

"No ..." His voice was growing fainter. "I made you ... strong. You needed to be strong, to be willing ... in order to fight him. I gave you ... the gift of rage, of anger ..."

"I won't do it," I said, shaking my head, looking down on his burnt, frail, thin body on the pavement. "I won't let you become a part of me, won't carry you with me for all my days like some sort of curse. You've abused me and my body enough for one lifetime, I won't give you a chance to do it again."

"Sometimes ..." he whispered, growing fainter by the second, raspier, "the hero has to do the hard things ... the cruel things ... in order to do the right thing. I had to ... teach you that. Make you ... willing to do ..." His voice trailed off.

"You don't sound any different than him," I said and drew my arms tightly around my midsection. "You *are* no different than him. And ultimately, what you leave behind will be exactly the same as him—just a bunch of graves all in a line, with the last one being your own." I turned on my heel and started to walk away.

"Sienna ... wait ... you can still ... beat him ..." the rasp grew fainter with each step I took. "You can't ... leave me like this ..."

I turned over my shoulder to look at him one last time. "Last time I saw you, you left me frozen and unconscious in the snow. Now I'm going to leave you burnt and dying." I turned away from him for the last time. "Seems like there's a karmic balance in that somewhere."

"I can still ... help you ..."

"Winter ... Erich ..." I said, not even turning around this time, as I walked off into the night, "... you can't even help yourself."

Chapter 44

Scott caught me just outside the outer wall of the science building, as the cool night air blew through gently. "You all right?" he asked, eyeing me cautiously.

"Fine," I said, and he fell into step beside me. "You heard?"

"Everything," he said. "You didn't really go at Sovereign at all. You buying into this idea of his invincibility?"

"I tried to drain him," I said, "that should count for something."

"Was that what that was?" He started to register understanding. "It all makes sense now, the bit about 'come inside.' I thought maybe it was—" He flushed and then looked down. "Never mind. I followed your lead."

"I figured as much," I said, my strides chewing up the distance between me and the headquarters building. "Since I didn't hear any sniper rifles bellow out in the night." I tapped the earpiece buried in my right ear. "Ariadne, call my mother. Get them back here, Sovereign knows."

"I heard," she said, "and they're already on their way. They're about twenty minutes out; I guess they decided to stay at a motel nearby, just in case."

"Well, that was stupid." I halted as we reached the pavement next to HQ, the quiet, wet swish of the grass silenced as I stepped off of it. "Maybe I was wrong for not going at him full out, but when I tried to attack him, he didn't even act like I was moving at him. When I fired my gun, he shrugged it off." I held my hand up. "When he touched me, it was like Andromeda all over again. Nothing." I looked up at the night sky above me, and saw a patch of lit clouds under the yellow lamp effect. "What the hell is he?"

"A lot of trouble," Scott said. "He fried Winter?"

"Crisped him," I said, and nodded my head back to the construction site. "He was still alive when I left. Barely."

"I heard that, too," he said. "You sure walking away was the best idea? I mean, if he had the answers and you could get them ..."

"It's what he wanted," I said then cursed. "He wanted me to absorb him, and I just ... ugh. I mean, I make decisions with my logical mind most of the time, don't I?"

"More than most people I've met, yeah," he agreed.

"I couldn't, this time, though." I put my hands on my hips and let myself sway. "Couldn't do it. Couldn't put aside my revulsion for him to let it happen."

"You could have locked him in a box for all eternity," Scott suggested. "Your own little version of imprisoning him for his crimes."

"I don't want to imprison him," I said. "He wanted to be imprisoned because he was too chickenshit to die. I don't want him in my head. Erich Winter is out of my life." I looked back to the wreckage of the science building. "He's out of life, period. Whatever answers he had were too toxic for me to want any part of." I folded my arms. "I'll find another way."

Scott looked down for a minute, shuffling his feet, then back up at me. "You sure about that?"

"Yeah," I said, staring up into the sky again. The stars were peeking out from behind the clouds, just faintly, now. "I have to."

Chapter 45

We sat around my office, just waiting, Li, Ariadne, Scott and I. I still had the smell of Winter's burnt flesh in my nostrils. I wondered if it would ever leave.

"Are we good now, Li?" I asked the question and caught the eye of the agent, who was sitting stone silent on the couch.

"I don't know what you mean," Li said, and I could tell he truly didn't.

"Your killers are dead," I said. "Security is scraping their scorched corpses off the lawn as we speak."

"Congratulations on sitting back and letting them become human s'mores for a supervillain," he said, giving me a dirty look. "I was after justice, not vengeance."

"Awesome," I shot back. "Tell me where in your system a meta gets justice. Please, point it out to me. Is it in the life sentences prescribed for all violent offenders?"

"I don't think this is going to get us anywhere," Scott said. There was a moment's pause. "Did you tell Senator Foreman that they're wrapped up?"

"I sent him an email," Li said. "I'm sure his colleagues will be pleased."

We settled into an uneasy silence, and Ariadne had her eyes anchored on me. "What?" I asked finally.

"You saw him die?" she asked.

"Security is bringing him in right now," I said. "You can visit him in the morgue, if you like, but I was assured by Dr. Perugini that it was indeed Erich Winter—going by genetic sample—that he is, in fact, dead, that the likely cause of death was burns covering one hundred percent of his body, and that he was going to, and I quote, 'Stink up the *maledetto* office if I don't get his corpse out of there soon.'"

"That fast, huh?" she spoke quietly, looking down.

"That fast, what? How quickly he died?" I remembered the sound of the shrieking, something so unlike the man I'd known as Winter. "Yeah, it was about as fast as could be expected."

"Can we talk about the giant elephant in the room?" Scott asked uneasily from the corner.

"Yeah, I know my decor sucks, but I'll get around to it sooner or later," I quipped, in spite of feeling not particularly witty. Bleh.

The door opened before Scott could have his say, and Reed entered, followed by my mother. "The dorm is still locked down," she said before I could say anything. "All our little metas—the few that remain, anyway—are all locked up tight with it."

"Thank you," I said.

"So," she said, "you met Sovereign."

"Yeah," I said. "Big surprise. He didn't try to kill me. Like, at all. He didn't even have a cross word for me. I'm a little confused."

"He didn't try very hard to kill me, either," my mother said, warily. "Which is worrisome."

"Count your blessings," Reed muttered. "He's quite content to kill everyone who's not a woman of the Nealon family."

I saw a haunted look on my mother's face as she looked at Reed, and I wondered what she was thinking. I closed my eyes and pictured Sovereign's face, the one I would have associated with Joshua Harding only a few hours before. I didn't know how to feel about him, whether to hate him or not. Then I thought about Erich Winter and realized I didn't really have the energy to hate anyone anymore. "Weissman will be coming," I said.

"We better come up with another plan, then," Scott said, "since it sounds like this one is blown. And about that elephant—"

"I don't know why, okay?" my mother said, turning on Scott.

"I don't know." She shot a guilty look at Reed. "I watched him kill people I cared about, and he spared me with barely a touch. He got angry, got aggressive, held me up in the air, handled me in a way I'd never been roughed up before. It scared the living hell out of me, but what was worse was that he told me he'd be watching and alluded to what he'd do if I ever had a daughter ..." she looked at me, and I saw the guilt lace through her, "... but he didn't hurt me. Not really."

"Am I the only one seeing the obvious motive here?" Scott asked. "Clearly, he—"

There was a knock at the door that interrupted Scott right in the middle of his thought. I gestured toward it and Reed turned the handle, letting the door swing wide to reveal Kat, standing just outside, her body partially obscured by the doorframe. "Oh," she said. "I didn't know you'd all be having a meeting this late."

"It's fine, Kat," I said, leaning my head back on my headrest for the millionth time. "Come on in. Might as well join the party; it'll be like a reunion."

"Even more than you think," she said, and started to come in, shuffling slowly. It took a moment for her to clear the doorframe and a second longer for me to register that she had someone with her, leaning on her, getting her assistance to walk. His body was smaller than when last I'd seen him upright and moving, but it was him, nonetheless, and I felt a shot of warmth as I stood.

"Janus," I said, and felt a little tingle of joy despite my weariness. "You're ..." He looked up, his expression hangdog as any I can ever remember seeing, as Kat brought him into my office and helped set him on the couch in front of my desk. "You're awake."

"I am awake," he said, "but only barely." He held a hand up to his head as though he were experiencing great pain. "I have had some troubling nightmares, as you might imagine. Terrible dreams. Things that I wouldn't wish on my worst enemies, though

I am told that list is not so long as it might once have been."

"So you remember?" I asked, watching his lined and sagging face.

"I remember a great pain in the back of my head," he said, "and little else after that. Until just now, when someone ... touched my mind. Someone who should not be able to touch my mind." He looked concerned. "Sovereign."

"Sovereign?" I asked. "He woke you up?"

"I believe so, yes," he said. "With the words, 'Someone should tell her.'" He blinked. "Which was ironic, since I was about to tell you before Weissman so rudely interrupted me."

"Tell me what? How to beat Sovereign?" I leaned forward, hoping to hear something I'd been looking for, something I'd been longing for.

"Perhaps," he said, still looking dreadfully tired. "At the very least, something helpful. Some knowledge of what he represents. What he wants. What he—"

"I need to know," I said, standing, leaning over the desk toward him. "I need to know some basics. Something to start with. To defeat him. I need to know my foe." I squeezed my hands together, knuckles pressed against the hard surface of the desk. "I need to know what type of meta he is."

Janus started to open his mouth, his lip quivered, and he looked down. He folded his hands in his lap and lowered his head. "Yes. Yes, you do. You need to know. Very well, then," he said and looked up at me, face resolute, like he had committed at last to stepping over some line that he had sworn he would never cross.

"Sovereign is ... an incubus."

Chapter 46

Sovereign
January 21, 2012
Minneapolis, Minnesota

They pulled into the grocery store parking lot following the little yellow Volkswagen beetle. *Is this really it?* Sovereign thought as they parked the car a few hundred feet behind the Volkswagen. They were both following another vehicle, a sedan, one that had just burned out of a Minneapolis neighborhood in a big hurry minutes earlier.

"Looks like they're pulling off in this grocery store," Weissman said. He didn't look quite so oily today; he looked younger, was dressed in a coat and jeans, and his face didn't look nearly as old as he was. "Any idea why?"

"Because she's here," said the man who had worked the last six hundred years to be known as Sovereign and not the name he was born with. "They placed a tracker on the bumper of the car she escaped in; her brother, he works for Alpha, and he's inside explaining it all to her right now—all about metas, about our world."

Weissman gave it a moment's thought before pushing a stringy black lock out of his eyes. "Is she ... ?"

"Is she what?" Sovereign's eyes never left the front of the store, with its massive orange-lettered display. "A scared seventeen-year-old? Definitely."

"Is she a succubus?" Weissman asked. He kept his irritation in check, but Sovereign could feel it. It was there, always, stewing under the surface of Weissman's mind. *His black heart is just as dirty as his greasy hair.*

"She doesn't know," Sovereign replied. "Her mother dressed her like she'd be one, though. Gloves, heavy clothing, all that. She even made rules about it." He sifted around again, touched her mind. Even at a distance he could feel it, and it was unlike the ones he had felt before. *Damaged? Wounded,* he decided. *Like me.* "Mom wasn't too kind to her, it doesn't look like. Locked her up in a box whenever she was bad, tried to keep her contained." *Overbearing parent? I can relate to that.* He felt a little surge of elation at the commonality. *This could be it. It could be her, finally. After all this time.*

"Wolfe's just lurking over there next to the Beetle," Weissman said, pointing a long, thin finger into the distance where the Volkswagen was parked. "Can't believe he drives that thing." He glanced over nervously. "He can't see us, can he?"

"I wouldn't worry about Wolfe," Sovereign said, still staring at the front entrance.

"Hard to believe there are this many players after her and she's only just left her house," Weissman said.

"Omega knows what her mother is," Sovereign said, thinking it over. "They've been after another succubus for years."

"Why?" Weissman asked. "Do they know—"

"Of course they know," Sovereign said. "They're the ones who made the rules. Who put the constraints on our people, isolated us from other metas, pushed us out of the mainstream and acceptability. The minute Hades died, incubi and succubi became persona non grata in the meta world, and they were the ones driving the change." He felt a slight smile come on.

"They feared you," Weissman said. "What you could do if you were truly unleashed."

"I've been off the leash for quite some time," Sovereign said with some amusement. "They haven't seen fit to do a damned thing with— or to—me." He grew quiet, thoughtful. "I don't know that they can anymore."

"They're the problem with the world," Weissman said, looking across at him. "They run the show. They repress the people. They have all the power, but they just use it to pump up their own wallets."

"Yeah, yeah," Sovereign said. "I'd take that populist rhetoric a lot better if you weren't presently trying to involve me in a scheme that's going to result in more deaths than I can easily count."

"But to good purpose," Weissman said.

"Says you," Sovereign replied. He could feel the chill seeping in through the windows and probed toward the mind of the girl in the supermarket. *Sienna. I should get used to calling her by her name.* He smiled. *It's a nice name.* She was getting angry, now; she'd seen the men in black suits from the Directorate, wanted to question them. Her brother was fighting her on it, asking her not to.

"A girl like that shouldn't have had to live in fear for her life the last seventeen years," Weissman said, extending his hand toward the supermarket. "She should have been able to live without being caged by her mother. Things like that happen all over. They'll continue to happen unless we make this work." Weissman leaned in closer to him. "Look, unless we have your support, this ... it ain't gonna happen. I've got the framework in place, the basics, but the people I have need some ... motivation. Some inspiration, maybe."

"You want to put the fear of the gods in them," Sovereign said, crossing his arms over his chest. It was getting cold, the Minnesota winter seeping into the car.

"How better to put the fear of the gods into the old gods than by finding someone who's more powerful than they are?" Weissman's grin was dirty, just like the rest of him, and Sovereign only managed to nod politely.

There she is. She caught his eye, even from across the parking lot, striding across the wet, snow-covered surface with a purpose, her brother in tow. *She's ... beautiful.* He stared out the window at her. She was shorter than he would have thought and pale as the snows that covered the land. Her dark hair whipped with the stirring of the wind, and when he caught a glimpse of her eyes he thought of the still waters he had seen when last he was in the Carribbean—deep and blue.

"There goes Wolfe," Weissman said, and the beast leapt out from behind a car to grab Sienna's brother by his neck. He held the man aloft until the girl herself turned around and saw. Words were exchanged, and she hauled off and punched him, solidly in the belly, to no reaction. "This could get messy," he said, a look of unmistakable joy on his face, as if he were watching high quality entertainment.

"I'm going to help her," Sovereign said. He was already on his way out of the car, feet crunching in the thin layer of slush in the parking lot.

"Wait, what?" Weissman was behind him in an instant, doubtless hiccuping time in order to keep up.

"Follow my lead," Sovereign said, feeling the urge to crush Wolfe, to break his bones. The day in the Forest of Dean came back to him in an instant, and he pondered it, thought of making a show of it in front of her, to impress her. I could do it, too. *Make up for the decision to let that miserable creature live, end his reign of slaughter once and for all.*

He looked past the fury of Wolfe to the girl gripped within his hand, and caught a glimpse of her eyes, wide with fear. *It would be foolish. She's lived in a cage for years; gods and mighty forces sweeping down on her will do nothing but inspire her fear and suspicion.* A sting of regret, a remembrance of past failures burned his cheeks as the moment on the *Edmund Fitzgerald* came back to him. Then the night at the Agency came back him, when he'd let his haste for revenge cloud his judgment and led him to kill the father of the very girl he was looking at now. *No. I won't make the same mistakes this time.* He turned to Weissman and whispered a command. "Whatever you do, don't expose yourself or your powers."

"What?" There was disbelief in Weissman's reply. "What are you playing at?"

"HEY!" Sovereign shouted, and felt the anger boil in him. "You can't treat a girl that way! Drop her!" He held himself back, though, restraining himself to keep from attacking hard, from cutting Wolfe to pieces. He slapped Weissman gently on the arm, a *Let's Go* kind of motion that prompted Weissman to run forward.

They both took it slow, human speed, and Wolfe tossed aside the brother—Reed, his name was—slamming him into a parked car. Weissman came at Wolfe slowly enough to warrant a hard hit. Sovereign saw a glimmer of time displacement before the impact, enough that he knew Weissman had prepared himself, had paused time for a second to move himself just a hair farther away to lessen the power of the blow. He still flew across the parking lot, landing in the snow.

Sovereign went on, charging at Wolfe. *Play it slow, play it dumb. Grab me, you silly bastard.* Wolfe obliged, planting thick, terrible fingers around his neck, flesh to flesh, skin to skin. *Now just hold on for a bit.* Wolfe's fingers dug in, and Sovereign held his breath, tried to widen his eyes. *Let him think he's winning ... just hold on ... hold on ...* He could feel the first sense of the fire kindling in his flesh, the first burning of his powers stirring to work where Wolfe's fingers met his skin. He watched the girl hammer at Wolfe's hands, trying desperately to break them loose from around her throat. Finally, she reached down and pulled out a gun, firing it into Wolfe's face as Sovereign fell, released from Wolfe's grasp at last. *I bet you feel that, you son of a bitch.*

A dart poked out of his eyebrow, hanging on by the bushy hair. Wolfe staggered, and she fell from his grip then shot him again in the leg. He smacked the weapon out of her hand and it slid across the slushy ground.

"Little Doll," Wolfe breathed. "That's not a fair toy for playtime." His eyes unfocused, widening, his steps uncertain. "What have you done to the Wolfe?"

Sovereign could feel it, the shadow, the little bit of Wolfe's soul that he'd taken. *Let them think it's a dart. Like there's a dart out there that could penetrate Wolfe's skin.*

"Back away from her," came another voice.

"New playmates are not part of our game," Wolfe breathed quietly into Sienna's ear. Sovereign watched, laying still, willing the beast to run. *If he makes one more move on her, I'll just finish him myself...*

Wolfe took one last look at the two agents and ran, sprinting across the parking lot, bare feet slapping on the melting snow. The agents dropped down next to her talking, both at once, focused on her. Sovereign could sense their distress, their fear—*We failed an assignment, oh no. Old Man Winter will be so angry.* He smiled. *Winter, angry.* He was certain it was a pitiful sight.

"Hey, you!" the younger agent shouted. Sovereign looked up in time to see the brother stagger to his feet and run off through the rows of parked cars, bouncing off them until he reached his own. A moment later, the sound of an ignition turning over roared to life.

"We gotta get her out of here," the older agent said. "Get her to Dr. Perugini."

"Yeah," the younger one said, and swept her up in his arms, carrying her. "She's bleeding everywhere." He carried her off, cursing, running across the wet, cold parking lot to the black Directorate sedan that waited. Sovereign heard the engine turn over almost immediatcly, and they skidded out moments later, splashing mush into the air as they did so.

"I hope that was worth it," Weissman said, appearing at Sovereign's side. He rolled his neck from right to left, making an exaggerated motion with it. "That big bastard doesn't pull punches. Even with the time skip I pulled to cushion the blow it still hurt like hell.

"It was worth it," Sovereign said, picking himself up off the ground. There was blood underneath him, all over the place where he'd fallen. That hadn't happened in a long time. He watched the car running down the street outside the parking lot as it skidded toward the freeway. "I'm in."

"In?" Weissman was rubbing his neck with one hand. "You're ... you're in? Like *in*?"

"I'm in," Sovereign said. "You're right. Let's make the world a better place."

"You don't even know if she's a succubus yet," Weissman said cautiously.

"I'm sure she is, but it doesn't matter," Sovereign said. "I read her mind. I saw her story. I know what Omega wants her for, I know what Winter would want from her, and it's not fair. No, I can wait." He let a smile break across his face in the cold, icy wind. "Besides, girls are into older guys nowadays, right?"

"Yeah, immortal vampires are pretty popular with the teenage girl set," Weissman said, nodding. "Should we go get her then? Go on out to the Directorate campus and ... ?"

"No," Sovereign said, watching the last turn where the Directorate car had disappeared. "The last few times I screwed up because I came at them head on. There are ... so precious few succubi. Even fewer that you would actually want to spend a year with, let alone five thousand." He watched the freeway ramp, contemplating. "I don't want to screw it up again. I blew it with her mother and her grandmother."

"I heard the mother has a sister?" Weissman asked.

"Charlie? Ugh, no," Sovereign said. "No, it's her. Sienna's the one. But we'll just leave her where she is for now. Sooner or later, Winter will screw things up, Omega will come at her as head on and hamfisted as ever, and she'll be right where we want her. That'll be the time."

"Uh huh," Weissman said, and Sovereign could see the skepticism. "So you just want to wait?"

"I do," Sovereign said. "Because this one ... Sienna Nealon ... I think she's the one I've been waiting for."

Sienna Nealon will return in

DESTINY

THE GIRL IN THE BOX
BOOK NINE

Coming in 2014!

Author's Note

Well, that was epic and I hope you enjoyed it. It was probably the hardest Girl in the Box novel I've written yet because of the sheer number of flashbacks while trying to be as realistic as possible about the environments and locations mentioned therein. Also, managing the reveals on some things I've kept back but have hinted at for so long was just a little taxing. One of my beta readers wondered how I'll be able to keep the series going for the next two books now that so many cards are on the table. Well, you'll just have to tune in and see, I guess...

If you want to know as soon as the next volumes are released (because I don't do release dates - there's a good reason, I swear), sign up for my New Release Email Alerts. I promise I won't spam you (I only send an email when I have a new book released) and I'll never sell your info. You can also unsubscribe at any time. You might want to sign up, because in case you haven't noticed, these books keep showing up unexpectedly early. You just never know when the next will get here...

Thanks for your support and thanks for reading!

Robert J. Crane

About the Author

Robert J. Crane was born and raised on Florida's Space Coast before moving to the upper midwest in search of cooler climates and more palatable beer. He graduated from the University of Central Florida with a degree in English Creative Writing. He worked for a year as a substitute teacher and worked in the financial services field for seven years while writing in his spare time. He makes his home in the Twin Cities area of Minnesota.

He can be **contacted** in several ways:
Via email at cyrusdavidon@gmail.com
Follow him on Twitter – @robertJcrane
Connect on Facebook – robertJcrane (Author)
Website – http://www.robertJcrane.com
Blog – http://robertJcrane.blogspot.com
Become a fan on Goodreads –
http://www.goodreads.com/RobertJCrane

Other Works by Robert J. Crane

The Sanctuary Series
Epic Fantasy
Defender: The Sanctuary Series, Volume One
Avenger: The Sanctuary Series, Volume Two
Champion: The Sanctuary Series, Volume Three
Crusader: The Sanctuary Series, Volume Four
Sanctuary Tales, Volume One - A Short Story Collection*
Thy Father's Shadow: A Sanctuary Novel*
Master: The Sanctuary Series, Volume Five*

The Girl in the Box
Contemporary Urban Fantasy
Alone: The Girl in the Box, Book 1
Untouched: The Girl in the Box, Book 2
Soulless: The Girl in the Box, Book 3
Family: The Girl in the Box, Book 4
Omega: The Girl in the Box, Book 5
Broken: The Girl in the Box, Book 6
Enemies: The Girl in the Box, Book 7
Legacy: The Girl in the Box, Book 8
Destiny: The Girl in the Box, Book 9*
Power: The Girl in the Box, Book 10*

Southern Watch
Contemporary Urban Fantasy
Called: Southern Watch, Book 1* (Coming January 2014)
Depths: Southern Watch, Book 2*

*Forthcoming

Made in the USA
San Bernardino, CA
03 June 2014